EVE BRENNER
ZOMBIE GIRL

A. GIACOMI

Published by CHBB Publishing

This is a work of fiction. All characters and events portrayed in this novel are fictitious and are products of the author's imagination and any resemblance to actual events, or locales or persons, living or dead are entirely coincidental.

Edited by Jessica Meigs
Cover by David Walker
Interior Formatting by Dreams2media

This book is dedicated to the memory of my late father. He always en-couraged great imagination as well as great literature in our household. He would always say illness was a state of mind, and to this day I believe that his sort of positivity is what makes people persevere even in their darkest hour. He never wasted a moment and I don't plan to either, and here we are, my first novel, no regrets.

"Whoever fights monsters should see to it that in the process he does not become a monster. And if you gaze long enough into an abyss, the abyss will gaze back into you."

~ Friedrich Nietzsche

PART ONE

A MONSTER IS BORN

CHAPTER ONE

EVE

I can't really recall what I was doing a few seconds ago. There was ample light, and now there is perpetual darkness. My immediate impulse is to shout:

"Hey! Who turned out the lights?!"

When I begin to think about it a bit further, I realize that caves really don't have lights, thus making my argument moot. Plus, there is no one around to answer my snappy complaint.

Rather than focus on the darkness, which makes my palms sweat heavily, I force myself to think about what I was doing before I was consumed by this swift darkness.

I remember placing my bag on the ground. The torches in the previous room were lit, and I took to lighting the ones in the corner of this particular room. I knew full well I wasn't supposed to be down here in the first place. If I had to create my own light, it meant that it wasn't a "safe zone" for digging.

The excavation crew and my archaeologist wannabe buddies are in the mess tent by now consuming some sustenance, and here I am, stupid me, I'm here thinking I've found something miraculous. I think I've stumbled onto something new and groundbreaking; instead, I've stumbled into the darkness and tripped over about a dozen rocks in the past five minutes trying to figure out where the exit to this damn place is.

"Stupid, stupid me," is all I can utter between my clenched teeth.

No one is even going to bother looking for me until well after lunch. Here I was thinking that I would sneak away while the others weren't looking and continue yesterday's hunt for some amazing treasure. All I want to do is prove myself worthy. I am so damn tired of feeling like Doctor August's cute little apprentice for the past year; I really just want his job already.

My wonderful Professor took me on one other dig last year. It was a short assignment in Colorado, and all we did was look at rocks the whole time. It was such a bust! I needed something better than rocks, something exciting! I begged Dr. August to take me to Egypt with him. He said it was an extremely high-profile dig and the volunteers would need to be fourth-year anthropology students or higher. I was surprised when he finally said yes and even agreed to let my best friends tag along.

My thoughts shift to Cameron and Alex. I can just picture them finding me down here eventually and shaking their heads and laughing at me for even thinking for a split second that I would go and make an enormous, world-shattering discovery on my first big dig. They love me but know that I'm a bit impulsive at times, and never at the right times.

I press my hand over my mouth to stop myself from giggling at the thought of Alexandra raising a perfectly groomed eyebrow at me while Cam insults me with his sly wit. He is much too quick with the smart ass remarks, and I never have a good comeback for him.

When I feel a bit calmer, I begin to feel around for my bag in the darkness. I slip and tumble over another rock. My fear of the dark distracts me so well that I forget my footing and land face first right on the dusty floor; it is quite possible that I ate some ancient ash on the way down.

"Mmm, tastes like failure! Great! No one is ever going to take me seriously," I blurt out.

This hunt is a bust and an ego adjustment all in one. I always knew I had a big head, but I don't like to admit it. I hate when Cam and Alex remind me of it. I don't like to be reminded of things that I'm already aware of. Definite pet peeve. Don't treat me like an oblivious dumbass. I would always remind Cam and Alex:

"I'm aware. I just choose to ignore certain things."

I guess that's why I decided to ignore the yellow caution tape at the entrance of this place. However, I can't ignore the feeling that I'm not alone at the moment. I hear a scraping sound nearby. Maybe someone finally noticed I am missing?

"Hello? Can I get some help over here?" I wait and still hear something faint, but no reply.

This time, I yell, "Help!" a little louder, but it will take someone with supersonic hearing to hear through these thick rock walls.

Amidst my frustrated screams for help, I think I hear something shifting behind me. I hear it again, and my fear is confirmed: something is here and is as uninvited as I am.

I stop moving, breathing, and talking to myself all at once. I really hope I don't hear anything more. I'm terrified of the options—snake? Big spider? Ancient mummy back from the dead? I laugh out loud at the thought, and then there it is again. Something is dragging, scraping, or shuffling towards me along the dirt floor.

My mental narrative shifts from embarrassment and self-loathing to a general "shit shit shit." If Cam were here, he would say, "Pardon your French, Missy!" but I'm far too frightened to reflect on our inside jokes right now.

I can barely breathe, and I feel like I'm about to cry. I don't like not knowing, and I am quickly learning that my fear of the dark is worse than I thought. My chest feels tight, and my head is spinning. Not a good time for my phobia to intensify. I need to think.

I hear it again and again, and it's getting closer. The sound transforms. It is less like dragging or shifting now and more like nails or claws dragging on solid rock. I try to crouch into what I think is a corner and make myself into the smallest ball possible.

The wall feels oddly warm. I didn't think it could get that warm down here with all the darkness and rock, and the thought reminds me of the fact that I'm very much below the surface.

Without warning, the wall I lay against begins to move. As my body presses against it, I suddenly realize it's not an animal; I think it might, in fact, be human. I let out a muffled scream and quickly get up on my feet, my fists tight, ready to defend myself against whatever is waiting for me in the darkness.

My lip bleeds as I bite down on it to control my terror. If only I had a flashlight or a match or a cell phone, this not knowing is making my blood pressure rise and my nerves dissolve into goop. This is making it impossible to think of a good solution.

I feel hands gripping my shoulders and let out a bloodcurdling scream. I didn't even know I could make that kind of a sound.

The screaming is to no avail, because here I am being flung through the air in complete darkness, and the landing is rough and painful. I think one of my ribs may be broken.

"Who the hell are you?" I scream through clenched teeth.

I'm in pain, but I'm not about to sit here crying and waiting for someone to murder me. Which I now believe to be their intent—whoever is down here is very strong. I'm not exactly light and fluffy: I'm a solid 150 pounds and swim team captain, a title I wear like a badge of honor.

I shove my hands frantically around the floor, trying to feel for anything hard or weapon like. I lay my hands on what feels like a knife; it's a rather sharp piece of rock, what luck. I pick it up and turn to stand awkwardly in the darkness.

I listen in the shadows for the next move. I feel a whoosh alongside me and throw myself towards it. I make contact with something, and it gives a mammoth-like moan. I've injured whatever it is.

"Good," I say out loud in triumph.

I continue to listen for sudden movements or a welcomed plunk to the ground. I hope I got that son-of-a-bitch good!

What kind of sick joke is this anyway? Hide in the dark and seek to attack someone dumb enough to come down here alone? I guess I do fit the profile, I sigh with acknowledgment. Am I to be raped, robbed, beaten…or just made dead? What exactly is this douchebag here for? It dawned on me suddenly that maybe I have actually discovered something important; maybe this room I stumbled into was never meant to be found.

My curiosity gets the best of me, and I begin to scream questions into the darkness.

"Why are you here? What do you want?" I wait in silence, but no answers come.

I'm starting to feel a bit faint from the fear coursing through me. I hear that strange moaning again. It's frightening and not like anything I have ever heard before. I stand paralyzed in the darkness with no idea what my next move is. While my thoughts race in every direction, I feel something graze my arm, and before I can pull it away, teeth pierce my arm's soft flesh. They gnaw away at my arm as if it is a piece of barbecued meat. I feel a ripping sensation, and my arm begins to feel warm and wet. Something sprays my face, and I know the taste; it's my blood that's spilling.

I'm screaming in the darkness now. Something has bitten me. I can taste the tears mixed with blood that continue to roll down my face. I can't stop screaming and can't defend myself with only one arm available to me. It feels as though my arm might go missing soon. Another large chomp finds the bones in my arm. I feel another large gush of warmth rushing down my limb, and the chomping sensation continues.

I so desperately want to see what's going on. I look towards my arm, as if I will be able to see it in this dark tomb. Then there in the darkness, I see two glowing red spheres. They look abandoned and weary, but they glow with strength and purpose. Eyes, it has burning eyes.

My brain is useless; it is seized by fear. I need to take action, but all I can think is, *What is happening?*

"Help me! Please God, help me!" I scream.

I continue to scream until I can't quite remember when my screaming stops and my unconscious state begins.

CHAPTER TWO

CAM

As I pick up the last satisfying potato on my lunch plate, I hear something in the distance. At first, it sounds like a wolf howling, but as I listen further, it sounds more pathetic and needy.

I drop my cutlery and look up at Alex. She looks up from her plate and gives me a baffled expression. Maybe she heard it too?

"Alex, what is that?"

She looks to her right, which is where the tent's exit is, and still does not utter a word. There is a stunned silence in the tent. We've all heard something, but none of us are sure what it is. Suddenly there it is again, much clearer now.

Someone is screaming.

It echoes through the dig site like an injured wolf's cry. I drop everything and rise from my seat. So do a few others, including Alex, who seems to be reading my mind.

Without another word, we pick up the pace. Alex is now sprinting beside me in the direction of the terrifying screams. I think we both realize the same thing and begin to run even harder.

Eve had told us she was going to take a nap. I should have known better than to leave her alone. She's more curious than twenty cats! Alex points in the direction of the screams.

"It came from one of the excavated tunnels below."

I grab a flashlight and rip down the yellow caution tape, which was the only barrier between safety and whatever is lurking down there.

With Alex behind me, we begin our descent. The deeper down I go, the more I fear the worst. No one else has worked up enough courage yet to follow us, so whatever we are walking into, we will be walking into it alone.

My flashlight finds something staining the ground. I have stepped in some of it as well. It sticks to my shoes like goop. The light has uncovered a long trail of blood. That continues up ahead like something has been dragged through here.

"Dear God, Eve," is all I can say.

Alex takes a big gulp of air when she sees what has me horrified. She covers her mouth; I can see she's trying not to vomit. The trail of blood grows darker from this main room towards a narrower crevice in the corner of the tomb. My heart sinks. Only Eve would be suborned enough to come down here. Damn that Eve, why does she always have to go looking for trouble?

When we arrived in Egypt, Dr. August told her specifically to stay away from this portion of the excavation, and he reminded her again only yesterday when she asked for permission to look around. The area hasn't been cleared by safety inspectors yet. Why would Eve want to do something so stupid? I have to stop myself. Why am I mentally arguing with Eve when she might not even be alive for me to yell at later?

I take a closer look at the crevice leading into the smaller room; my flashlight discovers that I won't fit through there. I slam my fist on the wall at this realization.

Alex steals the flashlight right out of my hand and starts to squeeze through to the other room without warning. In a panic, I grab her wrist to stop her.

"No! We don't know what's in there. You could be the one screaming next."

She slides her arm free from my grip, rolling her eyes at me.

"If Eve's in there, I need to get to her. Make sure there are people ready for her if she's hurt."

I look into her eyes, pleading, but she's off without hesitation, squeezing through to the other side. Just this once, I wish I wasn't such a tall or muscular guy. Today it's what makes me useless to both my friends.

In a moment, more of the staff and volunteers gather into the tomb with flashlights and lanterns. They look on with a combination of terror and excitement in their eyes, the same look most people have when they witness a bar fight.

"Sickos," I sneer as I give them the dirtiest look I can muster.

"She's here!" screams Alex from the other side of the wall. "But she's in bad shape. She's unconscious, and her arm looks mangled. I'm going to bandage her up the best I can so she doesn't lose more blood."

I say, "Okay," and then wait the most sickening five minutes of my life.

Alex finally yells back, "Okay, I'm going to put her flat on her back and pass her through head first. You are going to have to grab her shoulders and slide her through. Pull her while I push on the other end."

I am grateful again for my muscles, glad they can be of some service now.

I look into the crevice and tell Alex, "I'm ready."

The first thing I see is a mass of long brown hair. Eve's chestnut hair covers all of her face except her lips, which look pale. All I want is to brush the hair away and see her beautiful blue eyes open. That's when I will be able to breathe again.

Alex is trying very hard to be gentle, but it's a tight squeeze, and Eve gets a few new bumps she doesn't need right now. As soon as I can get my hands on her shoulders, I start to tug so I can get her to safety and the medical team as soon as possible. My hands find their way under her armpits, and I have a better grasp now. I can hear Alex panting from the other side. Alex is very tiny in stature, but she is determined.

With a few more pulls, I finally have her. She looks so pale as I push the hair from her face, dead even. My heart races as I hand her over to the medical crew for examination. They check a few things and then place her gently on a stretcher. I watch them carry Eve away. She is limp, and her body moves to the beat of every bump they walk over. I have to look away or I may die right here and now. Watching her move further from where I stand is agonizing.

Alex slips back through to the main room looking pretty rough herself. I hug her, and she hugs me back. We both feel the weight of the moments ahead.

When we release each other, I look at Alex, needing to know the details.

"What did you see in there? What do you think happened?"

She looks up at me, then back to the crevice she just slid through, and shrugs.

"Honestly, I have no idea. There was a lot of blood. It looks like something tore into her arm with teeth. Maybe some crazy dog was down here? I couldn't see how bad the wound was. It was just too messy, and my hands were shaking too badly to keep the flashlight still."

I don't look up at Alex just yet. I nod and ask another question. "Were there any clues we could follow to find what did this?"

Alex's continues with a touch of frustration in her voice.

"There was no sign of anyone or anything else. Whatever got her is long gone. What's really strange is that I'm pretty sure this is a trail of Eve's blood leading out this way, but she couldn't have made this trail herself because she was lying unconscious on the other side of the wall. Whatever attacked her left this trail of Eve's blood on the way out, but it's strange how there are no paw prints. It just sort of drags and spatters."

I shiver at the thought of Eve being attacked. This was supposed to be a nice little trip for the three of us to gain some archeology experience and knowledge or, on a more honest note, just to look at cool creepy stuff buried in some Egyptian tombs.

Our university professor Dr. Walther Hugo Augustus, or as we affectionately call him, Dr. August, offered us the volunteer experience of a lifetime. I'm not sure how Eve convinced him we were ready. He even told us that if we did well on the dig, we could study with him in Egypt for a semester and come in contact with some of his current research.

He always made everything sound exciting and intriguing, so how could we say no? We were aching for adventure, especially since we come from a very small town called Little Lake. This was our chance to actually explore somewhere new and exotic. Dr. August always had new top secret research he was working on, and he liked us so much, he would usually let us in on it if we begged enough.

Dr. August was recently in the news. He stumbled upon some human remains in a tomb in Hierakonpolis, Egypt. It made headlines all over the world. They think he may have discovered another Egyptian Pharaoh. We felt very lucky to even be considered to join such a high profile dig.

Eve, Alex, and I have been friends since high school. We naturally followed each other to the same university since we always loved the thrilling world of anthropology. It seemed so glamorous the way Dr. August explained it, and we just wanted a taste of it.

It feels ridiculous now, and I begin to lose sight of what this is all for. If Eve never recovers, neither will I.

I place my arm over Alex's shoulder, and we walk in silence towards the surface. The last few gawkers walk beside us, emptying the area gradually. With every step, I make a wish that Eve will be awake and well when we reach her.

***

This all feels too strange, like something out of a really bad, highly stereotyped mummy movie. Alex begins to shake me. I guess I spaced out for a bit longer than it seems.

"Cam, hello, earth to Cam?" She waves her arms in front of me.

"Sorry, Al. I just…I just can't think right now," is the only explanation I can give.

"Let's get out of here. They won't let us see her right now. They said they would call us if Eve wakes up soon, and then hopefully she can explain what happened."

I must look grim because Alex runs her fingers through my hair like I'm two years old. "It's not your fault, you know?" she says with care and concern in her voice.

I nod, and we walk back to the mess tent to kill time.

How does Alex do that? I think to myself as we walk. I can never understand how she just always seems to know what is on people's minds.

She tries to comfort me further.

"You couldn't have prevented this, and she's going to be fine, okay?"

"Okay." I sulk a little and hope she's right.

CHAPTER THREE

EVE

My eyes snap open. I have no idea where I am or how long I've been here. It's an odd feeling, not being able to account for things that have happened to me. I have had moments of missing time before, but that's only because I had a night out drinking and couldn't recollect how I got home. I did too much of that in first year trying to fit in and can't say that I miss it. I'm already over the party-till-I-puke days, and I am only in my second year.

I rub my eyes, willing them to focus. It feels a bit like I have been in a coma for forty years. What have I missed while I was out cold? Where the hell am I, and who are all these people?

I shake what looks like a nurse off me and then scream in pain when I realize she is stitching up my arm. They should have restrained me. If only they could have known I was an A type personality and total control freak. I don't like strange people touching me without an explanation.

After I slap the nurse's hand away, my natural reaction is to put pressure on my arm, and it hurts like hell.

"What are you doing?" I interject.

I press harder to relieve the pain, but I only open the stitch and make it bleed more.

The nurse curses me under her breath, and a doctor enters to check on all the commotion. He can tell I'm livid and tries to calm me with a smile and some reassurance that everything is fine, but I can't seem to calm down. I feel as though my veins are going to burst, and I can't even slow my breathing down.

What's wrong with me? Something doesn't feel quite right. I glance down at my arm; it looks like something took a bite out of me. I can't help it. I start to cry and scream.

"Eve, calm down!" the doctor says, placing a reassuring arm on my shoulder.

I have no idea what's going on or how I got here, and no one seems to be forthcoming with any information.

"Tell me what's happening to me! I don't feel well. I don't feel right."

I can't explain it any better than that.

The doctor looks a tad confused, but his voice remains patient and calm.

"Eve, you just had a little accident. You will be fixed up in no time, good as new."

I don't like being treated like a mental patient, so the smiling doctor makes me angrier rather than calmer. I don't want to be told to calm down; I just want to know what's going on.

I pick up a nearby syringe and hold it up.

"What's wrong with my arm? I feel strange. What did you give me?"

I don't know why I'm acting so paranoid and violent, but it just seems to come naturally at this particular moment. Where is Cam? Or Alex? Or any familiar face?

Time stands still for a moment, and I try to remember the last thing I did or saw or heard, but nothing is coming to me. This memory lapse makes me feel ill. I drop the syringe and bring my hands to my head, grabbing it forcefully, almost as if I am trying to squeeze a memory out.

Out of the corner of my eye, I see the doctor signal something to the nurse. The nurse gathers her courage and comes over to me; she pats me on the shoulder.

"There, there, dear, not to worry. I will have you all stitched up and you'll be good as new. Just like the doctor said."

I stifle back some tears and once again ask, "What happened?"

She glances up from the wound and whispers, "We're hoping that you can tell us that soon."

I sit back and let her stitch me up. I figure a stitched-up arm will look better, and maybe I will start to feel better too. I realize I must have looked insane for a moment there, and I apologize to the nurse and doctor.

"I'm not going to hurt anyone. Sorry for making your day more interesting than it needed to be."

The nurse gives me a look of forgiveness and tells me to hush while she continues her work. While she stitches away, I try to retrace my steps but find my mind is a blank. I don't know what happened, though I feel like I should; perhaps it's because I'm still in shock. I'm sure I will remember something soon. I begin to recognize my surroundings. I'm in the medical tent on site. It's not very big. It might hold two or three patients at a time. It was only set up for minor scrapes, but I sure am glad we have one at all! The closest hospital is hours away.

I feel immediately better when Cam and Alex walk in to greet me. Cam with his broad shoulders and large arms always gives the best hugs. He is the tall, dark, and handsome type. Alex looks so small in comparison; she is so naturally slim but eats like a race horse. Her long blonde locks look disheveled, which is out of the ordinary, but it will take a lot more than that to diminish her beauty. A smile sweeps across my face, and I almost want to jump up and attack them with hugs.

"Guys! Thank God you're here! I can't tell you how nice it is to see familiar faces! Do you know what's going on?"

They look at each other uncomfortably. Not a good sign.

"Listen, Eve, we really don't have much info for you right now. The police have been notified..."

Alex gives Cam a little nudge, essentially telling him to shut his face.

"Police? Why are there cops involved?"

I stare at them, and they are hesitant to go further in their explanation.

After a moment, Alex punches Cam in the arm and says, "Too much info too soon! She needs to rest."

I continue to plead with them. "I know you guys think I'm in bad shape, and I get that you are trying to protect me, but you need to let me in on what's going on or I'm going to go nuts!"

I already felt pretty nuts, and I'm sure the nurse would agree, but I wasn't going to share that right this moment.

I stare at Alex, sensing a moment of weakness. "Talk, Alex!"

She takes a deep breath. "You sure you don't remember anything?"

I shake my head and beg her to continue.

"Well from what we know, something attacked you in one of the tombs. We heard you screaming and came to find you. It looks as though you found a new tomb. There was a crack in one of the walls making a small entrance, and you crawled in, I assume. I didn't see anything in there when I crawled in to get you. It was very dark in there, so I didn't really have a chance to look around. I found you unconscious and, well, your arm like that..." Alex points to my mangled limb.

I stare back down at my arm as the nurse begins to wrap it

up. It's looking a bit purple. "Something must have got me good, something strong."

My arm looks so damaged. Looking at it makes me want to throw up, so I look away. I suppose I should just be grateful it is still attached.

Cam speaks for the first time. He looks so pale, and I hate to worry him. I know he thinks of Alex and me as his only family since his dad's a drunken bum and his mom died when he was eleven. We're all he has.

Cam begins, "I noticed a trail of blood heading out of the tomb, Eve. Whatever was down there escaped. I don't want you heading back in there alone until we figure this out. You weren't even supposed to be there in the first place. Dr. August is going to be so pissed."

I feel my cheeks turning red. "Do we have to tell him?"

Alex's mouth drops open. "Of course, we have to tell him! He's going to find out from the others anyhow. We might as well tell him."

"Shit." I try and think of ways I can smooth over my perfect disregard for his instructions and can't think of anything good to say.

"Guess he'll just have to yell at me and I'll just have to suck it up and listen. Shit, he might try to send me home."

That thought is altogether more terrifying than chunks missing from my arm. I can't go home early; that's just embarrassing. I only have a week to go! Going home means missing out on a great opportunity, and I have a feeling Dr. August won't invite me along on any future digs.

"I fucked up. Sorry, guys."

They give me a brief smile like it's already been forgiven. Before they can say another word, the nurse attempts to shoo them away.

"Alright now, Eve needs to get some rest. It's been a pretty traumatic day, and all of this can be discussed tomorrow."

I want to burn holes through the nurse with my eyes for sending my friends away. I could attack her again, but they may sedate me and send me home unconscious, so I can't protest.

I just don't want to be alone right now.

Cam and Alex reluctantly wave goodbye, and I'm left alone to my thoughts. My very empty thoughts.

The nurse offers me a glass of water, and I take it almost excitedly. I feel as though I needed something; perhaps it is water. When I glance back up at her, her eyes are burning red. She has a toothy grin on, and her mouth opens in a very inhuman way.

I scream as she comes right up to my face. Her hands are pale but strong, and she looks like she wants to devour me. I thrash around until I hear her speak.

"Eve! Tell me what's wrong? I can help...just relax!"

When I open my eyes again, she is the pleasant woman from before. I must be hallucinating.

"I'm so sorry. I don't know..." I can't finish my sentence. I just stare off, trying to recover.

The nurse looks from me to the heart monitor, her eyes almost bulging out of her head. To say that she looks a little worried is an understatement. I don't ask what she's thinking. I'm not sure I want to know. I am grateful when she leaves the room stating that she will find me another pillow. Before she can return with it, I'm out like a light.

✷✷✷

I'm running through a dimly lit tunnel that doesn't seem to end. I'm terrified; something is chasing me. I have no idea what it is. All

I hear is the sound of my panting and feet slapping against the wet ground. I don't have any shoes on.

Something breathes against my neck. I yelp and start running faster. I feel claws tear at the skin on my back. It only stops me for a moment. The fear is stronger than the pain, so I only force myself to run faster and weave through different alleys in the tunnel.

I hate the darkness. It seems infinite. I feel as though I've been running for hours, and then I hit a wall. A dead end.

All I can do is scream. I call out into the darkness for my mother. She appears looking young and unfazed by what's happening.

"Help me, please!" I squeak.

She replies, "Oh now hush, sweetheart. I can't help monsters. Critters like you deserve to be put down." She addresses me as though I'm a rabid pit bull that needs a shot of everlasting sleep.

I look down at my hands, and they're covered in blood. I'm panicking now. When I look back up, my mother is gone. All I see are two glowing red eyes in the distance. They are coming at me fast.

I can't breathe. I can't move. I am paralyzed.

The monster hits me like a brick and takes me down to the ground. I hear it tearing at my flesh. Oh God, oh God, I'm being eaten! Something is eating me.

I scream through the sound of tearing flesh and sputtering blood.

CHAPTER FOUR

ALEX

I arrive to sounds of Eve screaming at the top of her lungs. Where is the damn nurse when you need her? I try to shake her awake as she continues to scream. Who can even fathom what she's dreaming and what she's seen in the last twenty-four hours?

I smack her across the face, and she comes to. She stares blankly at me at first without recognition.

"Dummy, it's me, Alex. You okay?"

She shakes her head, trying to snap out of it. "I'm so sorry, Alex. I was having a nightmare. Someone was chasing me, and then they started eating me!"

She starts crying. Eve's not really a crier, but she's done a lot of that in the past few hours, and it's surely understandable.

She places her arms around her neck, searching for something with a look of panic in her eyes. I'm not sure what she's trying to say. Was it, "Look it…look out…locket?"

I don't ask her to clarify. She's not calm enough. Right now I just need to get her to relax. I stroke her head and hold her in my arms, wary of her injured arm.

"No one's going to get you here, hun. You're safe now. Shhh."

I'm also not usually the one comforting Eve, so this is actually quite odd for me. She comforted me when I broke up with that stupid jerk of a boyfriend, Chris, and every fight we had before that.

She comforted me when my parents separated for a short time and celebrated with me when they got back together. She was the only one who helped me search for my lost dog; she even made missing posters while I was inconsolable and hysterical for forty-eight hours. Eve was always there for me. It never mattered whether the dilemma was big or small. It's hard to believe we have been friends for so long. I met Eve in grade nine; we were only fourteen then. Now we are nineteen and nowhere near closer to more mature. Maturity is overrated anyway.

As I hold Eve in my arms, I feel oddly useful knowing that she needs me for once, and I'm ready to be her rock like she has been mine for so many years.

Eve sniffs back some tears and tries to pull herself together. "I don't know anything, Al. I can't remember. All I know is how I felt. I know I was scared down there, but I don't know why."

I continue to shush her and try to lull her back to sleep. It actually works, and I'm able to rest her head back down onto her cushion. She looks much more relaxed now, and I take this opportunity to examine her arm.

It looks god awful. It's definitely bruising nicely, and I'm sure it will leave a nice-sized scar. "Do they have land sharks in Egypt?" I say sarcastically under my breath. What could do this to her, and why can't we seem to find it or them? It's no use wondering. I simply keep thinking that, thank God, she'll get to keep her arm, although it will never look the same.

Eve is a very pretty girl, always has been. She has the glossiest brown hair and these sapphires surrounded by thick lashes. Her lips are full and luscious, and she has cheekbones that supermodels would kill for. She's also a bit of an enigma to me because she's girly in a sense, but her interests are sports, comic books, and action movies; she simply acts like one of the guys. She is most likely every man's dream girl, but she isn't even aware of it.

Eve is the kind of girl who likes to be pretty for herself; she doesn't care what others think about how she looks as long as she's happy with it. That's where her confidence comes from. If she feels she looks good, she can conquer the world, but a bad hair day can crush her spirits. I know this little imperfection will bother her for life. She smashed the mirror in her bedroom a few years back because she had a pimple that wouldn't go away quickly enough. I guess Eve is a bit vain, a bit stubborn, and a bit of a control freak, but the good really does outweigh all of these traits. She is always a true friend. If she makes a promise, she keeps it, and she's always truly happy for people's accomplishments and never jealous. She's honest at all costs, and I respect that. There are far too many people who lie to your face on a daily basis and think you're too stupid to know it. As Eve always says, "I love you enough to tell you the truth, even if it sucks to know it."

***

I leave the medical centre in a haze. I wish I could do something, anything, to make Eve feel better. All at once, it dawns on me as I recall Eve searching for something around her neck. Her locket!

I didn't think to look for it before; I was far more concerned with Eve. I need to go back and find it. It must have fallen off during the attack.

The locket holds a picture of her mother and a lock of her mother's hair that fell out during one of her chemo treatments. This is one of Eve's most prized possessions, and she goes nowhere without it. Eve has always been a little superstitious, the whole never letting a black cat cross her path, or not opening her umbrella inside, or donning jewelry with protective symbols.

Eve brings this locket with her everywhere, because once it was created, her mother was told that she was cancer-free. Eve believes the locket will keep the cancer from returning, and for what it's worth, I hope that little superstition of hers is true.

I lost Eve the year she found out her mother had cancer. She was simply a shell of herself. She couldn't and wouldn't believe it could take her mother's life. For that year, she hid away from us, spending every waking hour with her mother, living in constant fear that she might lose her. I can't blame her for feeling this way, and I completely understood that she needed the time, but I missed her and resented the fact that she wouldn't come to us for support or help. I felt left out of the loop and useless. I know that Eve never intended for Cam and me to feel this way, and we've never held it against her. We just wanted to be there for her like she has always been there for us, but that's Eve: she deals with things on her own. She shuts down for a bit and finds her own way back.

✳✳✳

I head to Eve's tent to check if the locket is there. It's not. I already had a feeling that was the case, but I was really hoping that the other option would not have to be explored.

"Fine," I sigh. "Guess I will just have to go back down there then."

I should probably call Cam for backup. I'm not sure if that "thing" is still down there hiding and waiting for its next victim.

As I head over to Cam's tent, I keep wondering why no one has found anything yet. Have the police even been notified about this incident? His tent is literally five tents over. When I arrive, I swipe the flap open quickly and see his bare ass.

"Crap, I'm so sorry. I should have knocked!" I giggle, knowing that tents don't have that option.

I give him a minute to put his pants on and then re-enter the tent.

"Jesus, Alex! Can't a man change without someone barging in on him? It's like the third time this week! I'm starting to think you like getting a sneak peek at this bod!"

I roll my eyes. "Sure, Cam, that's my goal in life—to see your full frontal."

He chuckles and then gives me the "what's up?" glance.

"Listen, Cam, you're not going to like this idea, but I need your help. I think Eve left her locket down there, and we need to go get it for her. You know how devastated she'll be if she doesn't get it back."

He stares at me like he's about to ask what the hell I'm thinking, but he reflects on my words and then sighs and says, "Alright fine. I'm just glad you didn't decide to go down there alone like Eve. You can both be so stubborn sometimes. I can't take it!"

***

We head towards the tunnels, which have been left unguarded since the incident. The only extra precaution they took was adding additional yellow tape. I roll my eyes at the sight of it.

"As if that would stop anyone!" I say, pointing at the bright lines of tape.

Cam covers my mouth as soon as I say it. Then I hear it too. There are people talking ahead of us. We weren't expecting company.

Two men appear with Dr. August at their side. The men are wearing suits that make them look like CIA agents.

I hear Cam whisper, "Suits in the desert? Are they nuts?"

One of the men looks like a football player on steroids; the other is quite small in build with thick-framed glasses.

The quarterback tells Dr. August, "Please make sure no one else goes down there until we finish our inspection. We warned you that it might be dangerous. You should have had security guarding the entrance."

The other man nods his head with stern agreement and adds, "This is a very important dig, Doctor. I'm still not sure why you decided to take a bunch of kids along."

I spit at the sound of the word "kids." We were nineteen, for God's sake!

Dr. August smiles and retorts, "Well, gentlemen, one day I will be dead and gone, and someone will have to take over where I left off. Who exactly is going to do that? These 'kids' may eventually be of use to you someday, so I suggest you have a little respect for their delicious curiosity. One day their work may even be greater than my own."

Cam and I fist bump at the sound of Dr. August's defiance.

"Thanks for standing up for us," I say in a whisper so that not even Cam can hear it.

The two men scowl at Dr. August and begin to leave. The skinnier of the two men turns back for a second and reminds Dr. August, "We'll be in touch."

When they are finally gone and Dr. August is alone, the defiant smile on his face fades. He seems bewildered? Angry? I'm not sure; I can't read faces or body language. I am of no use unless it's blatantly obvious. It took me years to discover Cam had a crush on Eve.

Cam and I stare as Dr. August pulls something out of his pocket; it's a rock in a very lovely shade of red. He lifts his arm as if he's about to chuck it off into the distance, but he rethinks this choice almost as quickly and places it back in his pocket. With his decision made, he begins to walk away.

***

When we begin our descent into the tombs, it's eerily quiet, and what's even more daunting is the fact that it doesn't seem like anyone has even revisited the area. Eve's blood still stains the floor. Have the police collected a single ounce of evidence?

Cam gives me this look of understanding. It's amazing how friends of many years don't even need to speak anymore, and they can just sense the other's thoughts.

I reach the wall. "Okay Cam, I gotta slide through there again. Pass me the flashlight."

He grabs my shoulders and looks at me with his stern dark eyes. "Please be careful. If you sense even a bit of danger, you get yourself out of there, understand?" He shakes me slightly while he says this. "I can't follow you in, so I'm begging you to make good decisions here. I don't need to lose anyone on this trip."

I shrug him off, trying not to let my fear show. "Okay Cam, jeez. Chill out, will ya? This will be quick."

I start to slide through the same crevice with the mini flashlight in my mouth. This makes it a little easier to feel my way around. When I enter the tomb, I shiver, thinking about what might have happened here. I shine the light around the room and locate Eve's satchel. I rummage through it. No locket. I run the flashlight along the ground. When I pull the flashlight back up, I see a figure in front of me. It looks like it's contorted and peeling away in some places. It's human, but the eyes are ruby red. Its neck twitches and cracks in an odd manner. I tremble and drop the flashlight. Screams fill the cave. They belong to me.

I can hear Cam on the other side. He is screaming with me.

"Alex, God dammit! Are you alright? Please answer me!"

I feel around on the floor frantically for the flashlight. When my hands wrap around it, I pick it up quickly and direct it at the corner that the figure was standing in. But it's not there any longer. My light traces every inch of the room, but the decaying man is gone. Perhaps I imagined him, but it is still enough to make my palms sweaty.

It takes me a moment to regain composure. All the while, Cam is still screaming.

"Alex! Alex! Alex!" he screams as I hear him pounding the wall.

"Cam, I'm okay." I take a deep breath before continuing. "I thought I saw something, and then I dropped my light. It was nothing. I'm fine!"

"You're fine. You coulda fooled me...you're fine..." He adds a "pfft" after that.

I can understand his frustration. I know he won't be able to squeeze through and help me if the need arises. He is much too large. He is built like a wrestler, which makes it hard to believe that his father ever abused him. His father was much smaller and out of shape, and Cam could take him but he was too kind. He never fought back. Something about his father paralyzed him and kept him from protecting himself.

When my body stops shaking, I continue my search. I see something gleaming in the middle of the room. When I move closer, I see it. It's here. I've found it. All I can think is, *thank God,* and I breathe a sigh of relief. We can leave now. I scoop it up and place it in my pocket.

I yell back to Cam, "I've got it! Coming back now!"

He shouts, "Okay," back to me, and I begin to squeeze my way through the crevice. I stop when I hear a noise. I fling the light in the direction of the sound instinctively, and there is nothing there. "Thank God," I gasp.

"Thank God what?" Cam yells.

"Nothing, Cam. Just thought I heard something." I turn to move ahead once more and flash the light in front of me. I see something there.

I scream and drop the flashlight again.

"Alex, what's going on? Come back now! Get out!"

I can hear the panic in Cam's voice; what the heck does he think I'm trying to do? Of course, I want out of here. I quickly retrieve the flashlight and speedily squeeze my way through the crevice.

He grabs me as soon as I exit. "What happened?"

I look up at him after taking a deep breath. "I thought I saw something, that's all. It's just my nerves getting the best of me."

He places his hands over his chest. "You scared the shit out of me, you know?"

I chuckle. "Yeah, I know. I scared the shit out of me too."

⋆

We head back up, and it's already dinner time. I didn't realize we were down there so long. I gleefully head towards the mess tent, triumphant and full of worth. Hopefully, Eve will wake up soon and be back to her old self. I can't wait to see her eyes light up when we return her most prized possession.

CHAPTER FIVE

EVE

I feel as high as a kite today, as the saying goes. I've been hopped up on meds for days so I won't feel the throbbing pain in my arm. They have it bandaged excessively now, especially after seeing the look of disgust on my face every time I peered down at it. I guess the nurses caught me peeking at it constantly and realized I was starting to become a bit obsessive with staring instead of resting.

The doctor says I can leave as soon as tomorrow, and I honestly can't wait; I've been going stir crazy. I have nothing to occupy my time except for my own thoughts, and they aren't pleasant. For someone with no recollection of what happened, I am plagued with nightmares.

The only distraction I've been offered appears in the form of Dr. August. He bursts into the med tent dramatically. I knew he would come to see me and ask if I recovered any of my memory from "the incident," as he calls it. I struggle to retrieve anything, but all I can remember is how dark it was in there. I remember my fear and nothing else.

In return, I ask Dr. August if they have made any progress with the case.

He sighs and furrows his wrinkled brow before saying, "There was really no evidence left behind and no trail to follow. Unfortunately, the case will soon be filed away as unsolved."

I bite my lip. I feel responsible for all of this; the same thing might happen to someone else, and I can't even help them figure this one out because I can't even remember what happened down there.

Dr. August is genuinely upset that one of his students has been hurt on one of his digs, but he is also sad that we will be leaving in a few days. His first love will always be discovery, but Dr. August always makes us feel important, much like one of his colleagues. Even though we are just some young schmucks with no real experience, we share his lust for strange and uncharted territory, and that is enough to win him over.

I will miss him, his long gray hair, and his quirky smile. He reminds me so much of Mr. Rogers and a much older Brian Cranston all in one. His days are growing closer and closer to retirement, and I know he'll be spending his later years sipping on margaritas in Florida with his family as the golden years wear on. He mentioned leaving the university at some point next year, which means I only have another year with him.

I have a feeling he might miss his life of adventure, but he always avoids the subject by telling us that it's time to stop being so selfish and leave something for the rest of us to discover.

"I do remember one thing, Dr. August."

He looks intrigued. "And what's that, Eve?"

I look down at the ground. "I owe you an apology. I didn't follow your instructions, and I'm sorry. I'm sure I've gotten you into some kind of trouble. All I can say is I'm an idiot, and I won't do it again."

That was very hard to get out, but I have to say something. I feel like complete shit about it. I know someone will be breathing down his neck about the girl who got injured on his watch.

Dr. August simply smiles and says, "Don't even worry about it. I'm mostly just interested in how you're feeling." He pats my hand and then leaves my side without saying another word.

***

While digging around in my thoughts, I don't even hear Cam and Alex come in. Alex has this huge smile on her face and tip toes towards me in a goofy manner.

"What is it, Al? What have you gone and done?" I raise an eyebrow, a little concerned with her abrupt display of happiness.

She smirks again before pulling something out of her pocket very carefully. When my eyes meet with the golden object in Alex's hand, I squeal, "My locket!" I nearly jump out of bed. "Where did you guys find this? Oh my God, I could kiss you both so hard right now!"

Cam blushes a little with the mention of the word "kiss." I often wonder if he still has a thing for me after all these years. It is no secret that he had a huge crush on me back in high school, but I thought he had long forgotten about it, or maybe he had and I'm just reading too much into things.

Alex hugs me with a triumphant grip. "I went back to the tomb to get it."

I can feel my face turn green. "Alex, why did you go back down there? It's not safe! You could have been attacked or worse!"

Alex just rolls her eyes at me. "You didn't think we'd let you leave without your lucky locket, did you? Now just admit you're happy to have it back and shut up, okay?"

I smirk a little. "I'm still mad at you, but thanks, guys. I don't know what I would have done without it."

Cam comes over to the edge of my bed and sits down. "So you

get to leave this sterile little place tomorrow, eh?"

"Yup, guess I do, but you know I've become quite accustomed to living in a large tent. Might have to get me one of these when we get home." I wink at him, and he turns a tad redder.

"Maybe I will just have to organize a camping trip?" Cam and Alex stare at me in silence; they know full well I'm not the camping type. Egypt was even a stretch for me. I spend most days running from large bugs. Cam cracks only a smile first, but he can't hide the laughter rising within him.

"I'm sorry," he begins to laugh through his words, "but I can't even picture that." He laughs even harder, and it becomes contagious. Soon we are all having a good laugh at my expense, and in that moment I know we all feel the same thing: very blessed to have each other safe and sound.

Once Cam and Alex leave, I squeeze my locket in my more capable hand and drift off to sleep. Tomorrow I will be free. Let the countdown begin.

✳✳✳

The next morning, I'm overjoyed to be out of that hospital bed but a little depressed about having to start planning my departure. I talk to myself as I organize a few items.

"Packing is one of the greater nuisances of our time," Aristotle would say. Okay, maybe he wouldn't, but I hate it. No, actually I despise it like an axe to the face. Maybe I'm exaggerating a bit, but that's in my nature.

I see Alex packing her things so neatly across from me. I don't know how she manages to squeeze a shitload of items into one luggage. I can't understand how she gets it to look that way and how mine looks like airport security has already rummaged through it.

Alex is more dainty and girly than I am. I like make-up, and I like looking good, but it's an effort for me. She looks amazing so effortlessly. Alex always says I'm the prettiest thing she's ever seen, but I think she's just being nice because she loves me. I admire how elegant she can look even when digging in the dirt; she must have royal ancestors somewhere in her lineage. I always feel like the unrefined tomboy next to her—I certainly have poor table manners. But she seems to love me anyway.

I decide to break the silence. "I hate to leave knowing that we found nothing."

Alex looks at me with a mirrored expression and nods. "I know what you mean. I came here hoping to find something magnificent. Well, I guess I did find this rock." She pulls a tiny rock out of her pocket. I take it from her hand so I can examine it.

"It looks like a little elephant," Alex says cheerfully.

"Actually, it does. I guess you found a natural wonder," I spit back at her sarcastically.

"Har har, you're so funny. Well, I thought it was pretty cool, and it's my souvenir, okay! Even Dr. August collects rocks. I saw him holding a beautiful red one when I was on the way to get your locket."

I never knew Dr. August to collect such small items; he's more into collecting larger treasures like a mummy, or a golden sarcophagus. I throw a pair of clean undies at Alex, showing my disinterest in her rock story.

"Ewww, Eve, so unhygienic! Honestly, sometimes I wonder why you weren't born a man!"

I laugh really hard until my ribs ache, and then I continue to pack. In a way, she was right; what souvenir do I have other than a nasty scar? I suppose I will always remember this trip. I rub the bandage on my arm, aware of it for the moment. Tomorrow our adventure will be over before it even began. I continue packing, feeling very sorry for myself.

CHAPTER SIX

CAM

It's our last day on the dig site. Eve hasn't been cleared to dig anything today. In fact, Dr. August pulled us aside earlier and told us not to let her out of our sight and make sure she doesn't attempt any work today.

Eve decides to kick up dirt in frustration while watching Alex and me dig and uncover some more pieces of pottery. So much for interesting finds; Eve isn't exactly missing out on anything. I think pottery might be the only thing I found this whole trip, and if I'm lucky I might have found enough pieces to complete one artifact and then someone else can have the pleasure of gluing it all back together. It would be a pretty awesome puzzle, though. A puzzle with no map to go by, so it's better handled by professionals.

I start to become annoyed with Eve when the dirt starts flying in my direction.

"Eve, can you stop kicking around that dirt? It's starting to get into my eyes and mouth," I cough out at her.

"Sorry, Cam, I'm just so bored. It's the last day here, and all I'm doing is standing, inactive, useless!" The little crease in her brow is cute when she does this; it always includes a little pout that makes it all the more adorable.

"Stop being so overdramatic, Eve." I chuckle to myself and watch her crumple down to the ground like a tantrum is about to ensue.

As Eve sits on the ground, she stretches her long legs out in front of her, and they glisten in the sun. God, she has hot legs. Must be all the swimming she does. I glance from her toes all the way up to her midsection, where a bit of skin peeps out between her denim shorts and her tee shirt. I gulp, trying to compose myself, but my eyes don't leave her. They move up to her chest and then rest on her face. It's extremely warm, and Eve is dewy from sweat. She flips her hair back in an erotic way. I'm not sure she means for it to look so sexy, but it does, almost as if she does it in slow motion. My heart is ready to do back flips, and I force myself to look away, but not soon enough. Alex catches me gawking and rolls her eyes at me before returning to her work.

I feel my cheeks grow warmer and decide to get back to work myself. This is not the best time to daydream.

When my eyes feel it's safe to shift their gaze back to Eve, she is looking at the tunnels a few feet away. *I wonder what she's thinking.* I go back to digging, assuming that Eve is occupied by her thoughts.

When I look up again a few moments later, I notice Eve is closer to the tunnels. I drop my tools and run after her. She doesn't try to move further ahead. She just stands there, frozen. "Eve? Where are you going?" She doesn't answer; she just continues to blankly stare at the tunnels.

I'm starting to think there is something wrong with her, so I grab her shoulders and give her a gentle shake. She speaks without looking at me.

"I need to go back down there, Cam."

I give her as stern a look as I can muster and say, "No way!"

She looks so desperate it frightens me. Her eyes are wide and insane looking. I swear they glow a strange hue that I can't explain.

"I need to find out what's down there. Aren't you the least bit curious, Cam?"

She must be joking, I think to myself. "Why would I be curious about getting eaten down there? Stay here where you're safe!"

By this point, Alex notices our squabbling and appears at my side.

"What's going on, guys?" Alex waves her hands in front of Eve's blank stare, which has not moved from its focus on the tunnels.

"Guys, I have to…" Eve stops talking abruptly and continues to walk forward almost as if she's possessed by something. Her eyes are fixed on her destination like someone is summoning her towards it.

I stand in front of her, trying to block her path, and she gives an animalistic snarl. *Well, that was strange*, I think, but I hold my position. She continues to move forward, and I continue to stay in her way as if we're performing a strange dance.

Eventually, her frustration builds, and she begins trying to push me out of the way. Her shoves feel similar to a football player's charge, and I feel slightly winded. I attempt to restrain her with my arms and notice her body goes limp when my limbs connect around her.

"Eve? Eve?" I shake her with vigor, but I can tell once I lower her to the ground that she is unconscious.

Alex looks down at us. "I think she fainted, Cam. Quick, set her flat on the ground and elevate her legs on a crate until she recovers." Alex quickly drags an empty crate over to us.

A few seconds after making Eve comfortable, she opens her eyes.

"What happened? Why am I in the dirt?"

Alex and I look at each other, very confused by what just happened.

"Eve, you were demanding that you had to go back to that tomb. I wouldn't let you go, so you attacked me, and then you fainted."

Eve's eyes go wide. "I did what now?"

I can tell none of this sounds familiar to her.

After some stunned silence, Alex speaks up. "Eve, maybe we should go back to the nurse. She can just check…"

Eve interjects without letting her finish. "No way am I going back there! It's the stupid meds they're giving me. They make me feel crazy, and they'll just give me more. So we're going to pretend nothing happened, okay? I'm not going into the tomb, and you're going to forget my crazy little episode here. Deal?"

I look at Eve and reluctantly say, "Okay deal, but if you wander off again, Alex and I will drag you to see the nurse, got it?"

Eve nods and crosses her heart as a promise.

Alex and I go back to digging, and Eve sits in the dirt in front of us without another word. Can meds really do that to someone? Maybe steroids. I've never taken a single drug in my life and barely drink alcohol since my dad was such a violent drunk. I'm glad that Eve is okay, but I keep a closer eye on her this time around. I'm not sure I trusted her right now.

CHAPTER SEVEN

EVE

It's almost time to leave. I let out a groan of disappointment. I know Cam and Alex are waiting for the bus with some of the other volunteers. I can only assume they are chatting about their finds or lack of, and I can't join in on that just now. I zip up my luggage, throw on a hat, and leave the tent for a moment.

I go off in search of Dr. August. Although I have seen him every day, I have not had an opportunity to say a proper thank you for the opportunity. My eyes search the grounds, and I find him in the distance looking at a map and discussing it with a colleague of his.

"Dr. August!" I wave and shout over to him. He waves me over, and when I'm closer, I blurt out what I came here to say. "Dr. August, I just wanted to say thanks for everything. I know you don't usually take second-year students, and I hope I'm not a total and utter disappointment to you. You know I love this work. I won't mess it up again."

He looks down for a moment before responding.

"No, Eve, I'm really sorry about everything, dear. I know you hoped for so much more on this trip, and you especially didn't expect to become a victim out here."

He truly looks upset as he crinkles his entire face into a frown. It's as though he can't even put into words how upset he is on my behalf.

I shake my head. "Honestly, I'm fine. I learned a lot, and I hope to do a dig again someday. I know this may be one of your last digs, sir, so it's been a real honour to have worked alongside you. I know you're retiring next year." I hope he doesn't hear the sadness in my voice; I don't want him to think me pathetic. Instead, he appears touched by it and a bit misty eyed.

"You're a great student, Eve. I will miss you when I retire. I'm not sure if you have any classes with me during the fall semester, but if not, I hope you will drop by and visit me on campus soon." He's about to return to his work but then adds, "I do hope even after I retire, I will be reading about your adventures someday, huh?"

I smile. "I would love that, sir." I give him a quick, awkward hug and turn to leave.

***

As I'm walking towards the crowd that awaits the shuttle to the airport, I feel around in my pocket and realize my locket isn't there.

"Crap!" I mutter to myself.

I better go double check the tent. Alex and Cam didn't go through all that trouble only for me to lose it again. That would be the icing on this miserable cake. I run in the opposite direction, away from the crowd, and catch a glimpse of Cam and Alex looking confused by my sudden change of direction and pace. I don't have time to explain.

Once I reach the tent, I search the nightstand and under the tiny bed. Thankfully, there it is, gleaming under my cot. I guess it fell out of my pocket during my half-assed packing job. As I reach for the locket, the bandage on my arm catches on something, and the fabric falls away. *Great! Now I'm going to have to refasten it and waste more time.*

As I reach for the bandage, I notice there is no pain. *That's odd.* I look down at where the nasty gash in my arm should be and am horrified to find that there is no gash, not even a scar.

I feel around, grabbing every inch of flesh, thinking I'm seeing things. Have I gone completely mad? Where is the wound? I'm scared all over again, but there is no time left to freak out. As I look down at my watch, I see that it is departure time. The bus will be leaving at any moment.

I quickly throw on my cardigan, since getting the bandage back on in time is not an option. I just hope my cardigan will help me avoid answering any questions about this strange healing.

I stand outside the tent in a cold sweat, panic staining my underarms. I want to talk to everyone and no one at the moment. Is this all a strange dream? I better wake up soon or I'm going to puke. I stand outside rubbing my palms on my shorts and trying to calm my nerves.

"Act normal and you'll be fine. No one is going to notice," I repeat over and over to myself until I begin to believe it.

While having my little freak-out session, as I pace outside of the tent, I hear wheels approaching and then someone hitting the breaks. "Shit, the bus is here!"

In the distance, I see Cam and Alex waving me forward telling me to hurry up. I start to run and make it over to them. I notice that we are the last ones to join everyone on the bus. "Sorry, I took so long, guys. I just wanted to double check the tent in case I forgot anything. You know I can't pack to save my life."

They both smile and board the bus. *Phew, they bought it.* Now I just need to pretend everything is fine until we get home. I hope I can pull this off, but I'm aware that I may look as tense as I feel. Cam looks over at me, and I think he senses it already. I flash him a big smile, and he accepts it and moves on. *Double phew.* For the rest of the bus ride, I pretend to sleep. I am also able to avoid conversations with everyone through the airport and onto the plane.

***

Once on the plane, I feel a bit more relaxed. I feel that going home will make this all go away like some big bad dream. There is some comfort in returning to something familiar. I try not to think about explaining things to my parents. Maybe I won't have to tell them anything since there is no evidence on my body that anything was ever wrong. I'm not sure how I can keep this secret from Cam and Alex for long. They know me too well, and sooner or later, they are going to want to see how my arm is healing.

Just once during the long flight, I go to use the restroom and bravely decide to check the former wound. It is still gone; I didn't just imagine it. My fear makes me sob a little, and I grab some toilet paper, ready to wipe away my tears.

When my eyes meet the mirror, what's looking back is not me. There stands a bony and pale figure. Her skin looks rotten, and purple veins appear on every inch of her. The eyes that burn red are the most terrifying part of her; they glare at me as if they want to pounce.

"But it's just a mirror. It can't hurt me," I try to convince myself.

I place my hands on the mirror in an attempt to wipe the image away, but it doesn't budge. Instead, the grotesque figure opens its mouth to reveal a dark smile that begins to turn red. Blood begins to pour through the spaces of each tooth until it fills her mouth and then begins to pour down her chin.

I cover my mouth and fly backward, smashing the back of my head into the wall of the small space. The back of my head throbs, and I fall to the ground shaking. I want to scream, but I must keep up the appearance of normalcy, at least until I'm home.

I rub the back of my head and pull myself together.

"Snap out of it, Eve," I whisper to myself.

I rise slowly so that my eyes lift above the counter and catch the mirror first. Blue eyes are glancing back at me, and I breathe a sigh of relief.

When I am in full view of the mirror, I see me again. I inspect every inch of my body to make sure whatever I see before isn't staining me. I convince myself that I'm seeing things, but my gut tells me there is something more to that. First my arm, now the mirror…something isn't right, and I know it.

When I get back to my seat, I am determined to sleep until we land. I try to let nothing bother me and convince myself that there is nothing but blue skies ahead.

Cam passes me as I struggle to act naturally in my seat. I lean back and try to look sleepy. He eyes me inquisitively. It's a shame and a blessing that he can sniff out any irregular patterns in my behavior. I wink at him, which is within my realm of "normal" conduct. He smirks and continues on. *Thank God*! I slam my eyelids shut and feel a slight bit of triumph. I'm such a pretty little liar sometimes.

CHAPTER EIGHT

EVE

Here I am. My front door. I'm not ready to enter yet. It's been a long trip, and my parents are most likely about to dissect me with a question and answer period. Delaying does nothing but postpone the inevitable, so I finally open the door and shout, "Hey, I'm home."

I drop my bags at the front entrance as my first greeter, our dog Winston, approaches, wiggling his almost nonexistent tail. He's a lovely little Scottish Terrier that just adores a good tummy rub. "That a boy, did you miss me? What a good boy," I say as I playfully rub his tummy.

My mother is the next to greet me with her Cheshire cat grin. This woman never stops smiling; I think she smiled during every chemo session she ever had. I'm not sure she even knows what the word sadness means. She inspires me to be a more positive person, even though I can be really negative and bitchy sometimes. I'm sure people wonder if I'm adopted because we're not alike at all. I love my mom more than anything in the world. In my mind, she's the best example of perfect.

"Oh, Eve, you look great! What a tan you have on you! I have a pot of coffee ready and your favourite chocolate cake. We can have some while we talk all about your trip."

And here we go, the Q and A session is about to begin.

"Let's get this over with," I huff to myself.

She follows me as I stroll down the hallway to the kitchen and grab a drink from the fridge. I am sipping a Five-Alive when my father comes in with his garden gloves on. "Hey, Pops!" I give him a hug, and he squeezes the life out of me. That father of mine should have been a wrestler.

"So I guess you have been doing my garden gig while I was away?" I smirk at the thought.

"Yes, and keeping your plants alive isn't easy. I'm not sure they all made it, but I did my best. That's what you get for asking me to help." He chuckles to himself.

"Well, Mom would have killed everything for certain, so don't be so hard on yourself." My mother tosses a dish cloth at my head to protest the mention of her lack of green thumb.

As we laugh, I begin to forget my strange misadventure for a little bit. My body relaxes, and my mind slows down. I feel at ease. I am in the best place on earth. I am home.

***

Dinner is ready an hour later, and we have been chatting about everything from the arrival, to the dig site, to my professor, and of course the food. My parents always seem to look at me like I'm Indiana Jones or something; they think my stories are so fascinating when nothing really exciting ever happens. Sort of like a cop who only gets to patrol for parking offenses. The one time something really weird and sort of exciting happens, I can't even tell them about it or else they'll freak out! I can't tell them about the incident. My parents are the worst sort of worry warts; they'll want to take me to the doctor and check the wound, which I can't even produce to prove there ever was an incident. It's all better left unsaid. Buried in my subconscious.

My mother sets a plate of grilled chicken, a baked potato, and a vegetable medley in front of me. She definitely has a flair for food presentation. I see the wrinkles around her eyes and mouth deepen as she smiles; she knows she's a great cook. It looks so delicious, I dig in immediately. I finish my plate with as little discussion as possible. I missed my mom's home-cooked meals, which is very obvious from the way I polish the plate.

"I guess you liked you meal then?"

To which I reply, "Absolutely not! Worst meal I've ever had!" My mother smiles, knowing my sarcasm will never cease and pleased that I enjoyed the meal so immensely, or had I?

My stomach begins to lurch; I feel as though someone has just grabbed my intestines and tied them into a large knot.

My father notices first. "You alright, hun? You look all red in the face."

I look at my father and nod, trying to pretend to be okay, and excuse myself to go to the washroom. The pain is excruciating. I double over onto the floor of the hallway bathroom and grab at my stomach. I'm sweating from the jolts of pain sweeping through my body. I make it to the toilet and dispose of every piece of food I have in me to give. I continue to heave until nothing is left and I've made a complete mess of my mom's lovely pink washroom.

I lean against the wall, exhausted. That didn't feel like any puke session I've ever had before, and trust me, I've had some pretty rough drinking nights before that I wished never to re-live. Winston is poking his nose under the door trying to see if I'm alright.

"I'm okay, boy. Shhh, go to Momma." I take few more minutes to compose myself before presenting myself to my parents again. I cautiously look in the mirror and wipe the sweat off my face. If I had a tan before, I don't see it now. I look pale and defeated, but at least it is me staring back this time.

When I walk back into the kitchen, my parents look extremely worried.

"Honey, are you sure you're alright?" my mother asks.

Now is a good time for a little white lie. "I don't feel so good. I didn't keep the meal down. I think I need to go rest. I will have to skip dessert for tonight, Mom."

She looks down at the large cake with a sigh. "Okay, honey. Maybe you just ate your meal too fast. And yes you're right, you're probably just overtired. Go get your rest."

With that, I depart for my bedroom and throw myself onto the bed, hoping I never have to get up again. I immediately fall into a deep sleep.

✶✶✶

The monster with the red eyes appears again. He chases me down another tunnel. I feel blood trickling all over me; it's so dark I can't see the wound or wounds. My arm stings, my neck stings, and my legs don't want to work anymore. I stumble to the ground and begin to crawl. The monster's breath is on my neck; it's so close. This is the end. It will finish me off, and there will be nothing left but bones. I accept my fate, laying flat on the ground, no longer struggling. Let me die. Let it be over. My eyes close as the teeth plunge into my throat. All I hear is gurgling, sputtering, and crunching of bones. The monster lets out a horrid squawk; it's not a human sound at all. My eyes close.

Moments later, I awake in a white room. I'm not dead? Perhaps this is the afterlife. I get to my feet and look around, but there is nothing in this white room except a mirror. I begin to walk towards it and feel something tear apart. Blood starts to drip onto the white floor. The contrast is so frightening. I hear something thud to the ground; I look quickly to the right, where the sound came from. My right arm lies on the ground, fingers still moving. I stare at the stump, horrified. I wonder why it doesn't hurt. Blood continues to drip; I'm so terrified something else will fall off. I start walking quickly towards the mirror, because even though I am terrified, I need to know what is happening to my body. I need to know what's left of me. I want to run to the mirror and realize I'm only slowing down. The blood leaves trails behind me.

When I make it to the mirror, I start screaming. It's not me anymore. I'm looking at a monster! There is not much skin left. What is left on my face is peeling off, and there is blood all over me. Nothing human is left. The most horrifying part is my eyes. They are as red as fire. I want to cry at what I'm looking at, but I can't cry. I feel as though I am trapped in this new form. I continue to stare in the mirror, and every cry comes out as a shriek. I'm going mad. My disgust grows, and I feel the desire to feed. I begin to chew at my other arm; for some reason, it feels good. I chew feverishly until blood spatters on the walls of the white room. I chew until the limb crashes to the floor. I am satisfied.

I glance again in the mirror and no longer feel disgust. I feel power. I lick some of the blood running down my face. It tastes euphoric.

I am starting to love the monster within me.

✳✳✳

I jolt upright, and my face is moist. I wipe away several layers of drool. *Thank God it's only drool.* I may have been sleeping for what seems like a year, but when I check the clock, it has only been a mere hour and a half nap.

What a strange dream, or maybe it was the stomach bug making me hallucinate? I look around the room for the source that awakened me from my slumber. My stupid phone. *Why didn't I turn you off?* I think.

I pick up the phone reluctantly and hear Alex's horrified voice. "Shhh shhh, Alex, slow down so I can understand you completely."

She takes a deep breath and tries again. "He hit him hard this time, Eve. Cam's in the hospital. I really didn't think he'd do this again, especially not since the last episode."

I know exactly what Alex is referring to, and I grind my teeth.

Back in high school, Cam's dad had about as much to drink every evening that a small liquor store could stock. One night, Cam joined Alex and me for the Little Lake Music Fest, and we dropped him off at home afterward. Cam already told good old Henry about his whereabouts that evening, because he wasn't a rebellious kid; he respected the "my house, my rules" attitude that Henry requested. But in Henry's drunken state, he determined that Cam never mentioned this "little concert of his" and was home way past his curfew. I can only imagine his hands raising towards Cam and making contact. I squeeze my eyes shut and force the memory out before I can envision anything further.

Cam never says much about that night, but the bruises spoke louder than any explanation could have. He received a lovely black eye patch and many new shiny bruises along his arms and legs. After that night, Cam was ready to leave home.

He lived with me for a few weeks until his dad came around begging for his son's forgiveness and pleading with him, telling him over and over again that he would never lay another hand on him again. At first, Cam was hesitant, but he forgave his father, and apart from drunk nights where Henry passed out on the sofa, there was no more violence.

I resented Henry every day after that. Cam spent a lot of time taking care of his drunken dad instead of getting to be a normal teenager. I don't know why Cam felt the need to protect that loser. Maybe guilt? Maybe because he felt his mother would want him to? Maybe it was out of pity? It was such a role reversal that it boggled my mind. Cam's always been the father in that relationship. He takes care of Henry, even when he never reciprocates it.

I guess I can understand why Henry drinks so much. He lost his wife so horrifically, but it's no excuse to soil her memory by treating her only son like shit.

I snap out of my memories and refocus on Alex's voice.

"We need to see him." Her voice quivers.

"What hospital, Al? How bad is it?"

She's sobbing on the other end. Even though I can't hear it, I know it from the silence in between her sentences.

"He's unconscious is what they told me, and he's at the local hospital in Little Lake."

I don't need to hear any more. I tell her, "I'll be at your house in ten minutes. Be ready and we'll go see Cam together."

I run downstairs and find Winston blocking the doorway. He is snarling at me as if I am one of the neighborhood cats trespassing on Brenner property. *Strange.* Does he know something is up?

CHAPTER NINE

ALEX

I'm biting my nails as I wait for Eve to show up. I don't understand why Henry would do this to Cam after all these years. He seemed to be on better behaviour, although he still drank himself numb.

I can honestly care less about what happened to Henry. He is a bad father, and everybody knows it. I remember going over to Cam's house when we were younger, and Henry always left everything a mess. He left Cam to clean up after him. I wonder if Henry knows how others view him or if he cares. I wonder if he realizes how bad his addiction has become.

His wife died in such a tragic and unforeseen way, and sure, that will leave scars, but how can he do this to his son? Doesn't he know Cam has emotional scars too?

Cam's mom died in a car accident when he was only eleven years old. From what Cam has told us, she was a pretty awesome mom. She would always sit with him and help him with his homework; she loved to bake with Cam and taught him some recipes he shares with us sometimes.

Henry still drank when she was alive, but he wasn't so angry then. Cam tells us the night she died, she had a really huge argument with Henry about his drinking. She said she was going for a drive to clear her head but never came home.

A drunk driver struck her car, and she spun out of control. As a result, she hit a metal pole, splitting the car and herself in half. It must have been awful for little Cam, and how was he expected to cope with a father that was never there for him? I think the guilt from that night ate up what was left of anything good inside of Henry. Cam tells us that's when the worst of it started. His father became cold, distant, and abusive. He was so lost in his own pain that Cam was forgotten.

Rage is brewing in my mind. *Was his own pain so much more important to him than his son? What a selfish, no good sack of shit.* I take a breath, trying to douse the fire brewing within my chest. I feel heat flowing through to my fingers and pull them into fists, almost ready to punch through a wall.

In so many ways, I can't understand addiction; it just never seems like an addiction to the drug of choice but rather an addiction to self-destruction. Henry is doing a great job of that; unfortunately, he is taking Cam down with him.

I hear a honk outside. *Great, she's here.* I am glad to leave these dark thoughts for a moment and just get going.

"Hey, Eve," I say as I give her a hug, and we exchange worried glances.

I get in the car and notice she looks pale and her eyelids are puffy. I don't have to ask what's wrong. We share our anger and let it fill the car. We don't speak on the way to the hospital. I can tell Eve is very focused on getting us there as soon as we can. She may have missed a few stop signs, but I'm not going to question that at a time like this.

✳✳✳

When we arrive, the nurse gives us a bit of a hard time, seeing as we aren't family.

"But we are the best thing he's got!" I shout at the nurse. "Let us see him now!"

The nurse rolls her eyes and says, "I'll see what I can do."

We are truly all he has available to him. His dad is being held at one of the police stations, and rightfully so. None of his cousins live anywhere near here. Everyone else is dead. We are his family now, and if only the nurse fully understood that, then perhaps she wouldn't hesitate to let us in.

After some more threatening words from Eve—*man, she has balls*—we are able to see Cam. He is hooked up to some machines, and some parts of his face look a bit purple. I can't help it; I start to cry. Eve puts her arm around me and brings me closer to Cam, who is clearly still unconscious. Eve takes the hand free of wires and devices, and I simply sit beside her in a state of shock while she caresses his hand. We do this for about thirty minutes, and I continue to sweep through many emotions like pity and grief and anger. *That drunken bastard Henry should get beaten and made some guys bitch in jail for this.* My thoughts are not normally so cruel, but I am so livid that I can't help but think it.

I'm sure I pass out a few times while waiting because I jolt awake forgetting where I am. When it registers that I'm in the hospital, I look to Eve and see that she hasn't moved, or slept, and her hand still cradles Cam's larger hand. She looks like a statue, frozen in time. Isn't she tired? We just got back from a long trip and haven't even settled back into our lives yet.

I take a closer look; Eve's eyes are very intently gazing at Cam in an evil, vicious kind of way. I almost don't recognize her. Eve's eyes seem to glow a strange shade of red; conceivably it is just a reflection off of one of the machines in here. The ferocity in her stare must mean she is lost in her thoughts, perhaps plotting ways to kill Henry.

The look in her eyes terrifies me. My skin grows bumpy as a chill fills the room. I worry that Eve is stuck that way. *Why isn't she moving? Is she even breathing?*

I shake her. "Eve, Eve, what's wrong?"

She doesn't seem to snap out of it. *This is getting creepy.*

I stand up and clap my hands in front of her and shout again, "EVE!"

She snaps out of it as if nothing has happened. "What the hell, Alex? You scared the shit out of me! Will you calm down? Jesus!"

My mouth hangs open. I'm about to ask her where the hell she spaced off to, but the doctor comes in, and that means questioning Eve will have to wait. I tell myself she was most likely sleeping with her eyes open, but I am still pretty creeped out. I've never seen Eve do that in all the years I've known her.

"Hello ladies," the doctor greets. "I'm Doctor Bergum. Now this boy is a friend of yours?"

We both nod.

"Does Mr. Jackson have any family in the area that can be reached?"

I heard Eve mumble something to herself. It sounds like she says, "No, just a sorry excuse for a father."

I cut in before the doctor can make out what she's saying. "No, he doesn't have anyone but us, and we'll gladly take him in after he's released. What is the extent of his injuries?"

I'm not sure I want to hear the answer if it's bad news.

He glances at his chart for a second. "Looks like he received a forceful blow to the head resulting in a minor concussion. He has a broken rib and quite a few bruises. He will heal. We just have him on some pain killers at the moment. He will awaken soon enough."

I let out a sigh of relief. "Oh thank God, he's going to be okay."

The doctor nods towards me before being called away by a nurse in the hall. He is gone as quickly as he arrived. I still have more questions, but I guess they will go unanswered until Cam wakes up. *Dang doctor shortage.*

"Our government really needs to invest in getting more people working out here." I look at Eve and give her an exasperated smirk as I say it; she returns the expression, and we go back to our sitting posts.

At some point, my eyes close. As I drift off to sleep, I hear a hissing sound. I open my eyes to see Eve slumped over and sleeping like the dead. Cam hasn't moved an inch. Everything looks as it should. I close my eyes once more, but I continue hearing it. I convince myself that I'm just exhausted and imagining things. I soon ignore the sound and drift off into a deeper sleep.

CHAPTER TEN

CAM

There is a strange ringing in my ear when I awake. It causes me to twitch in my bed.

Wait, this isn't my bed. "Where am I?" I ask groggily.

I guess I said that out loud because a reply comes quickly afterward.

"You're in room 223, recovering from your injuries," Eve says with a matter-of-fact look on her face. *Now that's the kind of face you want to wake up to.*

She jumps up and smiles at me. For a moment, I think it's just us in the room, but then Alex materializes behind her.

"Thank God you're awake, Cam. We were so worried."

I try to roll my eyes at Alex to show my resentment for her pity, but I can't; it hurts too badly. I take a moment to observe my bruise-riddled body.

"Yeah, I guess you would be worried seeing me like this." I point from my face to my toes.

Eve comes closer, and my heart picks up the pace. Why does it have to do that whenever she gets closer? I try not to look into her cool blue eyes; I get much too lost in them. Her eyes change as she looks at me more seriously now; the slight grin she had a second ago is gone. "What happened, Cam? Why did Henry do this?"

It all happened so fast I need a moment to remember the events from the night before.

"I just remember getting home. I called around for Henry, but I didn't see him in the house. I started putting my stuff away." I scratch my head, trying to remember what came next.

"Then Henry appeared in the doorway of my room. He started yelling at me, things like where were you? How could you leave me alone? It's like he had forgotten where I was for the past month. Then he came at me with a baseball bat." I shiver at the memory of my father's enraged face.

I see Alex cover her mouth immediately after I make mention of the bat. She looks horrified, and Eve looks like she's on fire, prepared to commit an unspeakable act at any moment.

"I guess the shock of it all kind of messed with my memory, because I don't remember any pain or how he hit me or when I went unconscious. I really don't remember much more than that. It's a blur."

I try to move a little in my hospital bed to prove that I'm fine—I can't take them staring at me like that—but each movement is excruciating.

"Although I seem to feel the pain now. Can you call a nurse for more pain meds?"

Alex runs off to find a nurse, and Eve helps me get comfortable. She's so close I can smell her. Her arms wrap around me lightly as she fluffs up my pillow. I inhale a whiff of her dark chocolate hair. We are inches apart, and our eyes meet. There is a moment there; perhaps it's just awkwardness from close proximity or sexual tension? I'm not sure, but I wish she would just kiss me or slap me so I can stop guessing.

Eve clears her throat. "The doctor says you have a broken rib. Try not to move too much. I'm not sure how long you'll be in here, but you will come live with Alex or me when you can leave."

I stare at her blankly, not sure how to feel about my next question.

"What about my father?" I really don't know why I care, but I do. You can call it guilt, call it obligation, call it madness; somehow my father is still my father at the end of the day.

"He's locked up for the moment, and I don't think you're safe with him anymore, Cam. He's hit a new low, and I won't stand by and watch you suffer with him." Her eyes become glossier with each word, but she bites back the tears for my sake.

I close my eyes tightly, knowing she's right and trying to accept it. I can't go back home ever again. Even with the abuse, his lack of caring, and bad fathering, I still feel this need to take care of him. Like it is my responsibility somehow. My burden to bear.

He never hit my mother; I can give him that much. He loved her and she couldn't help but love him. I'm sure she still loved him the day she died, even though they had a few arguments. I always thought my mother would want me to look after him. I feel badly because he was never like this before Mom died; he was still an alcoholic but a better man than he currently is. Now he's simply haunted by her ghost and can't escape his pain no matter how many bottles of Jack Daniels he cranks. Eve is right. Screw him! It's time for me to have some kind of a life and be happy.

"You're right, Eve. It's time for me to move on. I can't save him from himself. I think I should have left years ago."

Shortly after our little conversation, Alex returns with a nurse. The pain meds are administered, and Eve and Alex leave me to rest.

I do try to rest but find my mind too full. I was happy when I woke to see them. They're the best thing I have going. I've spent most of my life taking care of a man I barely know anymore. My mother's death ruined him. Hasn't he noticed that I'm in pain too? Yet I didn't follow him on a similar self-destructive path. I just kept thinking of my mother and how sad she would be if she could see us both now and what's become of us.

I choke back some tears at the thought. I'm a man, after all, and know that tears do nobody any good. I force the thoughts out of my mind and focus on getting some rest so I can heal. Whatever that means.

CHAPTER ELEVEN

EVE

After dropping Alex off, I head home to explain everything to my parents and hopefully, finally, get some rest. We have a long conversation, and my parents wholeheartedly agree to have Cam stay with us since we have an extra room anyway.

I return to my bedroom, and although my head is full of angry thoughts, I try to sleep them off so that I may feel fully functional again. I fall into a deep sleep quickly.

***

I awake to my mother calling me down for dinner.

"Shit, have I slept that long?" I rub my eyes and hazily begin to wake.

When I sit up, I find Winston at the foot of my bed.

"Hey buddy," I say playfully and reach for him.

He looks out of sorts and is staring me down, growling again like I'm a trespasser.

"What's gotten into you, boy?"

I get off the bed and try to pet him. Instead of allowing it, his teeth clamp down on my hand viciously. I scream until I am able to shake him off.

I hear footsteps running up the stairs. My mother must have

heard the commotion because she is the first to come check on us.

"What's the matter, sweetheart?" she pants as she opens the door.

"Winston bit me!" I yell. "I don't know what's up with him, but he's been growling at me and acting weird."

Oddly enough, my mother doesn't look too worried. "Well, he probably just missed you and is a bit miffed that you left for a little while. Don't worry, honey. He'll get over it." She winks at me and ushers Winston out of the room and downstairs to have his supper.

Once my mother leaves, I check out my hand. It's bleeding quite a bit but really doesn't hurt. I manage to keep it hidden from my mom, but jeez he seems to have gotten me good.

I head into the washroom to clean my hands and begin rinsing them in the sink. To my horror, the gash is closing and healing at a rapid rate. The shock throws me backward, and I stare at my hands until the wound is gone. I think I stared for a long time even after the fact until I am sure there isn't anything left.

"Oh God, what's wrong with me?" I sob.

It is then that I realize that something awful is inside of me, and I don't think it is ever going to go away.

CHAPTER TWELVE

CAM

After a few days, the hospital decides to release me with a few bandages and some happy pills. Eve and Alex are there waiting to break me out.

We drive to my house first to pick up my meager belongings. My dad won't be there, obviously because he is in jail at the moment, but Eve and Alex refuse to let me enter alone.

Girls always worry about emotional scars and want to hug them all away. What they don't understand is that's not how guys work. We own our scars. They don't leave us, and we don't talk about them either.

I am happy to just grab my shit and get out of there, not that there is much to grab. I've never felt at home here, so I never bought things to fill the space, just my clothes, a toothbrush, and some family pictures. A little sentimental, I admit, but I can always say, *Hey, I had a family once upon a time,* if anyone ever asks where I came from.

I take a final glance at the small home. It doesn't feel like mine as I stare at the home I grew up in. It hasn't been maintained well, and I feel a pang of guilt for not helping with the repairs. The roof of the tiny bungalow needs replacing, the paint on the front door is peeling, and the single car garage door is dented, giving the home an abandoned look. The front yard doesn't look much better. The yard hasn't been landscaped in years and just looks like patchy dirt and dead shrubs. I felt a little like that front yard today: broken, patchy, and a little dead on the inside. I turn away and get in the car without another glance.

We drive off to Eve's house, and I simply feel angry. I know the girls feel my mood bashing around in the car's small space, and they keep giving each other worried glances the entire way. I can't help it; I let my father beat me. Me, a grown man of nineteen, like I couldn't handle myself? How did I not see it coming? Now I am to live with my best friend's parents until who knows when? I just feel like a frustrated loser and that everyone around me is making me their charity case. As soon as I can, I'll find my own place and stop burdening others. I'm not their problem.

"Okay, you need to say something, Cam. You're freaking me out. What's up?" Eve asks, because if there's one thing I know about Eve, it's that she can't stand not knowing what's on some-one's mind. If she could have any superpower, I guarantee it would be telepathy.

"I guess I'm just, I dunno, wondering what to do next. I feel like a puzzle, and I don't know where any of the pieces go or how they're supposed to fit."

"Well, that's mighty bleak!" Eve blurts out with annoyed honesty.

"Yeah I know, but I can't help myself, Eve."

Eve hits the brakes hard, which jolts Alex and me to full attention.

"Listen, you're going to live with me and stop feeling sorry for yourself. You're a good guy and deserve to be happy, so stop wor-rying. We'll figure it out together! You have two weeks left before we have to start back at uni, and we're going to have fun, goddam-mit, so suck it up and give me a goddamn hug."

See what I mean about the hugging it out thing? I know better than to argue with Eve. I laugh and hug her over the backseat. Somehow she always makes me feel better, even though she pretty much bitches me out. I suppose that is for my own good.

CHAPTER THIRTEEN

EVE

Cam really settles into his new surroundings nicely over the next few weeks. It probably helps that I have known him for so many years. He practically grew up with me anyway.

He became part of our family without ever asking to be. My parents loved him from the moment they met him, mostly because they knew he was a good guy and wouldn't try anything "funny" with their daughter the first chance he got her alone. Cam is indeed a gentleman, without ever even having the role model. I guess his father was a good example of what not to do.

Cam and I aren't like that anyway. Sure, we had flirtatious moments back in high school, but it was innocent stuff, child's play. I knew Cam had a crush on me years ago; I had one too, but I never told him, because I liked him so much I never wanted to lose him. *Relationships ruin the best friendships.*

I feel better with him in the house. Knowing he is near helps me forget about my little "dilemma." I have almost begun to think I'm fine. Winston hasn't taken another bite out of me, and I haven't had any more weird reactions to food and no crazy quick-healing thing. Although, I am secretly interested in seeing if it will work again. But that is crazy because I will have to cut myself, and that in itself is madness, so I ignore the urge.

I head downstairs and find Cam in the kitchen reading the

newspaper. His dark hair is getting a tad too long, and it covers his face while he reads.

"Hey, Cam, do you wanna head down to the lake for a bit? Alex called earlier to see if we wanted to go for a walk and get some ice cream," I say.

"Yeah sure, I could use some fresh air." He nods, wiping the hair away from his face.

Hopefully, this will lighten his mood. Most of our high school days were spent by the lake after school, or at lunch, or when we skipped class together. This was "our spot," and something about it comforted us. We could be big kids there and escape the world for a little bit.

I often thought I would love to get married by the lake because it has such a special place in my heart. Some of our best conversations were held here. Cam and Alex shared their dreams with me, their fears, and their gossip.

I feel very lucky to have Cam and Al along for the ride; they make being me easier because they love me unconditionally.

As I think of them, I feel a sudden twinge of shame. I haven't told them the truth about my arm or the strange dreams or the incident with Winston the other night. I haven't told them a single thing, and I always tell them everything! I will have to do it eventually, but with all that Cam has been through lately, now just doesn't seem the time.

***

I love our small town, because, within mere seconds, we arrive at the lake where Alex is already waiting in our usual spot with her roller blades on.

"Hey guys, nice of you to join me," she says sarcastically. She hates when we are late, one of her biggest pet peeves.

"We're only five minutes late, Al. Don't get your panties twisted," I say, sticking my tongue out at her.

I look around at the water glistening in the sunlight. It is a gorgeous day, and it seems like everyone is here soaking in the rays.

Once we have our ice cream, we begin to walk and reminisce about our trip to Egypt and how amazing it was, for the most part. I'm grateful they don't bring up "the incident" and even more grateful that they haven't asked to see how my scar is healing.

It's only a few days until we will have to head back to university and be back in our dorm rooms. Thinking of the dorm makes me moody because the space is so crammed, and last year I had to argue with administration just so I could room with Alex.

Guelph University is just under an hour away, so our hometown is never too far to visit on weekends, but it still seems like such a big city compared to Little Lake.

I force myself to stop worrying about it. It isn't time yet, and I'm determined to enjoy my last few hours before I have to snap back to reality and hit the books.

Out of the corner of my eye, I see Cam pull something out of his pocket. I watch intently as he retrieves it and then shouts with delight, "Oh my God, a super flyer! Where did you get that?"

Cam gives his best "aren't I awesome" smirk.

It is nice to see him acting a bit more like himself.

"I found it online a few months ago, thought it would be good for a laugh. I haven't played with one of these since grade nine; it was a fad for like a month, and then everyone moved onto something new."

Alex's eyes light up. "So are we gonna play or what?"

It seems like a good idea to me, and I think I smile so big that I time travel back to being about seven years old. I can be such a big kid sometimes; even my parents often ask if I will ever grow up. *Well nope, probably not.*

We are only playing for about ten minutes before we start to get a bit too competitive with our throws. I see Cam get this look in his eyes like he's thinking, *That's it, you're done for,* and since I don't enjoy losing, I give Cam an equally evil stare back.

"You're going down, son!" I spit out at Cam.

He winds up his muscular arm, and when he lets go, it feels like a torpedo is coming for me. *Damn boys and their upper body strength, curse him!* I squeal a bit out of fear but keep running backward towards the road, determined to get it no matter how far it goes. It feels like I am running backward for hours in slow motion, and then the fun ends.

It all happens so fast. All I remember is hearing some screaming and then hitting the ground like a ton of bricks. I can taste the asphalt, and then I continue rolling until I face the sky.

Shit, I was on the road. How did I not notice I had left grass? I was so focused on my mission and didn't think of cars. I feel a bit of pain and can't move. I begin to panic.

A man gets out of his van and runs to check on me. I catch him eyeing my injuries, and he looks about ready to throw up. *That bad, huh?* is all I can think.

The next faces I see above me are Cam and Alex. They look horrified. Cam is on his knees assessing my injuries in seconds.

He takes a look at my leg. "Okay, it's broken. Don't move, Eve. I can see the bone. How does the rest of you feel?"

I lift my head slightly and look down towards my shin, where I see bone jutting out. *Oh ew, why did I bother to look?*

"I don't feel anything, Cam. Honestly, I don't feel hurt. Could be the shock?" Then my mind trails off with a sudden crash of terror. What if I start to heal rapidly around all these people? I don't want to be a lab rat. No one can know about me.

I feel my bone snap back into place; it is an odd sensation, and I scream. This causes Alex and Cam to look at the injury that is now healing. I see their stunned and confused faces.

Okay, Eve, think. Think quickly. Cam will insist on going to the hospital, so I should ask Alex to take hold of the situation. She'll listen to me.

In a desperate attempt to get out of sight, I sit up and grab Alex by her tee-shirt.

"Alex, I will explain to you later, but cover my leg and get me out of here."

She is a bit shaken by my sudden recovery but nods. Without any hesitation, she takes off her tee-shirt so she's only wearing her tank top. She quickly ties it around my healing leg so people can't see it. *God bless her.*

Alex then runs towards her car, keys in hand, ready to go. Cam looks furious.

He whispers to me as the man who hit me paces back and forth, his hands tearing at his hair. "What the hell are you doing? Where are you sending Alex? We have to get you some help."

I knew he'd say that, and I really need to keep him calm. "Cam, I know you don't get it right now, but I need to leave. I'm going to be okay."

When our whispered conversation ends, the driver who hit me is still freaking out, wondering what to do. I can tell he's never hit anyone, probably never been in a car accident either. I look at him and try to smile.

"Sir, I'm fine. Don't worry, please. My friends here are going to take me to get checked out, but I think I'm good, so I want you to forget this ever happened, okay? I can see you're the type who will worry, but honestly, I'm fine. I'm going to get up now."

I'm not sure I've been very convincing because he still looks like a wreck. Perhaps if I'm able to walk away, he won't worry. I wink at Cam so he'll get the hint to help me up. He does so with a snarl. *Sorry, Cam, you'll understand later.*

I am up in an instant; I feel nothing but a bit of tingling. The man takes a deep breath of relief, realizing that it can't be that bad if I can walk away from it. I can see he is still having a mental debate, though. He knows how hard he hit me and knows deep down inside that this can't be, but he accepts it because he very much wants this to be true.

"Miss, here is my business card. Please contact me if you need anything. I sure hope you are okay." He looks a little relieved, almost happy that he will be able to walk away from this consequence free. He is most likely thinking, *How can I be this fortunate?*

I take his card and thank him. I am even more grateful when he gets in his car and drives away. Alex comes back seconds later. We get in her car and drive swiftly to my house.

***

They help me to my room, and I am thankful that they haven't spoken a word. I sit on my bed and lift my shirt to see bruises that look more like a few weeks old rather than fresh. I grimace a bit as I lower the shirt again. The rapid healing hurts quite a bit but probably not as much as real broken bones.

Alex and Cam look disgusted and intrigued. How am I going to explain this? I guess I should start from the beginning.

Cam finds a chair in the corner of my room suitable to sit and scowl in. I don't have to be a mind reader to know what he is thinking; he is wondering how long I have been guarding this secret. I never meant to hurt them with my secret keeping; I only meant to keep my own ass safe.

I take a deep breath, and I'm not sure what will come out of my mouth next. The words in my head jumble together, trying to form sentences that make sense. I decide not to look at Cam for the moment. I turn to look at Alex instead.

I try to start my story. "I don't really know what's wrong with me. I started to notice something was wrong when I got hurt back in Egypt."

I take another deep breath and continue. "I remember feeling weird, hot and dizzy and just not myself. I just figured that was shock from my injuries. You know you don't get bitten every day by some unknown thing. My wounds healed really quickly. I was hoping you guys would never notice, but that was stupid. I should have just told you right away."

I roll my sleeve up carefully and show them the part of my arm where the bite was, where a scar should be, and yet there is my exposed arm, simply flawless.

Alex comes in for a close-up look and touches my arm in disbelief. "I can't believe I never noticed. How quickly did it heal?"

I am so grateful they haven't stormed out on me yet, although Cam looks about ready to explode. I turn to look at Alex again.

"The marks were gone the day we left Egypt. I hadn't really checked my bandages much after the incident, so it could have been sooner. I don't know."

I sense Cam and Alex searching their minds for questions they can ask next, and not surprisingly at all, Cam is up at bat next.

"I'm not going to pretend I'm not upset you didn't tell us, Eve. We could have figured this out together. I'm not sure you ever would have told us the truth if not for something like today happening. Maybe you are dangerous or a danger to yourself." He shakes his head. "We head back to school soon. I want you to tell Doctor August everything. I have a feeling he can help us."

I chuckle a little bit. "Us? You mean me. I think I should be making the decisions here, Cameron." He hates when I call him by his full name, but I'm miffed and I want him to know it!

"If I go to Doctor August, how do you know he won't make me his little lab rat? I'm scared, Cam. I don't know what I am right now, but it's not normal. I don't feel very human. Do you really think telling people is the best thing to do here?"

I may have raised my voice a little, perhaps a bit on the hysterical side. I don't mean to act the diva today, but I feel justified.

Cam's dark eyebrows return to their scowl, which isn't much of a scowl, to begin with. He is gorgeous. Not that he thinks so. He looks more like he is doing a high fashion pose, but I get his meaning.

"Cam, do you understand what I'm saying here?"

He doesn't answer. Instead, he turns towards the door. *Okay, now who is being a diva?*

"Eve, talk to me when you're thinking a little clearer. You need help, and for that, you're going to need to start trusting people. You're right. What happened today isn't normal in the slightest, and who really knows how much worse it might get?" He looks away. "Hurt" is the best way to describe his expression.

Before I can apologize further, he takes his leave.

"He has a point, Eve. What do you really plan to do next? Keep covering up what's going on with you or actually seeking the truth and finding a cure? You have to do something. Let us help." I give her a nod of understanding because I'm tired of arguing my point and just want the confrontation to be over.

✳✳✳

Alex stays a bit longer. She decides to check my bruises and time my healing.

In the next hour, any evidence of my injuries is gone, and so is Alex.

I am alone. I guess it's a lot to process. They need their space as much as I do right now.

Cam has shut himself in the guest room, and my parents won't be home for a while. I take this opportunity to think about what I should do about my situation. I'm tired of feeling scared, and I should feel glad to finally share this secret with someone, but I only feel suffocating concern.

What if I am putting Cam and Alex in danger? What if I am dangerous?

I have been having very violent dreams, and although I'm not acting any differently, I do feel a building rage all the time. I've chalked it up to PMS, but I think it's beyond that. I don't know what exactly is happening to me. Cam is right: what if it gets worse and I start to hurt people? I can't predict what my body is capable of anymore, and that scares the hell out of me.

✳✳✳

Cam and Alex are still barely talking to me when it's time to drive back to campus. We at least decided on carpooling, and Alex graciously offered to drive.

I wait on the front porch with my luggage. I've already said bye to my parents and Winston, and I thought I would wait outside for Cam. When he meets me on the porch, he doesn't even glance my way. I feel invisible.

Alex arrives shortly and saves me from the awkwardness. She smiles from her car and yells out to me, "Eve, will you wipe that frown off? You're still alive, after all!"

Am I? Well at least Alex is acknowledging me; it's only Cam's silence that's killing me. I feel as though I might cry.

He was living in the same house with me but wouldn't look at me or speak to me. He would speak to my parents and then just look through me. Even my mother picked up on it but brushed it off as the "back to school blues."

As I load up the car with my stuff, I see my parents joining Cam on the porch. They wave goodbye to me, and I wave back. I can hear Cam thanking my parents for letting him stay. That makes me feel worse; my problem, not his aggressive alcoholic father, seems to be the biggest thing on his plate. Why does it feel like I am always hurting Cam?

I stand still, almost breathless, as he approaches the vehicle. He doesn't even glance up as he begins packing his things in the car. I wait for him to finish so he has his arms free, and then I tackle him with a hug, refusing to let go until his mood softens toward me.

I am desperate for him to acknowledge me. He has no idea how much I need him right now. He doesn't hug back at first, but then I hear the defeat in his heavy sigh, and he wraps his arms around me in an act of forgiveness. Cam gets my message, and I know it will be smoother sailing now.

Alex gives a smug little smile, shakes her head, and prepares to drive. Her body language tells me that she thinks it is about time someone breaks the ice, and we are all glad for it. The energy in the car feels lighter as we wave goodbye to Little Lake and head towards campus.

This is our second year of university. I don't know what

possessed us to follow each other into the same program. I will admit that Alex and I have always dreamed of being famous archaeologists like Indiana Jones or Laura Croft, but I always thought Cam got into archaeology because of his crush on me; perhaps I was wrong about his motives. He does enjoy being out at the dig site, maybe even more than I do.

I'm not sure where my degree will lead eventually, but Alex very badly wants to become a professor someday. She loves the ancient world, and I know she'll do a great job teaching it in the future.

My heart isn't in teaching. I want the adventure aspect more than anything. I want to be out there in the field and traveling the world. I know Cam wants that too, but his father holds him back. He is always worried about who will take care of him when he is away. I guess that won't be a problem anymore.

Out of all of us, I think Cam could be famous if he really went for it. He has the looks, and he always knows what to say. I always tease him about having his own talk show. He will be a cross between Dr. Oz and Maury Povich. Since Cam's a bit of a health nut, he can have shows about eating organic food instead of poison, avoiding sunlight and living under a rock, preventing cancer with mind powers, and all that dumb stuff.

My point of view always angers Cam, who is a more open-minded individual. I guess I'm just a cynic or too small town. I happen to think if you're meant to die, it will happen no matter what sort of prevention strategies you adopt.

I guess Cam and I will always butt heads. It has become part of our friendship. Every now and then, Cam and I will have some friendly competition going. We're both fairly ambitious types. We bet on who will have the highest marks each term, who can swim faster, who can run faster, who can eat faster. Sometimes it gets to the point of ridiculous, and all Alex can do is shake her head. But what can I say? It keeps things fun. If you can't laugh and be a huge goof, what's life really about anyway?

I look out the car window, twirling my mother's locket in my hand. This necklace always makes me feel calmer. I like to think it brings me luck, and I've cherished it every day since my mother got better. I shove it back under my shirt when I feel a sudden pain in my gut.

My stomach seems to be acting up. I remember having some fruit for breakfast and feeling great after. So what can it be?

Alex looks in her mirror and notices the grimace on my face.

"You okay back there? You're looking a little green."

Cam swings around immediately to look at me. His face creases with worry. Why do I have to keep worrying everyone lately? Jeez!

"Alex, can you pull over? I think I'm going to throw up." And as soon as Alex stops the car, I hurdle over to the nearest clearing and empty my guts out.

I remember feeling this way before. When we arrived home from Egypt, I had the same reaction to my mom's cooking. I threw up wonderful food for no reason. It was like my body was rejecting it, and once again it seems like my body isn't satisfied. Almost as though it needs some new fuel.

I have been feeling a bit weak lately and wonder if I need an extra little something in my diet now that I have this "rapid healing" ability. Maybe multivitamins?

Cam comes running out to check on me. I am glad he does because I can't feel my legs; there's no strength left in me to get up. I'm kneeling there until Cam lifts me back into the car.

CHAPTER FOURTEEN

CAM

Eve sleeps the rest of the way. While Eve snoozes, Alex and I talk about what's happening to her. Our theories range from normal—a virus in her system or radiation poisoning—to the crazy, such as a monster biting her and her transforming into one by the next full moon. I think we might be watching too many horror movies, though.

The only thing we know for sure is that something bit her, and now it is making her sick.

"This is all too strange, Al," I say because I don't know what else to say. We can't Google symptoms and find a diagnosis or take her to a doctor. I think the doctor would faint.

Eve is probably right; they'll make her into their little test dummy. The healing quickly trick is odd but intriguing. Who will be able to resist that? They might try and cultivate her blood to find cures to illnesses, which would be a horrible way to live. I can suddenly understand Eve's fear and understand why she might not want to tell anyone. But I still feel that if anyone can help, it is Dr. August.

Alex and I argue about telling Dr. August. I want to do it immediately, but Alex thinks we should leave it to Eve. Eventually, we agree that if Eve doesn't end up telling Dr. August, then we will. We need to get her some help; she hasn't been looking too great lately.

I glance at her lying down in the back seat. She has dark circles under her eyes and seems to have lost weight too. She is starting to look a bit like death, for lack of a better word.

Lucky for us, Dr. August knows all about viruses, and if that's what this is, then I'm sure he can cure it.

He has studied not only plagues of the past but the more recent H1N1, or swine flu, as some know it. If Dr. August can't help us, no one can. I feel we can trust him. I just hope my gut feeling isn't wrong.

CHAPTER FIFTEEN

EVE

I'm still not feeling much better since my little barf session in the car. Alex had to unpack all my things for me. Luckily, the school honoured our request to share a room, and she will be my roomie this year.

All I can do is watch as she sets up our dorm. I am in no shape to put clothes in drawers or even fit sheets to the bed. I feel a bit like a corpse, and Alex says I look like one too. I guess I am looking pretty pale these days, which worries me because I usually have a nice olive complexion.

I lay on my stomach, watching Alex as she starts putting up some really cute wall stickers that look like fancy chandeliers. The room is starting to feel like a five-star hotel.

Once Alex is done playing maid and interior decorator to the stars, she asks if I want to grab some lunch. The thought nauseates me, but I suppose I should at least try to eat something.

***

Cam meets us in the cafeteria. It is a big place with many tables and couches. The entire space is still pretty empty. It will most likely fill in by Monday when all of the students return from their summer holidays.

The food is always pretty good here. I often hear horror stories about the crap they serve people in cafeterias, things that look like they might already be chewed, but this place has some of the best pizza ever, and I love their chicken alfredo pasta.

My stomach lurches at the thought of food. I'm not sure if it's hunger or nausea. Cam heads over to select his food first and returns with a heaping pile of garlicky alfredo pasta. The scent is so strong that I decide to get up and take a walk around. I will have to try to eat something eventually. It sucks watching other people eat when I'm not eating anything.

Alex picks up a big Greek salad, and I finally decide on a small turkey sandwich.

I carefully take one bite at a time, hoping it will stay down. Thankfully, it does.

"So Alex and I were talking in the car about seeing Dr. August soon. I took the liberty of calling him when I got to my dorm room, but he's still in Egypt. His secretary said he's extended his trip and won't be back for at least another two weeks."

I drop my sandwich. "But what about his classes? That's not like him."

Cam shrugs. "I don't really know what to think of it. I hope he's okay, but I'm more worried you. If you get worse, what will we do?"

Alex frowns into her bowl of salad; she's been quieter these days, probably just worried.

"I'll be fine, guys. I get a bit of nausea sometimes, but I get over it. It's only happened after my healing trick, so I don't know if there is a connection, but maybe."

I don't really know what else to say, so I try to change the subject to our classes and Cam's stalker for the year.

Her name is Claire, and she's a little quirky but undeniably pretty. She's usually in at least two of Cam's classes—purposefully or accidentally, we don't know—but she always sits next to him and tries to chat him up, which makes Cam's classes quite difficult to focus in.

Alex and I laugh at the thought, and Cam grimaces and blushes at the mention of her.

"So you going to hide in the back again this year, Cam? Or pretend Alex is your girlfriend again?"

Alex rolls her eyes and inquires, "Why don't you just ask her out already? Maybe she'll leave you alone when she realizes how much of an idiot you are."

Cam gives us both the finger but smiles along with it, which doesn't make its meaning that effective.

Once we finish eating, we tidy up our table and leave the cafeteria in higher spirits.

✳✳✳

Alex and I walk Cam to his dorm since it's on the way back to ours. When we get to his room, his new roommate Mark, an adorable black man, very much an Usher duplicate, answers in nothing but a towel.

He is ridiculously attractive with abs that won't quit. Alex and I are barely able to muster a greeting. *Oh my, God, we are such nerds.* He smiles back at Alex, which makes her cheeks hot. "Sorry, ladies didn't know I would have company right now. Just got out of the shower."

He doesn't look very sorry to us. He seems like the type of guy who loves to flaunt his physique, and I can't blame him. He obviously worked hard for those abs. Wait, is that a sixteen-pack?

After his greeting, he looks to Cam. "Hey man, you had

someone try and reach you three times while you were out. Someone from the Guelph Police Department. You in some kind of trouble? None of my business, but they asked me to pass that on and tell you to give them a call." And with that, Mark decides to go finish his cleansing ritual.

Cam turns a little pale. *Wow, now we match,* I think, but this is serious and not a time for sarcasm. Alex and I both know this has something to do with his dad.

We stay while Cam dials. When the phone begins to ring, we hold our breaths.

"Hello, this is Cameron Jackson. I received a call." He pauses to listen for a moment and then replies, "Yes, that's my father... mmm hmm...yes."

It sure does suck only hearing half of a conversation.

"What do you mean, gone?" Cam asks the officer on the phone, and then he shuts his eyes and looks unsteady.

His next words explain it all. "Why would anyone let him out on bail anyway? He's a danger to himself and others!" Then Cam slams the phone down with venom.

We wait while he takes a few deep breaths. I know he will tell us what the hell is going on, but he needs to calm down first.

After a few more big breaths, Cam blurts, "He's out. Someone paid his bail. I don't know who because he doesn't exactly have friends. And the best part...he's gone missing. Yup, disappeared, right under their incompetent noses!"

I think my mouth drops open to the floor. "What?" is all I can piece together to say in my growing tornado of anger.

Alex approaches to give Cam a hug, but he brushes her away. I get the message and take Alex's arm, leading her towards the door.

Before we leave, she looks back at Cam. "We'll call you

tomorrow, Cam. So sorry about all this. We love you." Alex sort of squeaks the last part, clearly hurt about her hug being rejected, as I shut Cam's door.

I get angrier and angrier as we walk to our dorm. My legs somehow pick up speed, and I don't realize it until I hear Alex, who is very far behind me.

"Eve, slow down. I can't keep up!"

When we arrive back at our dorm room, I throw myself onto the bed. I know I can't do much for Cam right now, so I force my eyes shut and try to calm down.

I hear Alex get in the shower after awhile and hope we can both relax soon.

Sleep comes quickly, but so do my nightmares. I dream that I am a lion, ripping crowds of people into pieces until my hunger is satisfied.

The bizarre thing about my nightmares is that they seem so real. Often times I wake to the taste of blood in my mouth.

I never dreamed much before the trip to Egypt, and I never really experienced recurring nightmares, but these vivid dreams have now become part of my new sleep ritual.

CHAPTER SIXTEEN

ALEX

I wake in the middle of the night to Eve growling. Her snarls sound like a wolf gnawing at something. I decide to tiptoe over to her and poke her shoulder.

"Eve? You awake?" She doesn't answer, but the growling grows a bit quieter now.

It still terrifies me, and I can't really get back to sleep. I escape to the washroom to pee, glad for the moment of silence. I wash my face, which still aches with sleep, and I feel some relief.

When I return to bed, Eve is gone.

I panic and call her name a few times, knowing full well she can't hide in such a small space. It is very obvious she isn't here. I look around for clues.

"The window!" I pant as I notice that it's wide open.

My mind skips to the worst-case scenario.

"Oh my God! She jumped out the fucking window?"

I am afraid to look down but force myself to glance after counting to ten.

When I stick my head out the window, there is no body lying below in the bushes, but I can see a large dent in the bush directly below our window.

"Oh no! What is she doing?"

I know she survived the jump since she heals so quickly now, but why wouldn't she just use the door? Perhaps she is testing her new skills? I think it more likely that she has gone completely insane.

I don't know what else to do, so I call Cam.

"Cam...Cam...it's me, Alex. I need your help. I think Eve jumped out the window, and I don't know where she's gone to. I'm going to go look for her. Please come along. I'm scared."

I can hear his voice tremble on the other end. "Okay, meet me outside your dorm building. I'm coming now."

I get off the phone and dress quickly. I know I have a flashlight packed somewhere, so I rummage around until I find it. Then I run for the stairs and descend as quickly as I can.

Cam is there in record time, and I can see why. He is shirtless with his pajama pants on. The only item he'd managed to slip on were his running shoes.

"Really? You couldn't find a second to throw a shirt on?"

He shrugs. He knows his outfit is a bit ridiculous and apologizes but adds, "Hey, we have bigger things to worry about than a missing shirt. Let's have a look at the bushes below the window. We can start there."

The bush is almost completely flattened. Dark spots cover a few of the leaves, and there are trickles of a dark substance on the ground. I gasp, unable to conceal my dread; a trail of blood lay directly under our dorm window. This is going to be pretty hard to explain.

"Al, let's follow the blood. Maybe we'll find Eve at the end of it."

"Sounds like a good idea, Cam, but what if what we find isn't Eve anymore?" It hurts me to say it, but it might be true.

"Alex, that's ridiculous!" he retorts, but I don't think I'm being unreasonable with my claim. She might end up hurting us.

"Cam, you've seen what I've seen. She's changing."

Cam shakes his head furiously. "So what are you saying? That we don't bother looking for her? That we hide out in our rooms? This is Eve we're talking about. We need to find her. Come on..." He begins to follow the blood trail, and I have no choice but to follow.

We follow drips of blood for about five minutes, which leads us to the parking lot. I notice this is where the blood trail stops.

"Eve must have fully healed by the time she got here." Cam nods, looking on with despair. Well, this makes the search and rescue mission more difficult.

Somehow I am wrong; another obstacle appears out of nowhere.

"Cam? Oh my God, where is your shirt? Did you get mugged?" Claire quickly has her concerned and lust-filled fingers all over Cam.

Claire is our dorm leader and Cam's crazed stalker. She's not afraid to show her affection for Cam, and Cam has no trouble showing his disgust for her. Yet it never deters her, not once. *What horrible, horrible timing for her to be out and about.*

Claire is not known for keeping her mouth shut, and who knows what state we might find Eve in out here. *We do not need this right now! But wait! What is she doing out here anyway at this time?* Claire isn't exactly a party animal, so I decide to ask her just that.

"Claire, what brings you out here at this time of night? You okay? Cam's fine. We just decided to go for a walk, couldn't sleep."

She eyes me suspiciously. Damn Eve for telling her that I am Cam's girlfriend. She probably would like to see me drop dead. Claire probably thinks we're on a lovers stroll and most likely won't leave because she's just so nosy and jealous.

"Oh, I'm just checking out a noise complaint," she says smugly. I'm not sure I believe her. She always seems to know where Cam is at any given moment. I often wonder if she implanted a tracker on him when he was sleeping.

Once she's answered my question, she turns her attention back to Cam.

"Hey, Cam, since you're here, I just wanted to let you know that they are showing some old sci-fi flicks for movie night next week. I thought you would love that. Wanna go?"

Man, she's blunt! How did she know Cam liked sci-fi movies? Weird.

Cam just gazes on in horror; he needs to say something to get her off our backs. He looks at me, and we start having an eye conversation. I'm trying to smile and hint that he should say yes to her proposal, and then maybe she'll leave satisfied.

Cam is staring daggers at me, showing me how much he does not want to do this. He eventually starts to plead with his eyes, almost like he's saying, "Find another way," but I can't think of another way.

I pinch some of his exposed skin, and he yells, "Yeaaaahsss."

He rubs the sore spot I've created and continues, "I mean yes, Claire, that would be nice."

Claire gives us a bigger grin than I think her mouth is capable of; it's a little creepy, to be honest.

"That's great! I'm so excited. I will pop by your dorm and pick you up next week. The movie marathon starts at 7 pm."

With that, Claire is off. I suppose she doesn't want to leave any opportunity for Cam to change his mind. She prances away victorious, and I try not to laugh at Cam's misfortune. I should just be thankful she's gone.

"Well, that was close." I look at Cam, and he looks about ready to throw up. "Sorry, Cam, what else could we do? Maybe the date won't be too bad."

We sit in the parking lot for a few silent moments after that, trying to hatch a plan.

"What do we do next?" I shrug in defeat. I can't think of anything other than continuing to sit here, waiting for Eve to hopefully appear.

After a few more silent moments, Cam comes up with a plan. "I think we should get in your car and drive around campus for clues."

I grab the keys out of my pocket, and we run towards my car. Maybe we can still find Eve before she decides to do anything stupid. What if she gets curious about healing after a train hits her? Maybe she went to the tracks to try it out? But I keep those thoughts to myself. There is no need for Cam to deal with my epic paranoia too. He's been through enough already tonight. I giggle to myself, thinking about his upcoming date with Claire; I can't help it even though it's not the best time.

"Shut up, Alex," he snorts, and I comply.

We drive around for what seems like hours. We stopped a few times to check out some noises we heard. None of the noises were Eve, though. We did, however, find a really cute bunny and a really awful-smelling skunk.

We return to park my car and, without any further ideas, head back to our dorms in defeat. I pray Eve will return to her bed on her own.

As I lock the doors to my car, I hear something that sounds like a growl.

"Cam, do you hear that?" I look over at him, and he is staring at something in the distance that I can't see.

"Yup, I heard that alright."

I grab my flashlight and point it in the direction of the noise. Something speeds out of view hastily, not wanting to be seen by the light.

"Holy shit, what was that?" Cam yells as he returns to my side.

But I don't know what it is. "Cam, let's get a closer look. It could be her."

Cam remains right behind me; he knows we can't forgive ourselves if we don't at least check it out.

The snarling gets louder as we approach, which makes the flashlight shake in my hands.

Finally, we reach a car where the noise seems to originate from. Whatever "it" is decided to hide behind a pretty sexy-looking BMW.

Cam grabs the flashlight out of my hand, and I don't put up a fight. I don't want to be the one to do the big reveal anyway. He puts his finger to his lips to signal silence. Then he starts to count up with his fingers.

"One…two…three…" and Cam quickly shines the light around the car.

My heartbeat picks up speed and then relaxes when I see that nothing is there.

I am a little confused and even more afraid because now it is silent again. Where did this thing go?

I shine the light around the parking lot a few more times but find nothing.

"Fine!" I scream and kick the stupid BMW out of frustration, exhaustion, and just plain worry.

Cam takes my arm and leads me back to my dorm as I sob the whole way. He can tell I've reached my limits.

I halt when I notice someone sitting slumped against the building's main doors. I grab Cam's arm to steady myself. The figure looks contorted and motionless. I can't see a face in the darkness. Cam decides to shine the flashlight towards the figure. When the light rests on Eve's face, I lose it. Tears roll down my face. I feel joy since we've found her, but terror since I have no idea what is wrong with her or if I can even help.

As I glance at her face, I know it's her, but something's off. Her skin is a purple hue, and all the veins in her face appear swollen. Her mouth and clothing are covered in blood, but I'm not sure if it's hers.

Eve's eyes roll into the back of her head, and she begins spitting blood out of her mouth and breathing heavily as if she's been chased for miles.

My first thought is, *Oh my God, she's dying!* I want to hold her, but Cam restrains me.

"What the hell, Cam! Let me see if she's okay!" I push back.

"I'm worried you'll get hurt too. So excuse me if I'm being cautious," he spits back at me.

Suddenly, Eve flops lifelessly to the ground. I force my way out of Cam's arms and run to her. I grab her by the shoulders and pull her back to a seated position.

"Eve, look at me. What happened?" I'm tapping her cheek, pleading that she snap out of it, but she won't speak or look at me.

Her blank stare reminds me of something out of a horror movie. She looks into my eyes, but it's as if she doesn't know me. Her eyes look hungry, and her mouth contorts as more blood pours out of it. Before she can lunge at me, she goes limp and slumps to the ground once more. I don't know what to do, so I simply burst into tears.

"Alex, it's not that I'm insensitive, but this is not the best place for this. Quick, help me bring her to your room."

I nod and slide under one of Eve's armpits while Cam slides under the other.

Eve's feet barely touch the ground, and her head flops backward, giving the effect of a broken neck. I force myself to look away or I'll sob harder.

In the stairwell, Cam puts his ear to her chest, and his eyes grow wide.

"No heartbeat," he says with a whimper. He looks so tragic as he sweeps her into his arms and continues up to our room. I'm wearing a similar look as I stumble after them.

Once in the dorm room, he places Eve carefully in the bathtub and begins to wipe away the blood in her hair and her face and on her clothes. He does this gently like he's bathing a child.

Once Eve is cleaner, her face seems to settle into a more peaceful state. Cam tells me, "She's breathing." Eve is alive. Now all we have to do is wait.

Cam places her on her bed, and soon after that, we are all asleep. I hope this is all a nightmare and I'll wake up in the morning and find everything completely normal again, but I'm not sure normal is something I will ever experience again.

CHAPTER SEVENTEEN

EVE

I wake up with my eyelids feeling light as a feather and my body feeling energized and better than it has in weeks! I jump out of bed and stretch, ready for my day. As I look for some fresh clothes, I stumble upon Cam. He is sitting on the floor sleeping against the wall.

"Cam? What are you doing here?" My question makes him bolt upright, and he looks absolutely awestruck.

"Okay, really weird reaction, Camy. What the hell? Will you relax?"

Alex is now awake too, and she has much the same look on her face as Cam has.

"Okay guys, you're freaking me out." I give a fake shiver. "What's going on?"

Cam comes closer to me and, without a word, grabs my shirt and lifts it into my field of vision. I see that the shirt is stained crimson. A shriek of repulsion emerges from my chest, and I flee to the washroom.

"Oh my God, my clothes are covered in it. What the hell happened?"

I crouch into a corner of the bathroom and begin to rock back and forth, hoping it will jog my memory, but nothing is coming to me.

I feel Cam's big arms around me, and I ask him again, "What did I do?"

He whispers back, very gently patting my hand, "We were hoping you could tell us that."

I don't like being talked to like a kid.

"Why are you whispering? Speak up and bring me up to speed."

Cam rolls his eyes and continues. "We found you outside of the building covered in blood, and you had been gone for hours. We think you might have jumped out of your dorm room window to escape somewhere."

Oh no, this is getting bad.

I wish I can blame the memory loss on an entire bottle of vodka, but I haven't touched a drink since last term. Even then, I don't think I ever drank enough to erase an entire evening. I can't remember anything from when I shut my eyes last night to when I opened them this morning. I start to shake.

"Cam, I'm scared," is all I can say because I can't quite put everything I'm feeling into words right now. I sob and rock back and forth while Cam holds me.

✳✳✳

When I have enough courage to rise from the bathroom floor, I notice Alex looking out the window at a huge crowd gathered below.

"I guess they found all that blood from last night," Alex says through some nail biting.

I glance outside to observe a rather large puddle of blood and many splatters that form a trail towards the campus entrance.

"Oh, sweet Jesus! Please tell me that's all mine."

Alex looks at me. "We believe it's all yours. There wasn't anyone else with you. I think you ought to go shower and burn those clothes, Eve. The less evidence there is, the less there is to worry about."

Alex is right as usual, so I suck it up and try to pull myself together. I am starting to look forward to seeing Dr. August as soon as possible; this is getting out of hand now.

I head for the shower and throw my clothes into the metal garbage bin. I light a match that I normally use for my aromatherapy candles. Sweet Serenity Lavender sure won't help me now.

I gaze at the lit match and have an insatiable thought. I give into it. The match is now under one of my fingers, and I just let it burn. I cringe because I can still feel pain, even though I heal super well.

The match goes out, leaving me with a painful sore, which starts to heal and disappear immediately. Yeah, that's what I thought it would do. Just couldn't help checking it out.

I light another match and throw it into the garbage bin; the clothes catch fire rather quickly. As the small flames devour my shirt, I get in the shower and start to wash last night off my skin.

Blood pours off of me and down into the drain. I hope to hell it's mine, but how can I be sure?

CHAPTER EIGHTEEN

ALEX

While Eve is showering, I try to keep busy. I clean our room, because whenever I'm agitated, the first thing I do is pick up some cleaning products. I find cleaning soothing.

As I Windex our full-length mirror, Cam watches the crowd below our window. He mentions that police officers are checking out the scene, taking pictures, collecting evidence, and beginning to clean up. I try not to listen too closely or I may have a heart attack. I just pray that none of this will connect to Eve.

It is scary knowing that my friend is in trouble and I can't even protect her from herself.

As if I'm not agitated enough, the phone rings and makes me leap half a foot off the ground. I pick it up reluctantly. "Hello?"

Cam gazes over at me, his eyes begging to know who it is. "It's Eve's mom," I whisper as I cover the receiver.

Cam walks off to the other end of the room, muttering sarcastically, "Fantastic!"

Mrs. Brenner's voice is smooth and sweet as she delivers her news. "Hi, Alex honey, I'm afraid I have some bad news. Well, I guess it depends on how you look at it. Is Camy there with you?"

I make a face, which makes Cam look worried. I try to change it, but it's too late. It's obvious that this can't be good.

I hand Cam the phone and wait for the aftermath. This day really can't get any better.

After saying hello and listening for a few seconds, Cam begins to fight back tears.

Oh no, Cam never cries. I immediately go to him; he pushes me away, and I resort to sitting near him and waiting until he's ready for my support.

He covers his face, trying to conceal his pain and his tears. I wish I knew what the news is. The suspense is killing me.

I take the phone from him once I realize he's in too rough a state to continue talking to Mrs. Brenner.

"Hi, Jane, it's me again. Cam needs a minute. What can I do?"

Mrs. Brenner exhales a large sigh. "There is nothing to do. Next will be the funeral arrangements. Alex, his dad was found outside of his house in pieces. It's like some animal got hold of him. What animal does that? It's some kind of monster." I hear her choke back a few of her own tears.

I breathe unevenly and ask my next question. "Are they certain it was an animal? Is it possible he was murdered?" I'm not sure I want to know anymore. My hands shake as I wait for her response.

"Between you and me, I really don't think the cops will look too far into this. Henry wasn't a very good man. No one in town liked him much. So it would be a rather large list of suspects if anyone even cared to pursue it. They won't suspect Cam because he has an alibi. He's been at school, and you ladies can vouch for that."

"So that's it then?" I say with mixed relief and nausea.

"I think the case is closed. We're just trying to help with the funeral arrangements now. We realize this is a lot for Cam, so tell him not to worry. Momma Brenner will handle everything."

That woman must be some kind of angel.

"Thanks, Jane. I will talk to him when he's a little more stable. Bye." I hang up with a whimper. I don't think Cam has made the connection yet, and I am thankful for that. It will be too much for him to handle right now.

He is crumpled up on Eve's bed with his head in his hands. "Cam, I'm so sorry," is all I can think to say. They are probably some of the most useless words at a time like this, but I just want him to know I care.

He looks up at me and seems as lost as a five-year-old in a department store.

"I know he was a horrible, horrible man, and I'm stupid, so stupid for being upset right now. I just can't help it. He was all I had left, you know? He was still my father. Now I'm really alone. I have nothing."

Cam doesn't cry anymore, and he doesn't speak. He simply gets up and leaves.

I don't chase after him. I know he probably needs a long walk and then something to punch. I don't feel the need to be the second item on that list.

My thoughts are now back on Eve. Why isn't she done showering yet? We really need to talk. I hope she can remember something from last night. She needs to tell me she hasn't done this, but I feel very secure in the knowledge I possess. I just really hope I am wrong.

CHAPTER NINETEEN

EVE

I finally find the courage to step out of the bathroom and out of my pity party momentarily. As I exit, I find Alex lying on her bed staring at the ceiling. I notice that Cam is gone, and I get this strange vibe that something more is up.

I sit next to Alex, about to ask my first string of questions, but then there is a knock at the door. Our eyes dart towards the door simultaneously. I'm only in a towel, but I can give less of a shit right now. I stomp towards the door and pull it open so fast I think I startle Claire Madison.

Our snooty, prissy, stalker Dorm Leader—or Overlord, as I like to call her—stands before me. Just the look of her makes me ill. She always has a smug smile or a know-it-all grin on her face.

What a bitch!

"What's up, Claire?" I ask as impatiently as possible.

I feel Alex come up behind me in her watchful way. I know she is making sure I won't say or do anything stupid.

Claire still seems a bit stunned as I tap my foot, maybe by my tone or how viciously I opened the door. I really just want to slam the door in her face.

"Um, yes hi. Just wanted to check in on you ladies. I'm sure you've heard all the commotion downstairs? Quite a scene, huh? Well, I'm glad you ladies are okay."

Sure she is. I roll my eyes right in front of her.

She's not turning to leave, so I'm guessing she wants to say more. *Just great!*

"Is Cam here, by any chance? I wanted to drop off the sci-fi movie night flier for him. I checked his dorm, but he wasn't there."

What a creeper. She has no shame.

I grab the flier out of her hand and tell her, "Yup, I will absolutely make sure Cam gets this. Thanks so much."

I'm about to shut the door when I see her beginning to sniff the air.

What the hell is she doing? I raise an eyebrow and look at Alex. She shrugs.

Claire continues to sniff the air until she arrives at the bathroom door. She turns around and crosses her arms at us. "You ladies know the rules of this dorm, right?"

Oh, there is that smug-as-shit look again. I could just tear her face off.

"Why do I smell smoke coming from your bathroom? Smoking inside the dorm rooms is a safety hazard and is prohibited!"

My blood is boiling, and Alex knows that I'm about to flip out, which is why she's holding my arm in a very beseeching way.

Sorry, Alex, I have my limits!

"Okay, Claire bear, it's an aromatherapy candle, and you can bite me! I know you're hoping to find something scandalous, but you won't, okay?! Now leave before I…"

Claire only smiles more when I say this. "Before you do what, exactly? I'm just following protocol, and you just gave me a reason to watch you closer."

She turns to leave, but before her grand exit, she adds a platinum blonde hair flip and throws us a quick line.

"Oh and ladies, Cam really shouldn't be sleeping over. I better not find him here again. This is a ladies' only dormitory. You could be expelled, you know?"

With the final word, she makes her way out the door and down the hall.

She may not turn around or care, but I still yell some choice words after her. One of my favourites is "stupid tits." Not very mature, I admit, but I have never been the most mature person.

I know Claire doesn't want Cam here because she is a jealous psycho who doesn't want anyone else to have him.

Alex looks at me, horrified. "Was that all very necessary, Eve? I mean, we're already in a heap of shit over here. Do we need more enemies? Do we?"

I can see the truth in what she is saying and feel a little bad, but only slightly.

"Sorry, Alex, I'll try to control my temper a bit better next time. Why did she stop by looking for Cam, anyway?"

Alex bites her lip. "Well, he's sort of going on a date with her next week."

I think my head nearly pops off my shoulders.

"What?!" I exclaim in total shock.

Alex waves her hands in a "keep it down" manner.

"When we were looking for you last night, she showed up and wouldn't leave until Cam promised her some one-on-one time. He made the supreme sacrifice."

I slap my forehead in disbelief. "Oh, Al, how could you let him do that for me? Poor guy has to go on a date with his crazy stalker? Really!? Oh, we're terrible friends."

Alex hugs me with a bit of a chuckle. "Well, Cam's an extremely good friend, if you think about it... Look, Eve, let's forget about Claire for a second. We have more important things to talk about.

For one, do you remember anything about last night yet?"

I close my eyes and try to remember. I squeeze my brain hard, but all I can see is a vague image of me running. I can't remember a location or anything.

"No hun, I don't remember anything yet."

Alex looks at me, a bit flustered. "Well, I hope you remember soon. I really think you might have done something horrible last night, and I hope it's not true."

"Like what, Al?"

She looks at the floor and chooses her next words carefully. "Eve, I got a call this morning from your mom. She said Cam's dad is dead. Some animal attacked him and tore him apart last night."

The silence is heavy after that. I can understand what she's saying, but I don't want to believe it. I think I sit there horrified for a long time.

When I snap out of it, I ask, "Is my appointment still on with Dr. August tomorrow?"

She nods. "Yeah, it's still on alright. We need some answers before this all gets even worse. I sure hope he can help."

All I can think is, *Me too!*

CHAPTER TWENTY

The next day, I drag Eve to Dr. August's office. Cam doesn't join us; he doesn't feel like being around anyone yet. I understand but hope it will pass because I desperately need his help. I glance over at Eve before we enter the office. I can sense she's afraid to tell Dr. August anything, but we have to try something.

"Eve, it will be fine," I say, but she doesn't seem reassured.

Dr. August answers the door immediately and hugs us both like long lost family.

"Great to see you too, Doc," Eve says with a giggle, which I join in on.

Dr. August always knows how to keep things light, even things of a more serious nature.

"Come have a seat, ladies, and we'll talk about whatever you need to! I haven't seen you ladies in quite some time. We need to catch up!"

Eve looks a bit green. I don't think she'll start talking voluntarily, so I try to kick us off.

"Dr. August, we noticed something strange about Eve after we returned from Egypt. I'm sure you remember what happened to her?"

"Of course, I do! How is the scar doing, Eve? I hope it didn't heal badly. Let me see."

Eve immediately covers her arm with her hand, which leaves Dr. August with a baffled look on his face.

After a few awkward moments, I coax Eve to show him. She rolls up her sleeve and raises her arm to him without a word or any eye contact. Dr. August observes the arm carefully and touches its surface, almost intrigued. When he's done, he sits back in his chair with an air of disbelief.

"How did you manage to heal so quickly and without a mark to show for it? I must know your secret!" He says it half joking but must notice we don't share in his hilarity because he's quick to hide his smirk.

"Eve, talk to me. Tell me everything, dear."

She has trouble looking at him, but at least she starts talking.

"There's so much to say. Where do I begin?" She bites her lip nervously then begins her list of events. "I was healed by the plane ride home. It was so strange. Also, a few weeks back, I was hit by a car and experienced the same type of rapid healing. I burned my finger this morning and watched it heal faster than ever. I feel nauseous most days. When I eat I'm never full. Except for this morning, I felt great!"

I give Eve a look of disgust because I have a very good clue as to why she might be feeling so good today. *Ewww.*

Eve bows her head shamefully as if she's read my thoughts.

I look back at Dr. August to find that his mouth is hanging wide open.

"This is not possible, Eve! You must show me!" He looks a bit pale.

Eve hesitates for a moment, then shrugs. "Sure, what the hell. Hand me a match, Doc. I'll show you something interesting."

Dr. August shuffles through his drawer and finds a lighter. He hands it to Eve with shaking hands.

Eve ignites the lighter and holds the flame under her left palm. She cringes and moans as her flesh bubbles but keeps the lighter steady, making the burn as severe as possible. I gag as the smell of burning flesh fills the room; I have never smelt that before and will be glad to never smell it again.

It seems like she's holding the lighter on that one spot forever. She must really want to show us the full extent of this healing talent.

When she raises her palm to us, I almost throw up. Her skin is badly blistered, a bit charred, and bleeding. It looks disgusting.

"Now watch carefully," she says, as though she's a magician introducing a magic trick.

I stare as the blisters begin to shrink. The skin becomes pinker, and all evidence of injury disappears before I can say, "Mississippi."

We stare in disbelief and awe.

The silence is broken when Dr. August abruptly jumps out of his chair and begins to pace back and forth, mumbling, "This is not possible," over and over.

"Please, Doctor, tell us something. We need your help," I beg, hoping he will calm down and not call any other doctors to check on Eve.

When he finally sits back down, he does not look like the same cheerful man. He takes Eve's hand from across his desk. "I am so sorry, darling. If this is what I fear it is, then there is no cure. I must go now, ladies, but if you return tomorrow morning, I shall tell you, show you, everything."

He leaves the office in a hurry, leaving us wide-eyed and dumbfounded.

"He knows something, Alex. I can't believe he knows something."

Eve looks as though someone has just died. I can sense she may never be the same after tomorrow's revelation. What life can she imagine beyond this strange new illness? Blessing? Curse? I'm not a negative person, but I am realistic, and I know in my soul that this can only get worse.

***

I hug her as we walk back to the dorm. She accepts my embrace and my silence.

When we arrive back, I encourage her to get some rest, and as she naps, I pray that she may get some kind of normal back in her life someday. But how will that ever happen?

Eve can never return to her old life. I know this, and I cry in the bathroom with that realization. I won't dare let Eve hear my sobs of concern. I'm sure she has enough of her own tears to shed.

What Eve needs right now is strong friends, friends that can handle anything, and I am hoping I can be that for her. I don't know if she will still be Eve after all this, and I might not know how to save her, but that doesn't mean I won't try.

CHAPTER TWENTY-ONE

EVE

It's Alex's turn for a shower, and I am thankful for the time alone, even just to stare at the ceiling and not talk about my current state for a little while.

My favourite poster is positioned above me, and there is a small visitor climbing over it. A tiny spider crawls around in search of something, and I'm sure I watch him walk from one end of the ceiling to the other.

My spider-watch is interrupted by a knock on the door. *What now?* I really don't feel like answering, but I hope it is Cam, so I rise to check it out.

When I open the door, I am supremely disappointed to find Claire on the other side. *She really doesn't have anything better to do, does she?*

"Hi, Claire, what's up?" I try to say it in the politest way possible, but it doesn't sound as sincere as I intend.

She ignores my greeting and gets right to the point. "Is Cameron here?"

Oh right, she probably wants to discuss "date night" with Cam.

"You know he doesn't live here, right? Did you check his dorm?" She looks a bit frustrated. As frustrated as a kitten can look, I suppose.

"I tried his dorm. His roommate Mark said he hadn't been there all day. So I thought I would check here…" Her explanation continues, but I can't seem to focus on anything else but her mouth moving.

My glance moves all over her face. Her cheeks are full but not full enough. Her arms look fuller and soft. I think I stare too long and start drooling because Claire's pretty face looks especially concerned when I look back up.

I think I see her mouth the words, "You okay?" and then I lose it.

This insatiable hunger hits me all at once, and I can't resist tearing into that lovely fleshy arm. I feel my teeth hit the flesh, and it excites me. Something inside me is alive.

Claire screams loud enough for Alex to hear, and Alex comes sprinting out of the bathroom and knocks me on my ass.

I stay down, deciding it might be best.

I can hear Alex checking up on Claire. An obscure set of words pour out. "Are you bleeding...are you alright?"

Claire chimes in next. "What the hell is wrong with her? I'm fine, I'm fine. She didn't break the skin, but it might bruise."

I assume Alex is trying to check her wound at this point, but I don't think Claire is interested in anyone else touching her at the moment. I completely understand. It's not every day someone tries to chew your arm off.

I know Alex is fumbling around for an explanation. "Eve's not well. She ummm...well...had a car accident. Her ummm...back... was in so much pain, and they errr...gave her some really strong meds, and she seems to be hallucinating pretty badly. I had her in bed resting. I really didn't think she'd be able to get up and answer the door while I was in the bathroom. Totally my fault. I'm supposed to be watching her."

It is such a terrible a lie, and I am amazed to hear Claire buying it.

"Oh no, poor thing. Well, I'm sorry to bother you two. Will you let me know if you see Cam around?"

Alex promises to forward the message to Cam, and then Claire is gone.

"That was close, Eve! You're lucky she has a thing for Cam and she knows we're his friends, or she might have filed charges. She has a nice mark on her arm. It looks like teeth marks. Jesus! What were you thinking? Are you out of your fucking mind?"

Alex is almost yelling. She is losing her cool, and I don't really have a good answer for her. I just stay on the ground searching my own mind for an explanation.

I finally come out with, "I was hungry."

That is the honest to goodness truth; Claire made me feel hungry. *How odd.*

"Well, I guess she won't be stopping by anymore." I chuckle.

"Eve, this isn't funny. I need you to start taking this seriously!" she screams.

"Listen, I can't change what just happened. I wish you would understand that. I'm changing, Alex, and I will understand if you don't want to be around for that," I say glumly.

With that statement, Alex lets down her guard. "Eve, I don't want to leave your side. I'm just scared too is all. I don't know how to protect you."

That warms my heart. I'm glad someone cares about Eve the freak.

I change the subject for a moment. "Did you hear Claire say that Cam is missing? Should we be concerned?"

I get up off the floor at this point and sit next to Alex on my bed.

"We'll try and call him in the morning. I'm sure he just needs some time alone. He's been through a lot. I'm glad he wasn't here to see this."

I feel a dull ache in my stomach. It might still be hunger, but I'm thinking it's more like guilt and shame. I can barely remember what it's like to have a boring day, and now I long for it. Just one day where nothing bad happens. For the love of God, just one!

CHAPTER TWENTY-TWO

CAM

As soon as I walk through the door, my roommate Mark corners me.

"Man, where have you been? Some blonde girl was looking for you, and your pals called earlier on the phone. Are You doing alright? Maybe have a 'sleepover' with blondie?" Mark insinuates since I didn't come home last night.

I guess if a guy or girl doesn't come home, most people assume he or she slept with someone, did the deed, got laid. I can just say, "Yup," and get a high five from Mark, but I guess I should let him in on what's going on with me since I will need to head back home soon.

"Mark, it's been a crazy few days. I didn't come home last night because I didn't sleep. I couldn't sleep. I got a call that my dad was killed, either by an animal or person. They don't know yet. They're currently doing an autopsy."

Mark looks at me in disbelief. "Ah, Cam, you could have told me. I'm your roomie. You can tell me anything."

I accept this offer with a nod. "Well, there's more to the story, so here goes. He was in jail prior to me coming to school. I got a call shortly after arriving at school that his bail had been posted, and now he's dead."

Mark sits down at that point. "Oh, that is some real heavy shit, Cam. What did your dad go to jail for?"

This is the part I hoped to leave out. I hesitate for a moment and then realize there's nothing to hide. It happened, and I need to get on with it. Denial doesn't do anyone any good.

"Well, he beat me up badly in a drunken rage. My rib still hurts where he broke it."

I blurt it out because there is no easy way to say it, and wait for Mark's reaction.

"Holy shit! How can you be keeping all this from me, man?! Your dad sounds like a real douche bag. Sorry, but I had to say it. You think he was maybe mixed up with the wrong kind of people and someone offed him when he got out of jail? Oh man, and I thought my family was fucked up because they like to colour coordinate for our annual family photo."

I laugh. "Dude, that is fucked up!" He raises one eyebrow, pretending to be offended, but I think he feels triumphant that his attempt to make me laugh has succeeded.

I don't know why, but I continue to tell Mark my life story. I tell him about my mom's death and how my father became increasingly intoxicated after that. I even reveal my crush on Eve, which I immediately wish I can erase from his memory as soon as I say it.

"Let me get this straight. You've been in love with this girl since high school and still haven't sealed the deal? Dude, that's ball-less."

I stare at him, confounded. "What?"

Mark puts on a teacher-like tone and continues. "You know, ball-less. One that has no balls. You could also call them cowardly, spineless, pathetic…"

I stop him there; I get the point.

"Mark, promise you won't say anything to her, okay? She's one of my best friends, and if we were supposed to be together, we would be."

Mark punches me in the arm. "I won't say anything, but I think you should. That's all I'm saying."

I sigh. "Okay, onto the next topic. I will be leaving for my father's funeral as soon as the autopsy is done. So in a couple of days. I have some friends from my classes lined up to drop off my notes. Can you just stack them on my desk for me when they pop by?"

Mark nods, and I give him my thanks.

Mark is a really nice guy. I'm lucky I didn't get a real freak like last year. I swear that guy was stealing my boxer shorts. Once, I saw my Calvin's with the funky red pattern peeking out the top of his jeans when he leaned over. Those were my favourite pair. When I asked him about it, he totally denied it! Thank God Mark doesn't do that. I'm not sure I can handle two underwear thieves.

The only thing that concerns me about Mark is how good looking he is. Alex and Eve nearly dropped dead from the sight of him. Eve may not want to be with me, but I think it will hurt if she dates my roommate. I just hope she will spare me that. I will rather not know the guy she's dating, and with the way Mark is, he will give me all the dirty details too! I shudder at the thought.

"Hey, Cam, one more question. Where the hell did you go all night? I get that you couldn't sleep, so where does a guy who can't sleep go?"

I turn to look at him again. "I really just wandered. I walked around the whole campus; I know it really well now. I went to a bar for a bit, had a few drinks, and I'm pretty sure a man hit on me. I mean, he looked like a chick but so wasn't."

Mark has a good laugh at that last part and then walks towards the washroom, still laughing and shaking his head all the way there.

★★★

After getting lost in my thoughts for a while, I decide it's time to call Alex and Eve. I'm sure they're worried about me. As I pick up the phone, about to dial, there is a sudden knock at the door. I open the door without giving it a second thought.

"Hi, Cameron! I just wanted to remind you about our upcoming date. So glad I caught you." She flips her hair and gives me a large grin.

Claire really is a cute girl; I just don't feel anything for her. I search myself for even an ounce of feelings for her: love, lust, friendship? But I feel only numbness towards her.

"I'm sorry, Claire, but I will have to cancel."

Claire's face droops immediately. "Oh, I get it. Yeah, you have 'better' plans, I'm sure." She looks a bit miffed, which makes me irritated because I have a damn good excuse. "Your dumb friend uses me as a chew toy, and now you're dumping me." She gives a little sob as she says it.

I try to ignore the last part because how can I break up with someone I'm not even with? *What a strange girl.* I skip to the part that really intrigues me. "What do you mean, 'chew toy?'"

Claire pulls up her sleeve and shows me some teeth marks on her arm; it's starting to turn a bit purple. I rub her arm. She likes that a little too much, and I regret it since it is giving her the wrong idea again.

"Maybe you can help me feel better, Cam?"

I stare at her with the most disgusted look I can manage. Now seems like the perfect opportunity to tell her how I really feel.

"Claire, you and I are not going to happen. I'm not into you, and I really wish you would stop following me around."

Claire's lip quivers.

Great, I'm going to make her cry.

"Fine! I don't know why you wanted to go on a date with me anyway. Sorry to bother you." She throws a crumpled movie flyer in my face and then storms off.

I desperately hope she will leave me alone from now on, but somehow I doubt it. Claire strikes me as a bit of a closeted psychopath. Something about her terrifies me, and I'm sure I will pay for this outburst someday. I shiver, thinking of the many ways she might retaliate, and when I can't bear to think about it any further, I pick up the phone and dial Eve.

She picks up without delay and shouts, "Cam?"

How'd she know? "Yeah, it's me. Sorry if I worried you guys. I just needed some time to clear my head."

She gives a sigh of relief. "Cam, I'm just happy you're safe. Thank God."

"Yeah, I'm fine. Are you okay?"

Eve avoids the question and changes the subject slightly. "Hey listen, Claire came by looking for you, and she said you hadn't been around for a few days. Alex and I immediately freaked! God, it's good to hear your voice."

She pauses for a moment. "Cam, I bit Claire."

I chuckle. "I know! She was just here and showed me. It was a pretty good bite there. I don't think you have to worry about her retaliating. I think I just pissed her off more. I told her I don't have any feelings for her and to stay away from me."

Eve is silent, and then she begins laughing hysterically. "Oh God, she's going to blow a fuse and murder us both."

We both laugh hard, even though I'm sure we both believe it.

"I'm going to hang up now. I'm waiting for the results for my father's autopsy. I will stop by and see you girls tomorrow."

"Good, because I have to meet with Dr. August again, and I would love you to be there."

"I will be there, Eve. You know I will." With that, I hang up, hoping she doesn't hear the warmth in my voice. I will always be there. Even if only a shadow.

CHAPTER TWENTY-THREE

EVE

I am glad to have Cam and Alex by my side today, standing in front of Dr. August's office door. I hold their hands and squeeze them. I feel as though I'm borrowing their energy and their strength as I breathe in deeply.

When I push the door open, I see Dr. August sitting readily at his desk.

"Please sit down." He motions to three seats in front of his desk.

I sit down first. I am impatient.

"Dr. August, please hit me with the truth. Be blunt. Be honest. I'm freaking out here, and any information would be welcome. You see, I attacked someone yesterday. I need to find a way to control myself. I don't know what's wrong with me, and if there is no cure like you said yesterday, then can we find one? I can't imagine living like this forever."

I'm sure my words come out as a jumbled, sobbing cluster of thoughts. I just hope it makes enough sense to merit an answer.

Dr. August leans back in his chair and ponders my revelation carefully before responding.

"Well, the rapid healing can't be all that bad. It must have some advantages?" He winks.

I can't really appreciate the joke at the moment since it's at my expense.

Dr. August clears his throat, removing the grin from his face, and continues. "I hope you are all comfortable. This is a lengthy story, and I do hope you won't share it with anyone else. The only reason I'm sharing this information with you is because I deem you trustworthy, and Eve is going to need your help if anything happens to me."

"Why? What's going to happen to you?" I blurt out.

Dr. August shushes me. "Eve, most likely nothing. Once I reveal everything, you will understand what we're dealing with. So please…all three of you…promise me your silence."

We all nod our heads.

"Of course, we won't tell anyone. I wouldn't want anyone to be in danger because of me, and I'm very aware that my 'situation' may garner some attention. So I'm all for keeping things quiet," I say as fear and curiosity course through my veins.

Another question pops into my mind, and I can't stifle it.

"Dr. August…do you know what I am?" My voice cracks.

He glances at me with something that looks like pity in his eyes. His wrinkles almost become deeper as he frowns. *Frowning is not a good sign.*

"Yes, I think I do, and I'm sorry for it." He fidgets with his hands. "Eve, you are no longer human. There is something coursing through your veins that you can't even imagine. It is something that I was trying to keep contained, but it found you. If you're ready to hear the details of its origins, then I will give you every bit of knowledge I have, but you will have to be brave and listen carefully. This story is not a pleasant one. Are you ready?"

I nod, feeling a growing chill in the room.

Dr. August nods back. "Good, then let's get started. I hate wasting time."

My hands sweat profusely as Dr. August begins his tale.

PART TWO

ANGEL OF DEATH

CHAPTER TWENTY-FOUR

DR. AUGUSTUS

I had heard stories about Hierakonpolis. Rumors really. Something frightening was happening in the city, and it peaked my interest.

Curiosity can be such a dangerous thing.

Hierakonpolis was an important place that would help us understand the beginnings of Egyptian civilization; it was also the site of some strange attacks.

As you know, Hierakonpolis is also known as the City of the Hawk. It was given this name due to a large amount of Hawks that are native to the area. There were many hawks inscribed in some of the hieroglyphics found in the ancient city.

The Hawks were once an omen of good luck, but that changed when they began swooping down and attacking people on the dig site. Many people left because of it, uttering some superstitious nonsense about "a curse." Or what I once thought was nonsense.

The other rumor I had heard about Hierakonpolis was also true and much more frightening than birds. People were disappearing without a trace. Soon enough, no one would volunteer to work at the dig site. They feared disappearing or at the very least having their eyes gouged out by vicious birds.

When I began my work in Hierakonpolis a few years ago, it started out as a boring dig; I started to think the rumors were just that. I noticed that none of the locals would work at the dig site. I thought that a bit strange but shrugged it off as disinterest on their part.

Of course, none of the warning signs stopped me. I looked at it as an opportunity to take over where others had left off. This was my chance to discover something truly significant. With everyone else being far too afraid to even look around, I could stake my claim in any discovery I made. I was hungry for fame and respect from my peers.

I now wish I had listened to my fellow colleagues when they said that I should forget about Hierakonpolis, but the past had already happened, and I had to deal with the consequences.

At the time, I was working closely with another professor. I had invited him along on the dig as a guest for a month or so. His name was Dr. Vincent Engel. I had worked with him in the past and enjoyed his company.

He was born in Frankfurt, which is the same German city I was born in. He then moved to Canada at a young age, just like myself. We had a lot in common and quickly became good friends.

He was much younger than me and had so much ahead of him. I knew his wife and two children very well. I never had a son of my own and regarded him as family.

Together, we discovered a few new tombs. Each tomb held more history and additionally rare and precious artifacts. It became our obsession. We dug further and further, thinking each mound of dirt would lead us closer to fame and fortune.

One morning, we decided to head to the dig site early without any of the others. We couldn't sleep, not with all the excitement of discovery surrounding us, tempting us, teasing us.

We headed down to one of the tombs furthest in the ground

and noticed a crack in one of the walls. I remember tapping it ever so slightly with my flashlight, and a large piece of the wall crumbled to the ground. When the dust cleared, Dr. Engel and I saw that this was another entrance to another tomb. We squealed with delight, naturally, and entered the tomb.

There was a sarcophagus inside. *Bingo!* We both thought we had hit the jackpot.

Dr. Engel was quick to try and open the sarcophagus. He slid the top of the beautiful golden box open. Inside lay a rotten body, not very well preserved at all. We both found it very strange that the ancient Egyptians would place a poorly mummified body in such an extravagant casing.

I studied the hieroglyphics on the tomb walls, looking for any explanation as to the identity of the corpse in the casket. While I did this, Dr. Engel continued to prod the rotten corpse. He looked closely at the body, searching for any jewelry or clues to who this might have been.

The walls were covered in murals of hawks with pharaohs. While I searched the murals keenly with my flashlight, I heard a scream over my shoulder.

Before I turned to look in Dr. Engel's direction, I sensed another being in the room. When I spun around to find Dr. Engel, I could see that a monster had risen from its sarcophagus. Dr. Engel was trying to hold it down; he was trying to seal the casket with the monster inside.

I couldn't move. I stood there in disbelief. The corpse had risen. This couldn't be possible, I told myself repeatedly.

Dr. Engel was screaming at me. I couldn't make out what he was saying at first. I just couldn't hear properly or see straight. My body was rejecting reality.

When I started to snap out of it, I saw the monster's mouth wide and ready to take a bite out of Vincent, who was struggling to hold the monster back.

He screamed, "Help me, Walther!" and I ran to his side to try to hold the being down in his bed. His eyes, if you could call them that, burned red, and his mouth was a gaping black hole that opened and closed with a furious hunger.

We held it down and somehow managed to slam the top back on and lock it down in place with its latch.

I looked at Vincent and asked, "What the hell just happened?"

He looked at me, panting, and opened his hand to show me a brilliant red stone.

"I grabbed this out of its hand, and then it rose and began to attack me. It was trying to chomp at me if you can believe it."

At this point, I could believe anything; ghosts, witches, psychics, Santa, all of them seemed quite plausible after what I had just witnessed.

The being in the sarcophagus didn't move or make a sound now that the lid was closed again. It seemed like a good time to run.

"Let's get out of here. I don't know what we've done, but we have awakened something evil, and that rock you took must be evil as well. Leave it here, and let's get the hell out of here!"

He looked down at the rock, and I saw in his eyes that he could not leave such a finding behind, especially after tackling a corpse to get it. Vincent did, however, agree to get out of there immediately. He began racing towards the exit without me. I remember my voice echoing after him, pleading with him to leave it.

Greedy men always leave stained paths behind them.

***

Soon after the strange incident, we resumed our work and convinced ourselves that what we saw had all been an illusion, a figment of our very indulgent imaginations. It couldn't have been real, and who would have believed it anyway?

The days following were quiet, almost normal again. We didn't speak about our experience again, and we didn't head to the tombs alone again either.

***

I remember the last fateful morning on the dig site like it was yesterday. I relive it every day. I replay each and every moment leading up to that point in time and often wonder how I could have prevented it. I regret so much and have very little time to make amends if my maker would even grant forgiveness.

Dr. Engel and I were about to begin our work one morning, and we were discussing a possible vacation in our future, possibly Hawaii.

After our chat, we set out for separate dig sites. I could see him from my site, and we waved to each other in the distance. I remember seeing small shadows circling the ground; it took me awhile to realize they were hawks. I looked up and noticed quite a few of them in the sky. They headed towards Dr. Engel's site and circled him.

I watched the strange phenomenon inquisitively and could not have ever anticipated what happened next.

The birds swooped down and attacked him. I could see their beaks tearing at his flesh in a synchronized dance of feasting.

Without thinking, I dropped my tools and began racing towards him. I was not close enough; some damage would be inflicted by the time I got there. I knew it.

When I eventually reached him, the birds had dispersed, leaving my friend breathless and bleeding in the sand.

His face was barely recognizable with all the missing flesh. I could see one of his eyes had been pecked out, and I almost lost my composure and sobbed over him.

I tried to pull myself together, and I screamed for help as I put pressure on the deeper wounds of his body.

He was shaking under my hands, trembling from the shock. It took them ten minutes to reach us, but it felt like hours. All the while, I kept trying to tell him he would be okay, but I didn't really believe he'd ever be the same if he lived.

They took him off to the medical tent in a small jeep, acquired for such purposes. There was no room for me. I told them I would go by foot and meet them there.

After watching the jeep as it sped off, I looked at the blood-soaked ground around me, and there amidst the carnage was the radiant red rock. The red rock that the horrid being had been holding, protecting.

At that moment, I believed the rock to be cursed, and Vincent Engel was its victim.

I pocketed the rock and headed towards the medical tent at the quickest pace my shaking legs would travel. I would think of a way to dispose of the rock later.

✶✶✶

The medics would not allow me to see him right away. They worked on stitching up his wounds and making sure he didn't lose any more blood. I understood that I would only be in the way.

Once I was allowed in, what I saw made my stomach turn. He looked more like a creature and nothing like my friend.

I immediately thought of his children's faces if they could see him this way. They would scream at the sight of him, and this would break his heart, just as the thought was breaking mine.

Without a word, I approached his bedside. I wanted to rub his hand or his shoulder in comfort but soon realized, as I searched his body, that there would be no comfortable area for me to do this.

I settled for whispering to him. "How do you feel?"

He didn't reply, but what he did next was strange.

He growled like a mutt and exposed his teeth. I tried to calm him down, but that only made the growling grow louder. This alerted the medics, and they came running over to us.

It was good timing because he pounced on me like he was about to chew off my face. The medics held him down, but he wouldn't calm down. He fought against their restraining arms until his heart gave out. I watched the monitor flat line, and a scream escaped my lips.

A doctor ran in with a defibrillator seconds later.

For me, this was all happening in slow motion. My friend was dying right before my eyes, and all I could do was watch. I felt a pang of guilt for ever inviting him here.

They shocked him once, nothing. They waited for the next charge and shocked him again, still nothing. They tried a few more times before giving up.

The room was silent as I watched one of the medics start to detach all the monitors from his body. Another medic covered him with a sheet. All I could do was watch in horror.

✶✶✶

I made the call to his family later that evening. The doctor said he would do it, but I felt it should come from someone they knew. It took everything I had to dial the number and give that news. It was as if I was the angel of death, taking their loved one away. It was my fault, and I would pay for it the rest of my life in guilty penance.

I didn't know how heavy that payment would be just yet.

The phone rang, and Lita picked up. "Hello? Who is it?" she said in a pleasant voice.

I couldn't find my words at first. "Ah…hi, Lita. I have terrible news, I'm afraid. Please sit down for this."

She began crying immediately, which made the telling of this news all the more miserable.

"Lita, there was a horrible accident today. Some birds attacked Vincent. He lost a lot of blood…and I'm so sorry. He's gone, Lita."

She cried harder as my words made her world crumble.

When the call was over, I felt a darkness wash over me. This dig was supposed to bring us glory and fame. *Was it worth it?*

I should have stayed away, or I should have made this journey alone. I was selfish to bring Vincent into this. I had lost a good friend, as well as my appetite for discovery.

I would go home tomorrow. I never wanted to visit The City of the Hawk again.

✶✶✶

I went back to the medical tent to pay my final respects to Vincent before they boxed him up and sent him on his way home for burial.

I entered the tent with my gaze miserably set on the floor.

When I reached the bed, I slowly pulled down the sheet that had been covering Vincent, but he was gone.

I quickly surveyed the tent. There was no sign of his body.

I called in the medics. "Did you send Vincent elsewhere already?"

They all shook their heads and had to see for themselves. They all looked horrified when they noticed that the body was gone.

"Who would take a body?" was all one of them could say.

I left the tent furious with their incompetence. Why hadn't they been watching his body? What if a body snatcher had taken him for parts? There were people terrible enough in this world to do it!

As I stood in the warm night air, I saw a figure stumbling out into the distance towards the tombs. I started running towards it. I suppose I had a manic moment of hope that Vincent was still alive.

When I reached the man and swung him around, I realized that it was Vincent, but something, besides his disfigurement, was abnormal.

His eyes shone red like the corpse we had seen in the sarcophagus. His head eerily twitched sideways as he examined me.

He dragged his body awkwardly towards me and growled. I had a moment to react as he dove at me, baring his teeth. I placed my arms up to hold him back, but he was strong and took me down to the ground. In seconds he was on top of me, trying to gnaw at any flesh he could reach. I used all the strength in my body to hold him off. I was screaming and fighting for my life.

I was able to get one of my knees under him and forcefully push him off of me, launching him onto his back in the dirt.

I rose and so did he. "Vincent, stop! This isn't you. Stop. Let's get you some help."

None of what I said registered with him; he just continued to twitch and head towards me again with a snarl.

I didn't want to hurt him, and I tried to think of a way to prevent his approach. Then it dawned on me. I still had the red rock. I didn't know what possessed me to use it, but I knew there might be something powerful about it. I pulled it out of my pocket and held it in front of me. It shone such a vivid red that it blurred my vision as I tried to observe Vincent.

The glow coming off the rock seemed to stun Vincent. He stood motionless for a moment, staring at the glow, almost trance-like. Then he began to retreat towards the tombs.

I didn't want him to go. "Vincent, come back, please. What about Lita and your children?"

He turned back for a moment when he heard her name. He looked at me with those dead burning eyes, and he seemed to have a trace of sadness in them.

He gave a scream that was both inhuman and melancholic. Something in that final scream said that he understood he couldn't go back to his ordinary life.

He stumbled away as I watched on.

In a few seconds, he was gone, and that was the last I ever saw of Dr. Engel.

✶✶✶

Most people packed up and left that very night. The staff was horrified when they began to hear the story of the man cursed by hawks.

I could scarcely blame them.

They heard he had died and then rose from the dead. I even overheard some medics saying he must have been "infected" by the birds.

This gave me an idea.

I approached one of the doctors in the medical tent and asked if they had any samples of Dr. Engel's blood. The doctor gave me a paranoid look and then took the vials out of his pocket and handed them to me. He told me that he was going to dispose of them, and as he placed the vials in my hand, he advised that I should do the same.

Something in Vincent's blood was rotten, something I couldn't explain. The doctor refused to give me any answers about the vials of blood and exclaimed that he was getting out the place since it was giving him the creeps. He walked off, probably to pack his things; I wouldn't judge him for his lack of bravery. I wasn't sure mine was intact either.

I was going to take the blood back with me and study it. It probably wasn't the smartest choice, but I couldn't leave Vincent behind. So I took part of him with me.

***

The next morning, I was woken up by the sound of many vehicles approaching the site. I quickly put on some shoes and stood outside of my tent to see what all the commotion was about.

Some men climbed out of a big SUV and began approaching me.

Once they were close enough, I could see from the pin on their suits that they were some men from CSIS. Someone must have informed them about what happened here last night.

The only question I had was why Canadian Intelligence would come all the way out here. Why hadn't they sent a local team?

"Are you Dr. Augustus?" one of the men asked, and I nodded.

"We have been asked to return you home safely and brief you on a case we are working on. We require your help."

"And what if I refuse to go with you?" I retorted, which was an error on my part.

You don't want to offend an agent.

One of the men took off his sunglasses and came very close to me and whispered, "I suggest you cooperate. It will keep you comfortable."

I understood that it was a threat and that I had no other options. The warning was loud and clear: "comfortable" meant alive.

They were here as requested by our government to seek me out. They didn't seem the type to fail. They would do what they needed to do at any cost.

The same man spoke again. "Dr. Augustus, let me make something clear. Anything you saw here, well...it never happened. We will be sending Dr. Engel's ashes to his wife."

I gave them a confused look. "But Dr. Engel went missing. How can you..."

And then I understood their meaning. They were going to send some counterfeit ashes home, and I didn't want to know who was going to play the substitute.

I kept my mouth shut and complied after that and ever since. These were powerful men; they could do anything they wanted. I feared what they might do to my family if I didn't cooperate.

I followed them home on the first flight out of Cairo.

***

When we arrived back in Canada, there was a black limo waiting for us. Inside, I realized that the windows were tinted so dark that I couldn't see the outside at all. They didn't want me to know where we were going, clearly.

After about an hour's drive in silence, one of the suits decided to speak. "We are headed to a high-security zone. Don't try anything funny. I assure you that you won't get away with it."

I was growing tired of threats and just rolled my eyes and remained silent.

I could feel the limo dipping down on an angle. It felt like we were driving down a hill for a good ten minutes and then stopped very abruptly. I had a sense that we were somewhere underground.

One of the men said, "We're here. Follow me please, Dr. Augustus."

It was so unnecessarily polite. He knew very well that I had to follow him.

When I came out of the car, my surroundings looked something like the Bat Cave. Was Batman lurking within? Or some other superheroes? I chuckled out loud at the thought and then asked, "May I use the Bat Phone please?"

My two new CSIS friends scowled at me. I guess they didn't have much of a sense of humor, and I guess I expected that too.

Finally, I was led into a room and asked to sit in front of a man at a big desk.

The man observed me closely before speaking. Was he simply looking to confirm that I was Dr. Augustus? Or was he worried that I might have contracted something similar to what Dr. Engel had been infected with?

After all the staring, he introduced himself as Agent Williams. He was fairly young to be in such a high position, and I'm sure he'd done some terrible things in a short amount of time to get there. Quite frankly, Agent Williams frightened me, even though his smile seemed so welcoming.

"These men have brought you to our underground research

facility. I am in charge of this facility and have requested your visit," he said with an air of superiority.

I squirmed uncomfortably at the thought that no one would ever find me down here.

"Why do you need me here?"

He gave a cheerful grin. "Well, you have experienced some strange and dangerous phenomena first hand, have you not?"

I nodded. He could definitely say that.

"Well then, we need your help to find its source and stop it from contaminating others. Let me fill you in quickly. Hierakonpolis has fallen victim to a strange virus that was first found in local hawks. These birds carry the virus and attack humans, thus contaminating them, just like your friend Dr. Engel. We have been studying the site for a few years now, and we have been trying to keep incidents quiet while we conduct our research."

I furrowed my brow. "Why would you simply wait for more incidents to happen? Why not just eliminate the threat? Shoot all those hawks out of the sky and save people?"

Agent Williams continued. "Negative, we can't kill the birds until we discover what this virus is capable of. Each victim has reacted differently when exposed; we are still looking to find some similarities. One victim began shedding limbs and growing them back. Another victim began to rot away until there was nothing left of them. The latest victim took to eating other humans and hiding in the tombs waiting for his next meal. We need your account of what happened to Dr. Engel to help us understand this virus. We also know you acquired some of his blood. This will help us do some further research."

How had they known I'd acquired some of Vincent's blood? I

could only assume that they had questioned everyone at the dig site. *Damn!*

"What do you plan to do with this information exactly? I want your word that you would never use it as a weapon."

Agent Williams looked offended. "Of course not, Doctor! We want to understand it so that we can find a cure. If this virus ever spread, we would have no defense against it. Plus...your friend, he's not really dead. We may be able to cure him."

My eyebrows shot up involuntarily. "How is this possible? What have you done?"

"We haven't done anything yet. We know you let him wander out of your sight. I guess you thought it was kinder than having to explain to his family that he had become a monster."

I sunk in my chair, feeling heavy and exposed. He knew my mind. Agent Williams was right. I didn't want to break the news to Lita.

Call me crazy, but that night that Vincent wandered into the tombs, I saw a strange pleading in his eyes, almost as if he were saying, "Let me go, Walther," and I did just that.

After a few seconds, Agent Williams continued. "What if we can cure him? We believe that he is still lurking in the tombs according to our intel. He seems to have had a few, snacks, like our last victim."

Oh no! I thought. He could attack others. I hadn't thought of that when I let him go. I was now starting to panic with this realization. I guess I sat there fretting for a long time without speaking because Agent Williams piped in again. "Well? What is your answer? Will you help us without research?"

I bit my lip and looked him straight in the eyes. "What do you need me to do?"

Agent Williams sat back and smiled. He looked so pleased with himself. Had I just made a pact with the devil?

✴✴✴

I spent the next few weeks at this secret facility being briefed on their gruesome findings and having them outline the details of my mission. I was to study Vincent's blood samples with a team of scientists to see if we could come up with a cure.

The only thing we discovered from the blood samples was that the virus had some similarities to the Avian Flu.

We tested the virus on hamsters and found that they became cannibals. They no longer had heartbeats, and some of the hamsters had a strange ability to re-grow their limbs. We tentatively named it the Azrael Virus. It manifested differently in each victim, but the one thing that all the infected had in common was that they were all dead in the medical sense.

No heartbeat and their bodies would rot if they didn't resort to cannibalism.

It sounds ridiculous out loud, but these sounded a lot like a new breed of zombies. I could see why this research would mean more than just saving Vincent. We would be preventing a zombie apocalypse.

The second part of my mission was to return to Hierakonpolis periodically and look for clues.

Every time I visited, something terrible happened. Someone new became infected or disappeared.

I never found Vincent, but I knew in my heart that he was still out there and still feeding. Some of these poor people might have been his victims.

Those who became infected were burned, and we sent home

fake ashes to every family, saying that the cause of death was related to an occupational accident. I guess you could say that was sort of true. A half-truth.

I felt terrible that I couldn't warn people of the dangers, but CSIS was threatening me, saying they would hurt my family if I didn't keep my mouth shut. So I did.

I knew I would be under tight supervision until our mission was complete, but the mission's purpose became more and more ambiguous as time went on.

In the back of my mind, I kept thinking there was something Agent Williams was hiding from me, but I was hiding something too.

I never mentioned the red rock that I carried with me at all times. It offered me protection that night with Vincent, and I have never been attacked since.

There was something special about the stone, but I hadn't fully figured it out yet. It didn't protect Vincent, but perhaps that had something to do with him stealing it from a mummy.

Hierakonpolis was a cursed place, and although I feared its dangers and was forced to be there against my will, I still needed to know what happened there.

I still want to know.

Even after all this time, even after all the horrors I've seen, I still needed to solve this mystery, even if I died trying. I owed it to my friend, and I owe it to the people who will continue to suffer if I don't stop this virus from spreading.

It could mean the end of us all.

CHAPTER TWENTY-FIVE

EVE

Dr. August's "history lesson" leaves me breathless. I can't believe what I am hearing.

Azrael Virus? Zombie Apocalypse? Magical red stone?

This all seems like something I would see in some B-class horror flick.

I am trying to let it all sink in, but it's a lot of information to process. What I got out of the whole story is that there is no cure, at least not yet. My body has become infected by a virus that kills you and then forces you to kill others.

I am officially a monster. Human no longer. This is hardest to take.

Not human. The two words swim around in my mind, making me lightheaded.

I hold my hand over my heart. *No heartbeat? Never again?*

"Will someone please check my pulse? I just need to know…" My hands are too busy shaking to check for themselves.

Cam walks over to me, his eyes bleak. I cross my fingers as Cam presses on my wrist. He waits thirty seconds and then decides to press his fingers to my throat instead. He waits another thirty seconds and then removes his hands, slowly shaking his head.

Dr. August and Alex look on with wide eyes. I can smell the fear on them, and the scent is delicious. What Dr. August has said is true. My heart has stopped, and I have ceased to live.

I am a living dead girl.

I get up from my chair unsteadily. "Dr. August, I think I've had all the information I can stand for today."

He nods. "Eve, we will need to test your blood and see how your manifestation of the virus differs. You weren't bitten as badly as some of the others. There's hope."

I look at Dr. August with anger racing into my cheeks. I feel as though I'm boiling. I must look scary because he moves back in his chair slightly.

"Hope? You really think I want to talk about that right now? Hmmm, let's see…You're perfectly safe. You brought me to that hell hole with the 'hope' of adventure, with the 'hope' of finding something groundbreaking. Now the only 'hope' I have is that I don't eat anybody, and the way I'm feeling right now, I may just want to start with you." I point venomously at Dr. August and then turn to leave.

As I'm walking towards the door, I hear Dr. August whisper behind me, "I'm so sorry, Eve…" and I slam the door before he can continue.

The glass on the door shatters, adding a nice dramatic effect to my exit.

I keep walking, because if I stop, I fear I might turn around and go eat his face off!

I can feel the hunger within me growing, and I need to find a distraction fast!

✳✳✳

I go to my dorm room and find my hiking boots. Hiking is always a good head-clearing activity.

I leave my cell phone behind. I really don't want to talk to anyone right now. No one will ever need to check up on me again anyway; I can't die if I'm already dead.

I hop in my car and head to the nearest hiking trail, about forty minutes away from the dorm. I used to love hiking as a leisurely activity. Now I think it will be a necessity. I don't want to eat people and should probably stay away from them as much as possible. Luckily enough, the trails are clear when I arrive.

I walk quicker than I remember being able to. I am faster and stronger. It feels like I can take down a tree with my bare hands but am too scared to try it.

In no time, I reach the top of the hill. I think I will need to climb it twenty more times if I am to burn off some real energy. I am not satisfied, and I am not tired.

I stand peacefully and admire the view at the top. All the beautiful trees below and the hills in the distance are simply stunning. A rock behind me offers me a place to sit, and for a few minutes, I can admire the view before continuing the hike.

I have only been there a few minutes when I hear voices. Damn! I don't want people around right now. I need a t-shirt that says, "Dangerous, stay away," or a sign that I can hold up saying, "Don't feed the animals," with an arrow pointing to me.

I bite my lip, hoping they aren't coming this way.

I see them rounding the corner. Why don't I ever get my way?

It's a couple going for a romantic hike. They look so happy. I lick my lips at the sight of them.

They see me and then sit next to me.

Why, God!? Why?!

They smile at me and say hello in unison. I nod in their general direction, trying to seem in deep thought. But the woman keeps trying to make conversation.

"Isn't this the best viewpoint? I love it right here. You can see trees for miles, and it's amazing if you come and watch the sunset." She makes googly eyes at her beau.

I assume they plan to stay and watch, and I can't be trusted near them.

"Well, I didn't come for the sunset today, just for some exercise. You two enjoy."

I am turning to leave when she grabs my arm.

"No really, stay. It's gorgeous. Don't leave on account of us."

Great, I found a real friendly one. I hate to be rude, so I say, "Okay, I will stay for a few minutes, but then I really must get going."

The woman smiles at me, pleased that I'm staying. The whole vibe of this moment is extremely strange.

After a few seconds of staring off into the distance, she starts making out with her man.

How incredibly awkward. You want me to stay, but then you start making me feel uncomfortable? What a weird chick.

I watch as they lock lips. It reminds me of eating the way she nibbles on his lower lip playfully. I start to get hungry and know I should leave, but it's too late. My mind is now on one thing only. It's almost as if my body goes on auto-pilot because I know what I'm about to do is wrong, but I can't stop myself.

The woman looks over and notices me watching. She smiles and asks her boyfriend if he would like me to join in. He nods with excitement.

What guy wouldn't want to make out with two girls at once? Stupid question, lady.

She points to me and motions me to come closer with her finger. They are making this too easy for me.

I am over there in a split second. She points to her lips, and I start feverishly kissing her. I hear her boyfriend say, "Alright! This is awesome!" as he watches.

She smells so good, like a perfect steak. One kiss becomes a nibble, which she doesn't seem to mind. It's when I start to nibble harder that she tries to push me away, but I'm too strong. I push her to the ground and tear into her lips. The blood pouring down her throat muffled her screams.

I have my back to her boyfriend, so he still has no idea that his make-out session has turned into a feast. I'm sure from his angle it just looks hot.

I begin to feast on her cheek meat. It is so tender that I give a moan of pleasure. She still fights underneath me, and I'm not one to play with my food, so I go in for my final bite. I chomp down on her throat. I chew the flesh and suck the blood flowing out. When she stops moving, I no longer have a desire to chew. Now that she's dead, she smells like week-old garbage.

I'm still hungry, and the closest living thing is luckily right behind me. I stand and turn to face him. He's smiling from all of the excitement, but it quickly fades when he sees my blood-covered face and clothing. He screams. The scream is very girly sounding, but it excites my hunger even further. I pounce and tear into his throat like a rabid dog. I chew until the screaming stops.

I dump his body beside his girlfriend and sit there, satisfied, as I watch the sunset. It is really beautiful. Such a shame they'll miss it. I close my eyes and savour the taste in my mouth.

✳✳✳

What seems like years later, I wake up on the ground. I squint in the darkness and can see the faint outline of trees surrounding me. My mind is fuzzy at first, but I force myself to try and remember the preceding events.

That's right, I was on a hike earlier, but why didn't I go home?

I stand, feeling very filthy and gooey. I rub my clothing, noticing a dark substance everywhere. When I raise my hands to the moonlight, they are stained red.

I give a silent scream and look for signs of life. My worst fears are realized when two bodies lay inches away from me.

I run towards them. There is no mistaking it: they are dead.

Their faces are almost chewed down to the bone. *Oh God, what have I done?* I sit in the dirt, sobbing and rocking back and forth.

This is the most terrifying thing I have ever witnessed in my life, and I am to blame.

I am a murderer! This realization makes me cry harder.

As I sob inconsolably, I hear a strange noise. I hope it's a hungry animal that will devour me and put me out of my misery. *That will be some sweet justice, won't it?*

I wipe my tears away and look for the source of the strange sound. There is a gurgling noise coming from one of the bodies.

"Holy shit! They're alive?" I turn towards them again.

The bodies in front of me sound like they are moaning. I smile with a glimmer of hope. *Perhaps I'm not a murderer just yet.*

I crawl over to them quickly and hear the moaning louder now. They still seem pretty dead, but then again dead people don't moan.

Their bodies start to twitch, and this frightens me so much that I crawl backward as speedily as a crab.

The next thing that happens is straight out of a Dracula film. *They rise!*

They lift their heads and then their torsos off the ground.

Soon, they are standing and slowly walking towards me.

It dawns on me that I may have transferred the Azrael Virus to them, and they are now full-fledged zombies looking for food. I am that food.

Crap! I better do something quick.

I am surrounded by rocks and start by throwing some at them. It's not working. It's not even slowing them down. The male approaches me first and grabs at my clothing. I hold him back; the virus has made me strong, but I won't be able to hold both of them off.

As my back pressed against the tall rock wall of the mountainside, I get an idea.

I smash his head against the rock wall as hard as I can. I hear a crack in his skull, and he crumbles to the ground. *Guess all those zombie movies came in handy after all.*

The next zombie comes at me with a chomping motion; I can hear the "clack" of her teeth. She looks famished.

I grab a big rock and run at her, smashing the rock down upon her head and taking her down. Then everything is silent again.

I try and take in everything that just happened. I know I did this, but I don't remember how. I seem to keep blacking out when I feed, and the worst part is whoever I feed on seems to come back. I can create zombies if I'm not careful. I can start a whole epidemic because what I create is very different from what I am. I still have feelings, I still look human, I can still talk, and I can heal. I wonder if these two can heal...

I wait for an hour, and when they don't rise, I figure it is clear.

My hands are shaking as I move the bodies under a tree. They are side by side like an adorable little zombie couple. I ended their relationship and their lives. I feel guilty leaving the bodies out here in the open instead of burying them, but burial mounds out here will draw some attention. I hope police will deem this an animal attack.

As I walk towards my car, I think about Cam's dad. Henry died from an apparent animal attack. What if I was that animal? And what if he is one of the undead now? He could attack our whole little town. Our families and our friends are in danger. I can't believe I haven't thought of this before. I have to get back to Alex and Cam, and we need to get home now!

CHAPTER TWENTY-SIX

ALEX

Eve bursts through our dorm room door in such a panic that I think a bomb might be dropping momentarily. I am half right; she hits us immediately with a verbal bombshell.

"I killed two people," she sobs unattractively and slides down to the floor on her knees.

Cam and I stare at her with our mouths gaping open. *What do you say to that?*

Cam's shock wears off sooner, and he sits beside Eve on the floor. He holds her close. I wonder if he will still be doing that if he knew what I know. He may be hugging his father's killer right now. Mind you, I have no proof, but my gut tells me that Eve did it. I just don't think now is the time to discuss who "might" have killed his father.

I know Eve's our friend, but she is under the influence of the Azrael Virus, and that makes her no less dangerous. We have to be cautious. I don't think Cam should be near her right now, but Cam and I will discuss that later.

Cam hugs Eve closer as she sobs even harder.

"What happened, Eve? Tell us everything," Cam says in between her sobs.

As Eve unfolds from her fetal position, I can see that she's covered in bloodstains. I can't help becoming paranoid; did anyone else see her like this? God, I hope not, or we will all be in a lot of trouble soon.

"I went hiking on my favourite trail to clear my head. Then this couple showed up…"

She goes silent for a moment. I can tell she is reliving it as she tells us what happened. Eve's eyes are closed tight as she continues.

"I was so hungry. I kept hoping they would leave, but they wanted to make conversation. Then it got really weird. They wanted me to make out with them, like something out of a messed up porno…and that gave me an excuse to get closer. I couldn't fight it. I had to eat. It's like something took over. Guys, I'm a monster. If there is no cure for this, I can't go on."

She stops there. I know she is going to say she wants it to be over, she wants to die, but she doesn't continue because I'm sure she remembers that she can heal. Killing her will be impossible, which makes her all the more frightening.

Here is my best friend aching in front of me, and I am torn as to whether I should run or hug her.

"Eve, I think it's best you stay away from people right now. Maybe we can ask Dr. August if there is a more secure place for you to be."

She looks at me, a little hurt by my mention of quarantining her, but it is the best thing I can think of. Eve shakes her head furiously. "No, no, we need to go home. I need to check something out."

Cam is standing now, looking all sorts of confused. "Eve, you need to stay here so Dr. August can run his tests. You can't leave right now."

I nod my head in agreement. Eve looks at both of us desperately. "You don't understand. We have to go home or a lot of people might be in danger."

She really has our attention now.

"I haven't quite told you everything yet. I black out after a feed, and when I woke up to those mutilated bodies, they actually came back to life."

I cover my mouth in horror, and Cam simply sits down in a chair, stunned.

"Eve, you know what this means, don't you?"

"Yes, it means I can spread the virus. I had to smash their skulls in to make sure they were dead and wouldn't come back and infect others."

My palms are a bit sweaty as I ask the next question. "What did you do with the bodies, Eve?"

Eve paces back and forth a bit before replying, "I left them under a tree, and I hoped the cops would think some animal attacked them."

She looks directly at Cam when she says this. She fidgets and stands awkwardly. This is Eve's attempt at confessing something to him. She always fidgets in the same manner when she has bad news to share. She looks at him pleadingly, and Cam looks back very confused; he is searching his mind and starting to put things together.

When the pieces come together, he stands up with a slight look of disbelief on his face. "Eve, you didn't?" he says in a soft voice, almost as if he is about to crack apart.

Eve goes to hug Cam as an apology, and he shoves her away violently.

I'm startled by the unexpected rage and jump a bit.

"I'm so sorry. I'm so sorry...please...I didn't mean to...I didn't know..."

Eve is barely managing to put sentences together. I just stare as a stunned voyeur as their strange conversation continues.

Cam's voice becomes more serious and angry. "Say it, Eve! Say what you did! Say it now! I want to hear it!"

Eve keeps repeating that she is so sorry as she sobs on the floor. Cam's next action is most shocking. He pounces on Eve, wrapping his hands around her throat. Without thinking, I run to them and try to peel him off of her. "Stop, Cam! This won't help anyone."

He shoves me away with the same force that he used on Eve, and I bump my head on the edge of the bed on my way down. *Ouch, that really hurt.* I place my hand where my head is throbbing and then bring the hand towards my face to see a bit of blood. It isn't too bad, so I try to get up. Cam is still choking Eve. She is making strange straining sounds, trying to get air that won't come.

I'm screaming at this point. "Cam, stop! Stop! Stop!" He eventually looks over at me and sees my fear. This makes him stop. His anger has gotten the best of him. I have never seen him this way.

I crawl over to Eve's very still body. Her eyes are wide open, but she doesn't seem to be breathing.

"Oh shit, what have I done?" Cam looks at the bruises forming on Eve's neck.

I push him back. "She can heal, remember? Just wait. She'll be okay in a minute or two."

We watch in silence, waiting for Eve to come back to us. It seems to be taking forever, and I begin to panic.

Cam is inconsolable and huddles into a corner of the room. If she doesn't come back, Cam will surely kill himself.

"Come on, Eve, wake up!" I shake her a bit. I can't check for a pulse because Dr. August said that she no longer has a heartbeat. How am I going to know if she'll come back or not? I am freaking out now.

"Eve! Eve! Wake up! Don't be an asshole! You need to wake up now!" I continue shaking her.

Nothing works. I begin shaking with fear. Maybe this is it? I give up and sit on my bed. Cam and I are staring at Eve's body from opposite ends of the room, and I'm sure we are wearing the same expression.

I put my head in my hands and shed a few tears. The room is spinning. I feel as though I can't get any air. Then Cam says, "Oh my God, Alex, look!"

Eve has risen, well slightly. She is sitting up, looking straight at the wall with no expression or further movement. This looks like something out of *The Exorcist*. Will her head start spinning next?

Cam looks horrified as Eve's head jerks towards him. She rises so quickly and unnaturally. In seconds, she has a hand on Cam's throat and has him in the air. *Oh shit, this is it; she is going to kill us both now.* I run over to Eve and place my hand on her shoulder. She growls, but I stay put. "Eve, please don't hurt Cam. He's your friend. He loves you. Eve, you're going to kill him. Stop please."

It is that last part that brings her out of her daze. She doesn't want to kill. She puts Cam down and seems slightly more human as she sorrowfully utters, "I don't want hurt anyone. I don't want anyone to die."

She falls to the floor looking exhausted. This time, I embrace her. My guess is that she's exhausted from healing herself, so I tuck her into bed and deal with Cam.

"What the hell were you thinking, dumbass?"

He doesn't really answer my question; he just looks pitiful.

"Do you think Eve really killed my father?"

I sigh. "I don't know, Cam. It's possible. She loves you so much that she would kill for you anyway. So maybe the virus acts on her impulses too."

"I'm not sure I can forgive that, Al. That changes everything."

I can understand that. How do you forgive such a huge crime?

"You can worry about that later. Right now we have a bigger problem. What if Eve did attack your dad and he has come back as a zombie? Everyone in town could be in danger. Did you hear anything back about the autopsy?"

Cam shakes his head. "No, nothing yet. I wonder what's taking so long."

He is slow on the uptake these days. "Cam, come on! If his body 'disappeared,' I'm sure they wouldn't want you to know about it. They could be hunting down dear daddy zombie right now. Eve's right. We need to go home and find out what's going on before it's too late. We will also know if Eve did it or not. If your dad stayed dead, then Eve is clear, and you can decide if she has anything to even be forgiven for. Okay?"

Cam nods. "I'm going to pack. We'll leave in the morning." He leaves, and all I can think about is the fact that I'm stuck sleeping next to the zombie girl.

I crawl into my bed and pray for sleep. I look over at the peacefully sleeping Eve and whisper, "Please don't eat my face off while I'm sleeping. Okay, buddy? That would be great…Thanks."

I reluctantly close my eyes and at some point fall into a deep slumber.

CHAPTER TWENTY-SEVEN

EVE

When I open my eyes the next morning, I am slightly disappointed that I woke up at all. I did terrible things, and now my friends are afraid of me, maybe even hate me. I look over at Alex sleeping. She's curled up with her hands and blonde hair covering her face. It looks like she is trying to make herself invisible like her hair is an invisibility cloak or something.

I throw the bed sheets off me and pick up the phone. I want to talk to Dr. August so badly; he is the only one who understands what I am going through. I guess I am done being angry with him. He doesn't want any of this, after all; he is just as trapped as I am. I just pray CSIS won't find out about me. I'm sure Dr. August won't willingly say anything, but when someone threatens or tortures you, sometimes you crack.

I dial his number. The phone rings and rings, but he doesn't answer. The answering machine comes on, and I decide to leave a message after the beep.

"Hey, Dr. August. It's Eve. I really need to talk to you when I get back. I'm heading home for a few days to visit my family. Talk to you soon."

I really want to tell Dr. August the truth, but an answering machine isn't the place to do it. I don't even know if CSIS will be listening in or not, so I think I will be cautious.

I hang up the phone and look back over at Alex. *Crapola, still sleeping.*

I want to talk to someone, but I guess it can wait until Alex wakes up. I lie down on my bed and stare at the ceiling, which traditionally has a picture of Spider-man. I have had a poster of Spidey above my bed since I was eight years old. The poster changes, updates, according to new comics and movies, but always Spider-man. It makes me feel safe to know that Spidey is looking out for me, and it just continued into my adulthood.

"Hey, Spidey," I whisper. "How did you deal with being different? I know you didn't eat people or anything, but you weren't always admired either. WWSD? What would Spidey do? What if this is me forever? Maybe I can be a superhero and just eat bad guys?"

I chuckle. I must sound so stupid. I suppose if Spider-man answered back, he would say, "With great power comes great responsibility."

Yeah, I have some power alright, but I have no idea how I am ever going to control it. Maybe I can have a secret lair that I can hide away in. If I stay away from people, then they might have a chance of staying alive.

Alex quickly saves me from my inner discussion by greeting me, "Good morning, Eve. You feel more like yourself today?"

I nod. "Actually, I feel great, and all I have to do is eat people to feel this alive again,"

I say it too casually, and Alex gives me a raised eyebrow.

Alex comes over to me very slowly. She looks like she wants to hug me, but she is being very cautious because of last night, I'm sure.

"I won't bite you, Alex. I promise. I'm not the least bit hungry. I had two dinners last night."

She gives me a brief smirk and then embraces me. The hug feels great; it's nice to know someone cares about me, even if I don't deserve it.

"I'm so sorry about last night, Al. If I could control this, it would be so much easier, but it's like the virus takes over. It's stronger than I am."

She shushes me. "Eve, I need you to be strong and not sulky, okay? We won't make it through this if you don't try and fight against the virus. It doesn't have to win. I'm afraid that if you give up and let the virus run things, there will be nothing left of my best friend."

"I will try, Al, I promise." But what causes a deeper ache is Cam. "Al, do you think Cam's ever going to speak to me again?"

She shrugs, which isn't very comforting. I want to scream.

I am going to lose him, aren't I?

Cam and I never dated because I never wanted to lose him as a friend. If we ever broke up, that would be it. I didn't really care for the whole awkward breakup and then the "do we stay friends after" discussion. In most cases, the relationship ends badly, and no one wants anything to do with the other person afterward. I don't want Cam to ever be out of my life. Maybe that is love? A fairly stupid and cowardly way to show it, but still love. It doesn't matter now if Cam never wants to speak to me again. No point in pouring my heart out if it is only going to be one sided.

***

Alex and I start packing our things, which takes me about five minutes, but Alex the perfectionist needs about an hour. I bite my nails each time she perfectly folds a shirt and then takes it apart to re-fold when she notices it isn't perfect enough.

Oh my, God, that is annoying!

There is a knock on the door, and I freeze. I know it will be Cam, and I'm not sure if I am ready to face him. I look at Alex and signal with my head that she should head over and open it. When the door flies open, it's Cam, just as I suspected. He doesn't acknowledge me, and why should he?

"I'm all packed. I will meet you two by the car." And with that brief statement, he is gone.

His voice sounded wounded. If I could take back everything, I would. I would have never gone into that damn tomb.

I stand by the door, tapping my foot as I stare at Alex inspecting the items in her suitcase ever so carefully. "Can you hurry up, please? We need to move. People in danger, remember?"

She rolls her eyes. "Yes, I remember!" She slams her suitcase shut. "Okay, let's go."

Shoot, I pissed her off. Can't win for trying, can I?

We head downstairs and pass Claire on the way. She gives us a fake smile as she passes, and I fight the urge to shove her down the stairs.

Once we arrive at the car, Cam is sitting on the concrete with his back leaning against the side of the car. He looks so tired; I'm sure he hasn't slept at all. He stands when he notices our approach and looks at me briefly. The quick glance looks painful, and he has to look away quickly.

"I'm going to sit in the back. I'm exhausted and just need my space right now," he says.

Alex and I both nod. I'm not going to argue with him in this state, not even playfully.

***

The whole way home is awkward. If it was still beating, I'm sure my heart would be aching from the distance growing between us. Our friendship is slowly changing, and I feel Cam and Alex slipping away from me. They are fighting to hold onto who I was and are terrified of what I have become.

We listen to the radio to fill the silence. I like radio better than CDs or hooking up my iPod. Something about it feels like the songs are speaking to me or narrating my current state. We hear The Cranberries sing "Zombie," The Cardigans sing "Lovefool," and then "the song" comes on.

Oh, for the love of God! Not that song!

The one song that always seems to play when I'm at my lowest of lows. Daniel Powter begins singing "You Had A Bad Day." How did he always know? In this case, it's been a bad couple of months, but that doesn't have the same ring to it. I can't help but start singing along; it just sums up my sorrow. I am shocked when Alex joins in. She smiles at me, and we both sing harder together. Some sort of healing washes over us. Are we having fun? It has been so long since I've been my same silly self, and Alex is enjoying it too.

As we belt out the tune, I glance back at Cam, who is still sleeping. I wish he will wake up and join in or give us his classic eyebrow raise of disapproval.

After the song is over, I place my head on Alex's shoulder for a long while as she drives. I love her so much that I think I will die if I ever lose her. I guess I should stop using that word. Dying isn't really part of my vocabulary anymore.

***

When we arrive at my house, I grab my bag out of Alex's trunk and wait outside of the car for Cam to join me. It is raining, and he is taking his sweet time getting out, perhaps getting me soaked as punishment. I stare back in the window. "Well? You coming?"

Cam doesn't even glance at me when he shakes his head.

Alex turns to look at me and says, "He's going to stay with me, Eve."

"Oh," is all I can muster to say, and then I turn to walk towards my front door so they can't see the tears welling up in my eyes.

Alex yells out of the car window, "We'll call you later to discuss what to do next."

I don't turn around, but I wave her off, showing that I understand.

I walk through my front door, and my dad is the first to greet me.

"Oh hey, honey. We weren't expecting you until later."

I hug him. "There wasn't much traffic, and we didn't stop for food or anything, so it was really quick." I give him a fake smile.

He places his arm around me and leads me to the kitchen. I can smell cookies. My mom always bakes when she knows I'm coming home.

"Hey, Mom." I give her a quick peck on the cheek as she whisks some batter.

"Hey, honey, how was the trip back? The weather has been awful, and I was worried the roads would be so slow, but here you are...and early! I'm not even done baking yet. So sorry! I wanted to have it all ready when you arrived."

She gives a little pout as she says this. She's adorable when she does this, and I give her a smile because I can't help it.

"Don't worry, Mom. I have plenty of time to enjoy some cookies." I don't have the heart to tell her that I'm not really hungry, well not for cookies anyway.

"Hey Dad, where's Winston?"

Dad has taken out the paper and started to read it at the kitchen table, his daily ritual. He shrugs, looking up from his paper. "I don't know. He was here a minute ago."

I leave the kitchen in search of Winston. I check the front room, but there is no sign of him, so I figure I will head upstairs. I have to unpack anyway.

On the way to my room, I hear a whimper coming from my parents' room. "Winston? Here, buddy..." But he doesn't appear when I call.

I follow the whimpering sound into my parents' bedroom. I kneel on the ground next to their bed to take a look underneath, and sure enough, there is Winston.

He is as far away from me as possible. The whimpering gets louder as I try to reach for him. He is afraid of me. "You know, don't you, boy? You know there is something wrong with me."

I don't want to scare him any further. I pick myself up off the ground and leave the room. I remember going to pick him out from a whole litter of puppies. He ran up to me and licked my face when I crouched down to greet him. He picked me, he picked our family, and I loved that damn dog! Now Winston doesn't want anything to do with me. It feels like losing a family member; he's been by my side for so many years. He is always the first one to greet me when I get home, by running to the door and jumping up on me as far as he can reach. I shut the door to my room so I won't hear the whimpering anymore; I can't stand it.

I have every intention of unpacking but feel much too depressed at the moment. I lie down on my bed and stare at the ceiling. There is my trusty Spider-man poster, but he brings me no comfort today.

"Hey, Spidey, I'm too sad to talk right now," I say out loud and then turn onto my side to face my window.

My stomach growls so loudly that I think a demon might burst out of it. I hold it and tell it to shut up like it is a separate entity. I don't want to be this.

I get up and head over to one of my drawers to pull out a pair of scissors. They are sharp enough to slice through anything. I usually use them to cut fabric.

I throw them on the ground and stomp on them. The two blades come apart, and I take the sharper blade in my hand. The blade grazes my wrist, and it feels good; it's cool against my skin. I begin to slice at my wrist. I know I can't actually commit suicide, but I want to feel something, anything!

As soon as I make that first slice, it heals as quickly as I made it. I am so desperate to leave a lasting mark that I continue to slice at the wrist vigorously, again, again, again.

It goes on for a good fifteen minutes through my sobs, but I can't make a scratch that remains. I toss the blade on the ground; there is barely even any blood on it.

I dig into my shirt and pull out my lucky locket. I hold it in my hands and rub it like it's a magic lamp. I just wish I can be normal again.

✦✦✦

A few hours later, dinner is ready and I have to pretend that I love everything I eat. All foods taste the same now, sort of like ashes and dirt, not very appetizing. But people? They smell like turkey dinner, and they taste like candy. Sweet, sugary, addictive candy. My mouth waters at the thought.

I mostly stare at my plate and take a few bites here and there. I can see my mother's disappointment as she glances at my plate. She loves when I eat; it means that I enjoy the food. She is most likely wondering if it is any good, which I'm sure it is; she is a fantastic cook.

"Mom, this is so good. The chicken is the juiciest I've ever had! I'm trying to savour every bite."

That makes her feel a little better, and we start up some dinner conversation.

"So, honey, how's school treating you?"

I look at my mom and try to give the best impression of a happy version of myself. "It's going really well. I love all my classes."

"Great to hear it. And how about the swim team?"

Shit. I hoped she wouldn't ask about that, but how could she not? I am captain of the team, aren't I?

"It's going really well, too." She knows I am lying as soon as I say it. She always knows.

My dad chimes in at this point. "How come you haven't invited us to any swim competitions yet? You usually do. I enjoy that. It's like being at the Olympics."

"Thanks, Dad." He looks confused and shrugs. "What?"

I figure I should tell them the truth; they are on to me anyway.

"Okay, listen. I'm not the captain of the swim team anymore."

My mom looks a bit upset. "Why wouldn't they make you captain again? You are an amazing swimmer!"

I shake my head. "No, no, they wanted me to be captain. It's just…this year is really busy. I decided to step back from the swim team this year."

My mom and dad stop eating to look at me, absolutely shocked.

"Eve, you love swimming, and in a year, you will be really out of practice. It will take you forever to get back to where you are now. Are you still training at least?"

Cue my dad with the guilt trip. He means well but can be harsh sometimes.

"No, Dad, I'm not training. I'm taking a year off swimming."

He drops his fork and sits back in his chair in disbelief. "But what about your dream of going to the Olympics someday? That won't happen if you don't show them what you've got. How could you just drop swimming altogether? That's not like you, Eve."

I know that; he doesn't have to remind me. Nothing is like me lately, absolutely nothing!

I wish I can tell them the whole truth. That I can't swim unless the team feels like swimming in shark-infested waters. That I am too busy eating people. That I am too busy trying to stay under the radar.

My rising anger starts to make me hungry. I don't like thinking of my family as a meal, so I excuse myself immediately. I don't mean to leave them hanging, but I'm sure if the conversation continues I will only get angrier and can't be responsible for my actions. It is safer just going to my room and locking the door.

Almost as soon as I enter my room, my cell phone rings. *Thank God, a distraction.* The caller ID says it is Alex. "Hey, Al, what's the news?" I answer.

"Well, Cam met with the Coroner, and he said the autopsy is finished. The cause of death was deemed an accident. There have been a lot of bears spotted in the area, so they believe that is what happened. The marks on his body are very similar to a bear's attack style."

I am relieved to hear there won't be any further investigation into the matter.

"Did Cam see the body? Was it there?"

Alex hesitates for a moment. "Well, that was the hardest part.

Cam had to go see for himself. He just had to know if his dad was dead, actually dead. Cam said the body was so mangled he couldn't really imagine him ever healing and coming back to infect others. Eve, his dad was in pieces."

I feel so disgusted with myself. *Did I really do that?* I have no memory of it, but I was so mad about what Henry did to Cam that I wouldn't put it past me. My anger seems to trigger my hunger.

Since I don't say anything more, Alex continues. "Eve, the funeral is going to be tomorrow. Let your family know. Cam wanted to get it over with as quickly as possible. They are burying Henry at the local cemetery next to his wife."

"Okay, see you tomorrow." I hang up feeling miserable. I want to hug Cam. What he saw must have been awful.

***

The next is rainy as well. *Perfect funeral weather.*

My mother and father are waiting for me in the living room, all dressed in black.

"I'm ready. Let's go," I say, and we silently head towards the front door.

Winston is blocking our way. He sits, staring at us with concern. When he catches sight of me, he growls and runs upstairs.

"Winston has been so strange the past few days. It must be this weather. It's making him crazy that he can't go outside and play," says my mother.

"Maybe he knows about the funeral?" says my father. "Dogs are pretty intuitive."

I really just want to speak my mind and say, "*No, it's just your zombie daughter scaring the shit out of him.*"

It only takes us ten minutes to arrive at the cemetery. As we park, I can see Cam standing by the burial site with the priest. It tears me up inside that Cam is all alone; he has no other family standing beside him in support. His parents are gone, and he really isn't close with his other family members. He has some distant cousins that he's never spoken to, but that is it.

I get out of the car and head towards Cam. I hope he will embrace me; I need to feel the warmth in his hug. Instead, he hugs me with as little force as possible, just enough of a hug that my parents won't ask any questions. He then turns to my parents and thanks them for coming and for all their help. I can see the gratitude in his eyes.

We take our places around the grave.

Shortly after, Alex arrives with her parents and her younger sister Janna. I watch as Cam hugs Alex with the hug I hoped for. Their embrace makes me very envious. It almost looks as though they never want to let go of each other. I instantly feel ashamed of my envy. I deserve to be shunned, to be forgotten. We are all here today because of me; I won't forget that. I should just be thankful that Cam hasn't handed me over to CSIS. He has every right to do it.

The priest begins the burial ceremony. I can't listen; I just look at Cam's face. He has the kindest face I've ever seen, but today it is stained with exhaustion and sorrow. It is at that moment that I realize just how much I love him and that he will never love me again.

The priest asks Cam to say a few words. Cam takes a crinkled piece of paper out of his pocket and smoothes it out. He doesn't look at anyone as he begins to read it.

"Today, I say goodbye to my father. He was never the same after my mother died, so I hope he can be with her now. My father was a very flawed man, but he was still my father. My mother would always say give him a break, he had a hard life. I thought today would be a good day to do just that. I won't mention his vices. Those will be left to God's judgment today. I want to reflect on a few fond memories with my father.

"I remember when my father surprised my mother and me with tickets to Disneyland. I was eight years old, and it was a dream come true. All my friends had been and I just kept begging and begging. I really didn't think I'd ever go. That trip was one that I would treasure forever. It was the happiest my family had been together. It was perfect. I remember riding on my father's shoulders so I could see Mickey Mouse in the parade. He was a different man on that trip. He was the father I wished he could have been my whole life.

"When my mother died, he hugged me so tight. It was very comforting to know that we both loved something so much. It hurt us both equally and affected us forever after. I hope that he never feels that kind of pain or sorrow again. I wish my father peace. May his soul finally rest."

There is not a single dry eye to be found after Cam's brief speech. He did very well considering there wasn't much of anything positive to say about Henry Jackson.

The cemetery staff begins lowering Henry's casket into the ground. My mother's sobs are the loudest. I know she considers Cam family; she always treats him like he is her own son. Her heart broke when she first found out about my friend Cam, whose mother died when he was young. She invited him over as much as possible, especially after learning that his dad was such a heavy drinker. She wanted Cam out of that negative environment as much as possible. I know deep down she hopes Cam and I will get married some day, but any possibility of that is long gone.

Cam is offered a shovel. It is a tradition for a family member to deposit the first heap of dirt upon the coffin. A twisted tradition, if you ask me. But Cam accepts and then thanks, everyone again for attending.

Everyone begins to head back to their cars; they want to give Cam some time to say goodbye to his parents. However, I can't go; I can't leave the day this way.

"Mom, Dad, I'm going to go talk to Cam for a second. I will meet you guys in the car."

They nod and keep walking towards their vehicle.

Cam is sitting on the grass watching each shovel throw dirt in the hole. I walk up to him slowly. I'm so nervous my hands are sweaty. Without any words, I sit beside him for a minute. It's nice just to be in his presence.

I take his arm and place it around me like a scarf on a chilly winter day. He doesn't reject this. "Cam, I know you may never truly forgive me, and I accept that as a possibility. That doesn't mean I won't try to win you back, and you can't blame me for that. You are so wonderful, and I'm so sorry for everything. I would take it all back in a second. I miss you."

I don't wait for a response; I kiss him on the cheek, which is slightly moist. It takes everything I have to leave him, but I manage to get to my feet and walk away. I can feel his eyes following me as I leave. I hope that this is the start to fixing what I broke.

***

When we get home, I feel emotionally and physically exhausted.

"Mom, Dad, I'm just going to head to bed. I'm not really hungry for dinner right now."

They look at me understandingly, and they each give me a hug before I head upstairs.

Once in my room, I change into my jammies. The soft fabric on my skin makes me instantly sleepy. I crawl under the sheets and soon afterward fall into a deep sleep.

***

I am running so fast, through trees, through backyards. I'm not sure why I am in such a hurry, but something is driving me. I have a mission, a destination, a purpose tonight.

I travel in the darkness, snarling like a wolf. I can feel my anger mounting. When I reach my destination, I am almost excited. Something is about to happen, but I'm not sure what. I just know it feels exhilarating.

I glance through the bushes. There is a man standing outside of his house.

Oh, my, God, it's Henry Jackson.

He is pacing in front of his house. *Waiting for someone?* My question is answered when a vehicle pulls up. There are two men. One is the driver; the other is a very big man. The big man is the only one to exit the vehicle. He heads towards Henry.

Henry asks, "Do you have it?"

The big man nods. "Where's my money?"

Henry's hands shake as he digs through his pockets for cash. He pulls out many crumpled bills and places them into the big man's hands. The man then counts the money and nods. "Okay, man here is your stuff. I would say you order from me too much, but that would be bad for business."

The big man passes him a little bag and winks at Henry before getting back in the car and driving away. Henry watches as the car drives off. He waits until the car is out of sight and then empties the pouch into his hand. He is now holding pills. I can't be sure what kind they are, but I can't help thinking what a selfish man he is.

He drinks heavily, and now he does drugs? Maybe he should clean himself up so his son can have a father.

My anger is reaching uncontrollable levels, and I'm shaking. I rustle the bushes in my rage. Henry Jackson looks my way. He can't see me, but he knows something is there.

He slurs his words when he speaks. "Get out of here, ya dumb dog. I swear I'd shoot you if I had a gun. Stupid neighbours letting you shit all over my lawn. Get out of here before I kick you dead!"

He kicks up some dirt to show he's serious. I am no dog, as he'll soon find out. I watch a little longer, trying to control my rage. Henry downs the pills all at once. His eyes roll back into his head with pleasure.

Good, I think. *Then he won't feel so terrible when I rip out his throat.*

I watch as his happy pills kick in. He's laughing to himself. The laughter triggers something dark within me.

I walk out of the bushes towards Henry. I want him to see me; I want him to suffer as he made his son suffer. I walk up to Henry as he opens his eyes.

"Oh, hello you. What are you doing here?"

I don't respond. I just continue getting closer. He looks at me a little more closely and starts to become afraid. "What happened to your eyes?"

He starts moving backward, but it's no use. I can attack him in seconds, and he will have no time to escape. He knows this; he knows that I'm here to hurt him. He can feel it.

He crumbles to the ground and pleads for his life. I can barely make out a word. I'm so hungry, and it's all I can focus on. The sweat on his brow looks just as appetizing as the rest of him. The look on his face is pathetic.

The last words I hear him utter before I tear into his flesh are, "Tell Cameron I love him, and I'm sorry, I'm so sorry..."

***

I wake up in a pool of my own sweat. I want to scream, punch a hole in a wall, and cry all at the same time. I remember. I did it. I remember everything. Every detail floods back; even the taste lingers in my mouth. What is worse is I can remember how much I enjoyed it, how good it felt to rip him to shreds. I was fast, strong, and vicious. Whatever part of me is still human feels terrible after hearing Henry's last words.

I have to tell Cam the truth. He needs to hear that his father loved him, even if it is too little too late. Cam deserves that much and I deserve to lose him. I will never let Cam forgive me. I will never forgive myself.

I cry into my pillow as Henry's words play over and over again in my mind.

"Tell Cameron I love him, and I'm sorry. I'm so sorry..."

CHAPTER TWENTY-EIGHT

CAM

I feel like I haven't slept in months. I would say I feel like a zombie, but the word leaves a foul taste in my mouth, and I decide to banish it from my vocabulary.

I sit in Alex's guest room staring out the window. I didn't leave this chair last night. I may have dozed off in it a few times, but there was definitely no solid sleep. My body throbs with exhaustion, but I don't care about the ache. I feel little numb inside; something in me has changed.

I long to be the old Cameron again, to be happy. I want to forgive Eve and just move forward already. I guess I'm just not ready yet. I have to respect the time it might take me to mourn this loss. My mother is long dead, and I never fully got over that. My father is dead; he was an abuser and an alcoholic, and I should hate him, but I don't. I am just sad that I am alone. The last of my family. How has this whole family gone to shit?

All these thoughts swirl through my head like daggers. My painful thoughts haunt me, preventing me from being myself. Alex can see that I am crumbling; she makes every effort to spend time with me and comfort me, but I only want to be left alone. I am alone after all. I love Alex and her family, but they are not "my" family.

I continue staring out the window. It is another perfectly gray day, and the rain has begun. Last night, the weather report said that we will get some record-breaking rain over the next few days. There has already been some major flooding in the city center, but it hasn't affected our area yet.

As I look out the window, there seems to be a figure lurking in Alex's front yard. I stand and press my face against the window to get a closer look. There is a dark figure standing in the middle of the lawn staring up at me. I can't make out who it is through all the rain. Although it is raining hard outside, I force the window open to get a closer look, and standing there on Alex's rain-soaked lawn is my father. He stares back at me with fiery eyes.

I stumble backward.

I must be dreaming. I rub my eyes frantically and return to the window. There is no one there now. I really need to get more sleep or they might put me away for hallucinating. Next, I might start hearing voices. That thought really scares me, so I climb into bed and throw the sheets over me like a shield.

Please sleep. Please sleep.

***

About an hour later, there is a knock at my door. It is Alex. She looks a little pale. *Great*, I think. *What now?* What can we possibly have to deal with now? I don't display my annoyance. I just ask, "What is it, Al?"

She comes closer and is about to speak but stops when she hears something behind her. Someone is in the hallway.

Janna, Alex's little sister, pops into view. "Whatcha guys doing?" she says with a slight grin on her face.

"Janna, go away. Cam and I need to talk." But Janna doesn't leave.

"Talk about what? Can I talk too?"

Alex rolls her eyes. "No, Janna, it's personal."

Janna pouts and turns to leave. Once she's out of view, Alex turned to face me again.

Without looking behind her, Alex yells, "Janna, get lost!"

I hear Janna shuffle in the hallway. "Fine! God! I'm going!"

I grin a little. "How'd you know she was still there?"

Alex smiles back. "I've lived with her for thirteen years, and I know exactly how that brain of hers works."

We both have a little laugh. Even though most people seem annoyed by their siblings, I envy the dynamic between them. I wish I had someone to annoy.

Alex puts on her serious face again. "Look, Cam, I know you have a lot on your plate right now, and I'm so sorry to add to it, but this is really freakin' important."

I wish she'd just spill it already. I'm not into suspense these days.

"Al, can you just tell me, please? You're killin' me here."

She bites her lip and hesitates a bit, then sighs and continues. "Okay... I went to the cemetery this morning to place some flowers on your parents' graves, and when I got there, the graves looked like they had been dug up. Both graves were empty, Cam. I could see the caskets, and there was nothing in them."

Hearing this makes me feel as though I am about to faint. This can't be.

"Alex, take me there now! I need to see this for myself."

"Should we call Eve?"

I shudder hearing her name. "No! I don't want to see her right now."

I can see the hurt in Alex's eyes. She wants me to forgive Eve, but I don't have time for this shit right now.

***

When we arrive at the cemetery, I bolt out of the car and start running towards the grave site. I'm not even sure the car was fully stopped when I got out.

As I stand in front of my parents' final resting places, I can see that what Alex said is true. My father's grave has a hole in the dirt big enough for a body to slide through. When I look through the hole, down below I can see that the coffin under the soil has also been opened. It looks as though someone blasted through the wood, but how can that be? That takes an insane amount of strength. *Last time I checked, the guy inside was dead.*

I walk over to my mother's grave next. The marks look a bit different. It looks like someone dug down with their bare hands and then opened the casket, which is still fully intact.

I drop to the ground. I don't care that I'm sitting in mud. I don't even feel the coolness of the rain on my skin. I am totally and utterly lost. *What do I do now?*

"Al, did you tell anyone?"

She shakes her head. "No...I didn't know what to tell anyone. Hey, some bodies are missing? Or it seems like we have grave robbers? Or one possible zombie just stole a corpse? None of those make me seem very sane. Especially here in Little Lake, nothing interesting ever happens here. They would think it was some prank."

We have to tell someone. I have to find out what happened, but I won't be able to do that on my own. Once we're back in Alex's car, I pull my cell phone out of my pocket and place an anonymous call to the police.

"Hi, Little Lake's Cemetery seems to have been vandalized. There are two disturbed graves on site that you should look into."

After transferring that brief piece of information, I hang up.

"Come on, Alex. Let's get out of here before the cops show up."

She nods, and we speed off in her car.

As we drive away, I ask Alex to stop by and grab Eve. She's a little surprised by my request.

"Look, Al, we're going to need Eve's help, bottom line!"

This is true. Eve is the strongest thing I know. She will be useful in our search. I keep my other motive hidden from Alex. I really just have to know if she did it. Did Eve take them? Maybe she did her crazy sleepwalking thing and dug up my parents thinking it would please me? I suppose anything is possible these days.

When we arrive at Eve's house, I knock on the door. Eve is shocked to see me, but there is no time for apologies or forgiveness. I just need her to come with me.

"Eve, we have a problem. I can't talk here. We'll talk in Alex's car. Come on."

She nods, noticing my desperation, and yells back into the house to inform her parents of her departure.

When we get in the car Alex starts driving, and after a few awkward moments, Eve asks to be brought up to speed. I tell her about the empty graves, and before I can tell her my theories on what happened, she begins crying. She is sobbing so hard that I can't continue.

Alex pulls over so we can coax Eve to tell us what is wrong. I feel she knows something that can help us. In that moment, I don't care if she did it. I just want to know what happened so badly.

Through the sobs, Eve starts to form slurred sentences. "I did it...I have my memories back...I...I...attacked Henry. I killed him. I remember now. I'm horrible."

I don't know what to say to Eve's confession. I already sort of knew she did it. Now I just want to know if she took my parents' bodies as well.

"Eve, did you go the cemetery last night?"

She shakes her head. "No, I didn't take the bodies, Cam. I didn't do that, but I have this feeling that your dad might be back. He might be infected. I don't know what he'll be like now. He could be more dangerous than before. He has nothing to lose now. He's already dead."

She has a point. My father the zombie could destroy this whole town with one little bite. The Azreal Virus would spread like wildfire!

"But why would zombie Henry take Cam's mom? What would he do with her?"

Alex makes another good point: what does he want a dead body for? He won't eat her, and he won't be able to bring her back. Or can he? The thought terrifies me.

"Eve, do you think my father would even remember his life before being a zombie? I know you're infected, but all your memories are intact."

Eve's eyes are swollen with sadness. This is the first time I have looked her in the eye in days. I feel a stinging in my chest; I do feel bad for her. I never looked at this from her angle. It must be terrifying, and all I've done is forsaken her. I will fix this later, but right now, we need to make sure my father stayed dead.

"I'm sorry, Cam. I don't know what your father will be like. That couple I infected seemed like movie zombies. You know the dragging feet, brain eating, monster type? They didn't seem like their former selves."

Okay, that didn't help me much.

"Alex, let's go to my father's house. Maybe he's hiding out there if he remembers his old life."

Alex speeds off; she knows we have no time to waste.

***

Alex stops in front of the old house. I hate visiting it now. We all get out of the car, and I'm sure we're all thinking the same thing. We are hoping that we don't find anything terrifying inside.

I head around back and find that the door is open. Someone has definitely been here. I step into the house first, and Alex and Eve follow. There is a foul, rotting smell in the house. I instinctually pinch my nose. Eve must smell it too because she starts growling like a dog. Alex and I stand back and let Eve lead the way. She's trying to sniff out the source. She stops when she reaches the basement door.

I reluctantly open it. We all get a whiff of stench that almost knocks us down. The smell is stronger down there. I don't really want to find its source; fear is getting the best of me.

Eve doesn't hesitate; she is almost drawn to the stench.

The basement is dark and unwelcoming. I try to turn on the light, but it only flickers, creating a very eerie glow. I see a pile of something near the base of the stairs. I keep walking towards it.

With each step, the stench becomes more and more unbearable. I get close to the pile, and the flickering light only allows me to see pieces. I can distinguish teeth, hands, legs, and a single eye. I dash backward, repulsed and unsteady.

"There are pieces, pieces of people in a pile over here," I say, much quieter than anticipated. *I must be going into shock.*

There is no need to warn them. When Alex starts screaming at the top of her lungs, I know they are seeing it too. Eve just stares at the pile, looking hungry.

We hear a noise, and Alex goes silent. There is a shifting sound behind us. It makes us simultaneously turn. I don't see anything, which makes it all the more terrifying.

Eve starts heading towards the sound. It is easy for her to be fearless when she can't die. I follow her closely. I want to protect her, even though I am positive she doesn't need anyone's protection.

When Eve arrives at the source of the sound, she turns towards me and hugs me with such a force that she almost takes me down.

"Eve, what is it? What do you see?"

She looks me in the eye. "Cam, don't look. Please let's just go."

She tries to hold me back, but that only makes me more determined. I push her out of the way and am horrified at what lay in front of me.

"Mom?"

I look closer at the figure lying on a metal table. There are stitches all over her. Her arms are sewn on, but they don't match. Her torso is covered in her favourite dress. My eyes flood with tears, and I hold the corpse's hand. It obviously does not belong to her, but my sorrow craves her touch.

I scan lower to see her bones exposed from the torso down. I glance back at her face. It looks like her, except for the eyes. One is blue, and the other is green.

Someone is rebuilding her.

I scream, feeling like a million daggers are piercing my heart. I never heard myself scream before. I sound wounded. I suppose I am.

***

I don't remember how I left the basement, but I somehow make it outside, where I throw up all the contents in my stomach. Eve is beside me, rubbing my back.

"Cam, I think your father remembers who he is. What we saw down there is proof. He thinks he can bring your mother back by giving her a new body, but he is hunting others and taking parts he needs. He needs to be stopped. There were three bodies down there. Who knows how many others there will be?"

I nod, still not feeling well enough to stand.

"Cam, there's something else I need to tell you about the night your father died."

Oh no, please, no more bad news.

I wipe my mouth. "Okay, Eve. It really can't get much worse— it's already unbearable—so just say it."

She doesn't look at me as she speaks. "Cam, as I attacked your father, he knew it was me. He had a message for you. He asked me to tell you that he loved you and that he was sorry."

The words feel like a ton of bricks falling on my chest.

"He said that?"

Eve nods.

"He loved me?" I am shocked.

I always thought he hated me and that's why he drank so much. I often thought if he had the option of trading me for my mother, he would.

Eve helps me off the ground. "Cam, I'm not leaving your side until we find him. If he remembers everything, he will come for you. I'm absolutely terrified that he might try and use you for parts as well."

I look at Eve and ask, "Is there even a chance he could bring her back?"

Eve shakes her head. "Dr. August said you have to die from being exposed to the Azrael Virus in order to come back from the dead. Your mother died in a car accident, so there is no way she will rise. Your father doesn't know that, and I'm sure he'll do whatever it takes to finish building her. We need to keep our eyes open."

I give Eve a bone-crushing hug. I catch her off guard. I have been so horrible to her; I even attacked her. She can't control the virus any more than we can.

CHAPTER TWENTY-NINE

EVE

After driving around town for three hours, we decide to call off our zombie hunt. There are no signs of Henry Jackson anywhere.

I know Henry will come looking for us eventually, but I don't want it to come to that. If I am hungry, I'm sure Henry is ten times hungrier. Every minute that passes is a missed opportunity to save someone. I don't want anyone to go through what I'm going through.

Here I am acting so self-righteous when I am the one that caused this mess. I don't think it's fair that I get to play the hero *and* the villain in this crazy saga. But what is fair anyway? Is it fair that I was bitten? Is it fair that I now need to eat others to survive? Is it fair to Cam and Alex that they have to guard my secret? None of this is fair.

I keep thinking it will be better if I just disappear, but not today. Today, we have a zombie to catch.

We end up at Alex's house after our car ride, and I decide it will be safer if I stay with Cam and Alex tonight. I may be a bit of a cannibal, *kind of an understatement*, but there is no question that I am strong enough to protect them. This whole Azrael Virus comes with a few perks, which I haven't thought about until now. *You can't hurt what you can't kill.*

As we sit in Alex's kitchen trying to think about our next move, we hear the door burst open, and we all jump.

"Damn this doormat. I swear I trip over it every time, Dina. Can't we just get rid of it? It's hideous anyway. It's a damn cat that says 'home is where the cat is,' and we don't even have a freakin' cat!"

Thank goodness it is only Alex's parents.

"Well, the cat on the mat is so cute! If you can find me something cuter, then I will consider getting rid of it."

Ah, Mr. and Mrs. Dashkov, they are always so entertaining with their petty arguments. Most arguments are so laughable I have to excuse myself from the room or burst out laughing in their faces.

Back in high school, the Dashkov's were considering getting a divorce; they fought so much they thought they should try therapy to save their marriage. Therapy ended up being another thing to argue about, and it led to a brief separation. I know Alex was so worried they would get divorced, but I knew they would stay together; they were much too similar. How would they ever find another person who liked arguing just as much? Turns out that's just how they show they love each other. I roll my eyes at the thought.

I don't really understand their relationship. They constantly seem like they hate each other but insist that their fighting is "normal" for couples. I agree that most couples argue; I just don't think it is "normal" when it is 24/7. They don't really leave any room for romance, or respect, or happiness really.

I bite my tongue and never mention my true feelings about Alex's parents. I just hope Alex won't be tainted by their strange relationship. I want her to have so much more. A lover, a friend, a partner in crime. Someone who will make her feel special instead of pointing out her every flaw. I don't think that is too much to ask for in a relationship. When Mrs. Dashkov snaps out of her silly squabble, she notices the three of us standing there awkwardly and tries to break the ice.

"Oh, hi guys! It's nice to see the three of you together. It's like old times. Eve, you should stay for dinner. We're having pork roast and baked potatoes."

Behind her, I can see Mr. Dashkov rolling his eyes. He mumbles something sarcastic about the meal being his favourite.

"I heard that, dear. You can have some air for dinner if you prefer."

Mr. Dashkov gives her a fake smile and leaves the room.

Why do they have to make everyone feel so uncomfortable? I want to crawl under the table.

I speak first. "Sounds delicious, Mrs. Dashkov. I can help set the table…"

She shakes her head. "Nonsense. You three can hang out. I'll call you when it's all ready. I'll have Janna set the table. She needs to have something to do or she'll get up to no good."

I am glad to leave the kitchen.

We retreat to Alex's room, and we pass Janna on the way.

"Hey, little sis, Mom wants you to help set the table,"

Janna replies with sticking her tongue out at her big sis and then continues downstairs obediently.

When we get to Alex's room, she shuts the door behind us. We wouldn't want anyone hearing our strange conversation now, would we?

"So what's the plan?" Cam asks impatiently.

"I don't really have a plan, Cam. We checked the cemetery, we checked your old house, and we drove around the entire town. I think the best thing to do is see if he will come to us. Tonight, we will wait and observe."

Cam looks disappointed. "But what if he doesn't show?"

I shrug. "Well then, we are no worse off than we are right now."

***

We try to eat dinner rather quickly. I want out of the dining room as soon as possible. Mr. and Mrs. Dashkov are at it again, this time about table etiquette.

"Arthur, I've told you countless times that you need to pass the food to the guests first. You're not supposed to serve yourself first. It's rude!"

Mr. Dashkov starts taking food off his plate and putting it back on the serving trays.

"Is that better, Dina? Can we start again so I can do this properly?"

Mrs. Dashkov rolls her eyes. "That wasn't necessary. I was just trying to teach you the right way to do it."

Mr. Dashkov is starting to get angry now.

Wow, this is getting mighty uncomfortable.

"Dina, if I wanted a teacher, I would hire one."

I tune them out after that. If I keep listening, I might lose my mind. I wish they'd both just shut up already.

I really don't even know how they work together. Mr. and Mrs. Dashkov actually met at work. They both work for the pharmaceutical company Med-Trust. I'm sure they just avoid each other at work; how else would they get through the day?

I decide it's time to excuse us from the room.

"Thank you so much for dinner. Cam, Alex, and I are going to go for a little after-dinner walk. The rain has stopped, so we thought we'd take advantage."

Mrs. Dashkov looks a little disheartened. "But you haven't had dessert yet."

Crap, I want to leave now!

"Well, maybe we can have some when we get back? The walk will help us make more room for dessert." I give a very fake smile, hoping she will agree to that.

"Oh okay, you three have fun. I'll leave some dessert on the kitchen counter for when you get back." She winks at us, and I stand to leave before she can say another word.

It's always an interesting dinner at the Dashkov house.

Our walk consists of neighbourhood watch duties. We spy on our neighbours and look for anything suspicious. The only strange thing we see is a creepy black cat that not only crosses our path but hisses at us on the way by.

Un-believable! I don't need any more bad luck these days! Stupid cat!

We head back to Alex's house empty handed. Since I haven't been feeding, I feel exhausted. I request an early bedtime, and no one protests.

Sleep comes easily to all of us. We've been through a lot together, and it's all been so stressful.

***

My eyes flutter when I hear a bird. *Is it morning already?* I open my eyes to find it pitch dark out. I have to find out where the sound is coming from. My first instinct is to check the window, and right there on the sill is a crow. It's sitting on the window ledge making so much noise! I can't believe Alex and Cam are sleeping through this!

I fully open the window and shoo him away; he wisely flies off immediately.

"Good riddance," I whisper.

I am about to shut the window when something outside grabs my attention. I look down at the ground below me, and I see a dark figure lurking in the shadows, avoiding the moonlight.

"Who are you?" I ask.

The figure does not reply. Instead, it backs away further into the shadows.

Dang! I'm convinced it's Henry.

"Alex, Cam, wake up! I think he's here! He's in your front yard. We gotta go check it out."

They both look groggy, but they eventually manage to get up and follow me out.

We tiptoe downstairs as quietly as we can. I would hate to wake Janna; she might want to see what we're up to. Such a curious girl, I'm almost positive it will get her into trouble someday.

We quietly head out the front door and into the cool night air. I don't bother putting on any shoes, and I can feel the moist grass squish under my feet with each step I take.

We stand in the front yard waiting. I still see something moving in the darkness.

"Come over here. Come out where I can kick your ass!"

Cam and Alex give me a "what are you thinking?" look.

I shrug. "Don't worry, guys. I got this."

I'm ready for a fight; I'm thirsty for it!

The figure continues to move forward out of the shadows until he is in full view. It's Henry alright. He has a creepy smile slapped across his face. It's probably only creepy since most of his cheek is missing and his teeth are showing in a way that no living human can achieve.

I guess he can't heal as well as I can. However, the rest of him looks pretty good, so I guess he has some healing ability. Dr.

August did say that the virus manifests differently in each person.

Henry comes closer and closer. I put my fists up ready for a fight. I feel confident and excited for the chance to test my body. I don't really know my full capabilities yet. But I will get a bigger opportunity than I thought because as Henry nears, I notice five other zombies following him out of the shadows.

"Fantastic! A zombie gang! For shit's sake! Cam, Alex, get inside! I can't fight them all and protect you both. Get out of here."

I'm waiting to hear their retreat, but they stay. It isn't a good time to be stubborn.

"Please go! We don't need more zombies!"

Cam acts as though he doesn't hear a word. Instead, he pulls a wooden stake out of Mrs. Dashkov's garden. I look to Alex next, who is also blatantly disobeying my orders. She grabs a trowel out of the garden and holds it out in front of her in preparation.

I look Henry in the eyes. They are fiery; he's out for blood. I can sense this is no ordinary feed. You don't bring a posse unless you expect a fight or a bloodbath.

Henry stands there and signals his minions forward. The first zombie approaches and lunges at me. I head butt him, and he crumbles to the ground. I'm pretty sure I cracked his skull. The power I hold feels so amazing. I feel a sick pleasure coursing through me and point to the next zombie. "Come on, freak show, come get some."

The zombie tries to tackle me, but I grab both of his arms and pull up, instantly snapping the bones. His arms flail limply as he continues to try and attack. I kick at both his shins, and they shatter instantly. The zombie is immobilized. He kneels in front of me and is still hissing and growling. I put both my hands together to make one mega fist and smash it down onto his skull. The crunch is loud and satisfying.

"Whoo! Is that all you've got? The score is 2-0, my creepy friends. Who wants some more?"

I want to eat my words after the next zombie approaches. I guess this was a former body builder on steroids. He's humongous! With a light tap, I'm on my ass. Mr. Massive zombie grabs my throat and lifts me in the air.

The other two zombies head for Cam and Alex. I hope they can handle them because I'm a little busy at the moment.

The massive zombie launches me across the yard and into a tree. I feel the tree crack a little as I make a nice dent in it. I'm a little dizzy and breathless, but I can see him approaching again. He's drooling; I think I might be his next meal.

Quick, Eve, think. I look around and notice a shovel by the shed. That shovel could work; now I just need to get over there.

Big boy is already too close for comfort. He growls and shrieks in my face so that I can smell his rotting breath. I want to throw up, but there is no time for that right now. I try to push him away; even with my new strength, it's very difficult to keep him off of me.

Luckily I am able to get an elbow free. I lift my elbow as far into the air as I can and then rain it down onto his forehead. It stuns him for a moment, and he drops me. I make a run for the shed. The shovel is just in arm's reach when he grabs my legs and takes me down to the ground. I keep throwing my arms forward, hoping I can grab it as he tries to drag me backward. I'm pulling at the ground, trying to get closer to the shovel; a few inches will grant me salvation.

I turn to face him and continue to try and wriggle free. He's about to chomp down on my exposed ankle, but luckily I wiggle one foot free and kick him in the teeth. He is thrown back a bit. As he fumbles to recover his hold on me, I launch forward and grab the shovel. I shove it towards his neck. When the shovel buries itself into his neck meat, I press and lift it straight into the air with all my might. The shovel slices through like butter, and with a "pop," his head flies over the shed. The rest of the body lands right on top of me.

"Eww, gross, zombie blood."

I seal my mouth shut as the goopy blood pours all over me. I don't need to ingest any more of it. It's all over me, and I'm stuck struggling to shove this large body off of me. As I continue to struggle, I glance around, and my eyes find Cam and Alex still fighting off the other two zombies. I want to run over and help them. A different fire burns inside of me. It's not hunger; it's desperation.

I will not lose them. I will not fail.

Using my blood-covered body, I try to lift the body slightly and slide out from under it. Fortunately, the blood works as a lubricant, and I slide out from under him, one leg at a time.

Once free, I am running towards Cam but notice he has the zombie pegged to the ground. He then raises the garden stake and drives it straight through the zombie's eye, and it stops attacking.

Since Cam has everything under control, I turn to look at Alex, who has successfully stabbed the zombie many times with the trowel but hasn't managed a direct strike to the head.

A head wound seems to be the only way to stop them.

"Alex, throw the trowel over here."

She looks at me wildly, wiping the blonde hair out of her face, and then tosses it over the zombie's head. The trowel lands in my hand, and before the zombie can react, I hammer the trowel into the top of its head. The body crumples to the ground, and I can see relief spreading over Alex's face. Relief will have to wait; it isn't over yet. Where is Henry?

Cam looks out into the distance. "He's gone. Why would he come all the way over here and then not stay to watch?"

I look at Cam as he says this, and a startling realization hits me. "Cam, I think your father may be smarter than the average zombie. He seems to have a plan. He got these zombies to do his dirty work, and we know he is trying to re-build his wife. He's thinking."

A zombie that thinks. Now that is a scary thought. He has nothing to lose. Perhaps he even likes being a zombie. The more I think about the possibilities, the more fear I feel.

"I think we need to notify the police."

I raise an eyebrow at Alex. "I agree with you, I do, but how would we go about this without looking crazy? Alex, are we supposed to tell them that there are zombies walking amongst us? I'm fairly sure they will laugh hysterically."

Alex rolls her eyes. "I know we can't tell them that. I was thinking of making another anonymous call about 'strange occurrences' at Cam's old house."

Alex makes a good point. If they see what we saw in that basement, they may start looking around town for a suspect. Never in a million years will they guess that it is good old Henry back from the dead.

It is time to take action. I can't be afraid of being linked to this right now. What are the chances they will place me as the cause of this whole mess anyway? It is all so far-fetched.

As I look around the yard, I realize we have quite a bit of clean up to do.

"What should we do with the bodies?" I say casually.

None of us has ever hidden a body before, and it takes a bit of planning before we come up with a reasonable solution. Cam is the one to suggest we throw them down the sewer. It seems like a good enough plan. Alex grabs a crowbar from her parents' shed and hands it to Cam. He pries open the closest sewer lid; luckily, it is just down the road from Alex's house. He makes it look effortless. Cam is built like a Greek god. It is hard not to look at him in awe. I can understand why Claire is so obsessed with him.

Cam and I carry the bodies over one by one, while Alex keeps an eye out for any wandering neighbours. I don't want to have to explain this to anyone.

Our gruesome task is completed quite quickly. The bodies are rotting so well that the bones simply snap as we shove them down the manhole. The only one that is a little problematic is the massive zombie I fought off earlier.

Alex grabs another shovel from the shed and pummels the body until just about every bone in it is smashed. That makes it much easier to squeeze the body into the hole. It takes all three of us to accomplish this. We throw any of our bloodstained tools down the manhole and then seal it again with its lid.

After the bodies are taken care of, there is still the issue of blood on the front lawn. I quickly head over to the side of the house and grab the hose. I rinse the grass until it looks clean enough. It is a bit hard to tell in the dark, but I hope that I am able to rinse off most of it.

When we get back into the house, Alex places the anonymous phone call and then hangs up quickly so the call can't be traced. She takes a deep breath and regains her composure. Cam is the one having a hard time calming down; he paces back and forth in Alex's room.

"We need to do something. I'm sick of waiting around. I want to know what's going on!"

I pat Cam on the shoulder. "I know you want answers, but

we have to be smart about this. Neither one of you needs to end up like me, or worse. We can't just go zombie hunting when we're outnumbered!"

Alex looks at me with a raised eyebrow. "Why not? Why can't we zombie hunt? We have the best weapon available. We can use it to our advantage."

She winks at me. Of course, she is referring to me as their secret weapon, and though I am virtually indestructible, I am still terrified. I'm not afraid of hunting Henry; I am afraid that I will lead my friends to their deaths. I can't have their blood on my hands too.

"Okay, here is the deal. I will track Henry down myself. I don't want you guys out there. When I find him, I will call you for back up." They nod.

I don't really intend to call them; I think it will be best if I take Henry down on my own. A little white lie, but it is worth telling. After our little agreement, we all try to get some sleep, but I'm not sure any of us will ever sleep again without nightmares.

The next morning, Mrs. Dashkov knocking on the door awakens us. She sounds a bit perturbed as she asks to come in.

"Come on in, Mom," Alex replies.

When she enters the room, she is fidgeting with her hands and searching for her words. "Umm…the police are here to see you three…"

All I can think is, *Oh crap! Someone must have seen what we were up to last night.* I begin to panic and wonder how we are ever going to explain all this.

Mrs. Dashkov looks directly at Alex. "Do you have anything you need to say to me, Alexandra?" She is hoping for a confession, which means the police haven't told her why they want to speak to us.

Alex shakes her head and looks confused; that is some pretty good acting. Cam, on the other hand, looks like he has crapped his pants.

"Okay, come on downstairs when you're ready." And then Mrs. Dashkov shuts the door.

"Stay calm, guys. I know this looks bad, but we still don't know what they want. It could be anything! Maybe they just want to update us on Henry's missing body? Maybe they're just asking if we've seen anything suspicious?" I'm not sure I believe those stories myself.

In that moment, Cam and Alex look so lost. Alex bites her perfectly manicured nails, and Cam tugs at his dark hair, almost pulling out a clump. I can't let them get in trouble for my shitty problems. I can't help but feel I am destroying them somehow.

"Look, guys, if they do know about the bodies, I will take the blame…"

Cam cuts me off. "No, Eve, we're in this together. We always have been."

I could kiss him right there. It is nice to have someone on my side, even if I am the one to blame.

"Listen, Cam, we can't all look for Henry from a jail cell."

Cam hugs me tightly. He's so warm, I don't want the hug to end. As he holds me, he whispers, "Exactly, Eve. That's why I can't let you take the fall. It has to be me. You need to be the one to find Henry. You're the only one who can stop him."

He lets me go and bolts out the door before I can argue. Alex and I look at each other. *I guess we better follow that boy. Who knows what he's up to?*

We join Cam in the front room. He's already sitting in front of the two cops. One cop is a fairly pretty Latina woman. She is the type of cop many men would hit on, but I can sense she is a no-nonsense kind of girl. Her badge says, Officer Gomez. The man she's with is Officer Han. I know him fairly well. His family owns an amazing Chinese restaurant in town, and he helps with many local charities. I first met him when doing the ten-kilometer Run for Breast Cancer Awareness. He is a very nice man; he even let me call him Han Solo the day of the run, which makes him super cool in my books. I hope Officer Han will go easy on us today.

Alex and I take a seat on the sofa next to Cam. Officer Han begins our meeting while Officer Gomez stares us down with a look of repulsion. If she didn't like us before we opened our mouths, we sure as hell didn't stand a chance of her liking us afterward.

"I am Officer William Han, and this here is my partner Officer Martina Gomez. First off, I wanted to let Cam know that we are still doing everything in our power to find the people who dug up your parents' graves. It's an absolutely appalling crime, and we won't stop until we find them."

"Officer Han, how do you know that there is a 'them'? What if it was just one person who dug up my parents?"

Officer Han shakes his head in response to Cam's question and then continues. "There is no way a single person could have done that so quickly. They would need to be the Incredible Hulk to dig up all that dirt and carry the bodies all by themselves. Now for the second piece of business, we got an anonymous call earlier this morning about checking out Cam's previous place of residence for some suspicious occurrences. The person on the phone wasn't very specific, but I figured we should go over and check it out. I thought it might be connected to the grave site somehow. Officer Gomez and I went into the house and didn't find anything."

I want to jump up and ask, "But did you check the basement?" but I obviously can't say a word.

Officer Han becomes more serious when he asks his next question. "Do you three have anything further to add to the investigation? Is there anything else you want to tell me?"

I feel he knows something more. He is hoping we will admit to it and save him some trouble. We glance at each other and shake our heads; there is nothing we want to add willingly.

Officer Gomez stands and scowls at us. "Are you sure you don't want to tell us anything?" She stares right at Alex when she says it, which makes Alex tense. "You see, we traced the call from this morning, and funny enough, it led us here."

Dammit, I thought they couldn't trace a short call.

I can see Alex sweating; she is agonizing over how to explain the call. I hope she has a good answer because I sure don't.

Officer Gomez continues her scare tactic. "I really hope you wouldn't lie to us. That's a crime in itself, and it really wouldn't benefit Cam." She pauses for effect and then continues the mental assault. "Unless, of course, one of you ladies committed the crime? That would be a good reason to lie, but I can't see you two committing a crime like that, so I really do expect you to tell me the whole truth about who placed the call and why. I understand people do stupid things sometimes…"

She is really starting to make me mad. I feel a vein pulsing in my forehead. She isn't going to like me when I'm angry. How dare she suggest that we would take Cam's parents as some stupid prank? I am boiling, literally. I feel so hot that I think I might faint, and this isn't a good time to faint; it would seem like an omission of guilt. I try to stay quiet and calm myself down. If I get too angry, I don't know what will happen next. I'm pretty sure if I eat a couple of police officers, someone will come looking for me eventually. They don't usually let cop murders go unsolved.

Alex sighs and begins speaking. I am a little afraid of what might come out of her mouth. "I placed the call. I'm sorry I lied. I only did it because I didn't want to seem like a snoop. I had gone over to Cam's place the other day and heard strange noises coming from inside the house. I knew the house wasn't occupied, so I thought I would notify the police."

Not a bad story actually. Good job, Alex!

My blazing elation is quickly extinguished when Officer Gomez continues. "Why did you make the call at four a.m. this morning? Why didn't you call right after you left the Jackson residence?"

Alex looks baffled. "I don't know. I didn't really think about that. I just called because I thought it would be beneficial to your case."

"It didn't occur to you that it would be most beneficial if you called it in right away?"

Before the situation escalates further, Officer Han steps in. "Okay, Martin, cool it. I don't think they had anything to do with this. I think they were only trying to help."

Thank you, Han Solo. Someone had to tell this bitch to back down.

"We'll be on our way now. Please call us if you have any further concerns or leads. We will take what we can get. There wasn't much evidence left at the grave site."

We thank the officers as they take their leave. Officer Han shakes my hand, but Officer Gomez only gives us a cold stare before walking out the door.

She has every reason to suspect us. I know she is only trying to do her job, but I still want to rip her face off. I can tell she is going to be watching us very closely from now on.

CHAPTER THIRTY

As soon as the officers leave, I give Eve and Cam a look of relief and then start laughing like a lunatic. Cam smiles back, but Eve looks ill. She leans against the wall for support.

"Eve, are you okay?"

Her forehead is beading with sweat, and she's mumbling. Before I can get over to her, Eve slides to the ground. Her collapse triggers Cam into action, and he's by her side in a split second. He lifts her off the floor and brings her upstairs to my room.

She is so warm to the touch; I fear she may burst into flames.

"Cam, why is she burning up? What should we do?"

He looks stumped and walks out of the room.

"Cam? Where are you going?" I whisper after him.

He comes back a moment later with a cool wet towel and places it on Eve's forehead. She lets out a sigh of pleasure. Thank God that gives her some relief.

We sit waiting for Eve to snap out of it.

✳✳✳

Half an hour goes by before Eve begins to make slight movements showing her return to wakefulness.

"Welcome back to the land of consciousness," I say softly.

"What happened? Did I faint?"

I nod. "Yes you sure did, and you were burning up."

Cam comes over to her, his eyes still filled with concern. "Eve, when was the last time you ate?"

She looks at him sideways. "Last night. Why?"

He runs his fingers through her hair. "No, you dunce. When was the last time you really ate?"

He is referring to Eve's new favourite food, people.

Cam continues. "Eve, I think you need to feed regularly. If you don't, it seems to affect you. It may even kill you."

Eve shakes her head frantically. "No, I can't, Cam. I don't want to! I don't want to be a monster."

I know Cam has a point; she has to feed to survive. I hate the idea of her eating people, but I also can't stand the idea of losing her.

"Eve, you should listen to Cam. Tonight we are sending you out to feed. I really think you should stick to eating criminals, though. Not as many people will miss them."

Eve looks shocked. I think I shocked myself with that comment. *But hey! It is some sort of solution.*

We all laugh uncomfortably.

CHAPTER THIRTY-ONE

EVE

That night, Cam and Alex pretty much shove me out of the house. With their permission, I feel oddly less awful about my new eating habits. I look back at them in the doorway as I make my way down the street; these are the only two people who love me regardless of my secret. I'm sure other people will try to destroy me if they know what I really am. I often have nightmares about a town of people with torches chasing after me screaming, "Kill the beast!" As if I am Frankenstein or something. I am still me in my heart; although un-beating, it is still in the right place.

I walk the dark streets with my senses ablaze. Anything wicked will be my next meal; drug dealers, thieves, gang members, or murderers, they will be my tasty conquest tonight. I drool at the thought. I decide to head to a biker bar on the outskirts of town; there are usually a bunch of low life's there. I may even get to test my powers if they decide to pick a fight. I rather enjoy that aspect of my infection. Powers are a definite perk.

When I arrive at the bar, there are a bunch of biker guys out front. They are rather large, with long beards and leather outfits. I quickly realize that I do not adhere to the dress code. I am wearing jeans, my brown fall boots, and a pretty pink blouse.

Pink? I really didn't think this through, did I?

Next time I will remember to stick to all-black attire. The men out front watch me as I make my way to the front entrance of the bar. They whistle at me, and I pretend not to hear them.

The inside of the bar is packed. There are many girls in trashy outfits and many more men in leather. I stand out like a sore thumb. I bite my lip, trying to conjure some courage and continue towards the bar. I am painfully aware of all the stares I'm getting.

"Bartender, I would like some whiskey, please."

Maybe I shouldn't have added the "please." That makes me seem too delicate.

He raises an eyebrow at me but pours the Jack Daniels all the same.

I chug it and ask for another. The bartender laughs, amused by my stupidity, and pours some more. I take my time with this one. I sip it and observe the bar. Everyone seems like scum in here, and it makes me hungry.

As I continue to observe, a tall man covered in tattoos enters the bar, and everyone goes quiet. They appear to be afraid of this man. People clear a path for him as he makes his way toward the bar. It looks like people jumping out of the way of a speeding vehicle.

He is the one I want. I lick my lips.

He strikes fear in others, so he must be up to no good.

He sits at the bar and orders a beer, and by "orders" I mean that he yells, "Beer! Now!" and the bartender passes him one with trembling hands. I raise my glass to the heavily tattooed man and throw back the rest of my whiskey.

This gets his attention, and he makes his way over to me.

"Hey honey, what's your name?"

I didn't think of an alias beforehand, so I give him a version of my own name.

"I'm Eva. Who are you?"

He smiles a wicked smile under his perfectly groomed mustache.

Who even wears mustaches anymore?

"You don't know me, huh? Well, that's probably better for you. Around here, they call me Luci. It's short for Lucifer."

I want to roll my eyes and hurl at the same time—*that is so lame*—but I'm positive someone with that kind of a nickname must have earned it.

"That's quite the nickname. So are you going to buy me another drink? I'm all out." I turn my glass upside-down as an indication of this fact.

He looks intrigued. He likes me. I guess he likes his women rude. Luci asks the bartender for the entire bottle of Jack, and he places it in front of me.

I throw my glass onto the floor. "Guess I won't be needing that." And I begin to drink straight from the bottle.

Luci laughs and claps with delight. I think I'm in his good books now.

I finish the whole bottle of Jack and pretend to be drunk. I can't really get drunk with this whole healing deal, but I still remember how drunk people act.

"C'mon, Luci, letzz go outside, juss you ann me." I slur my words perfectly.

People whistle, thinking we are heading outside for something more enjoyable. Little do they know, this will be the last time they will ever see Luci, and I'm sure I am doing them a favour.

I grab Luci by the collar and pull him outside. He doesn't mind; I guess he also likes it when his women play rough.

"Letzz go out back. Itz more privacy."

He laughs as I try to get words out and agrees to go around back.

When we get there, he kisses me ferociously. I automatically think, *yuck*, but hey if this is how I can catch my food tonight, then I'll play bait.

The next part startles me; Luci puts his hands at my throat and begins to choke me. He's no longer interested in kissing, and by the look in his eyes, I can tell his intent is murder. He squeezes and squeezes. It's painful, but I don't fight him, and I eventually black out.

When I come back, I am angry as hell. My hunger has peaked, and there will be no stopping me now. I open my eyes slowly to find Luci smoking a cigarette looking mighty pleased with himself.

I get up, and as he turns to look at me, the cigarette drops out of his mouth.

"No, that's not right. I killed you. You weren't breathing. You had no pulse. You're dead."

Luci looks as scared as a spooked pup.

"Oh, I'm dead, trust me. I just don't stay dead."

I think I hear him scream like a little girl before I tear his throat open, but I can't be sure. I am too focused on how delicious he is.

I leave the body behind the bar. Luci's blood is still pouring out everywhere, making a rather large puddle. I might not have finished my meal, but I made a good dent in it. I think people will be hard-pressed to find a body in that mangled mess. I don't feel badly about any of it.

I wipe my dripping mouth in satisfaction and make my way home in the shadows.

CHAPTER THIRTY-TWO

CAM

It is the middle of the night when the door to my bedroom opens. In the frame of the doorway stands Eve.

How did she get in Alex's house? And why is she in my room?

She approaches me without a word. There is blood dripping down her face. I sit up to see if she's okay. I rub her face and find that it's not her blood. *Thank God!*

"Eve, what are you doing?" She still doesn't speak. She comes closer to my face, and her lips touch my cheek. Her breath is warm, and I lose all sense of my surroundings. Her lips find mine, and I stop caring about the blood on her face. I just want her to kiss me until the end of time.

She pulls away, and I snap out of my dreamlike state.

My eyes open, and I find myself making out with my pillow. I am such an idiot that I slap the pillow in my face a few times. Eve will never kiss me like that; she never even agreed to date me. I thought I was over her; I convinced myself time and time again that I don't love her, that I don't dream of a future with her. I am one sad sack of shit. I'm pretty sure Eve thinks of me as a brother and nothing more.

I get out of bed and decide to wash my face. My dream has left me a bit sweaty; I need to snap out of it.

As I rinse my face in cold water, I find my mind flooding with thoughts of Eve. I remember the first day I met her; I swear she shone as I asked her where one of my classes was. She was kind and funny. I loved her immediately.

She made me part of her family, she made me a priority, and yet she didn't love me like that. I always had an ounce of hope that she would love me back someday, but things have changed. How can we ever be together now? She ate my father, she eats people in general, and I can't forget the most important obstacle: she is dead.

Even with all these new horrifying realities, it doesn't stop me from loving her. I wish I can tell her all this, but I am much too focused on keeping her safe. We don't know what this Azrael Virus is capable of. I may lose Eve altogether, and that thought is more horrifying than anything else.

I go back to my bedroom after freshening up. The moon shines through the window, and I am drawn to it. I have loved looking at the stars ever since I was little. Constellations are my favourite things to study.

As I look up at the sky, I hear a rustling below. My mind immediately rushes to my father. Is he back? Now might be the perfect time to end this nightmare. I look around the room for something to use as a weapon. I spot a hockey stick in the corner. *Perfect!* I grab the stick and head downstairs and out the door.

I hold the hockey stick in front of me like a spear, readying myself for any attack.

I hear the rustling noise again and head towards the sound. My heart is racing; I'm not sure I am ready for this confrontation. Can I even really kill my father? I guess I will find out.

I stab the hockey stick straight into the rustling bushes. A rabbit runs out. I think we are both badly startled. I sigh with relief. I guess I overreacted.

I turn to head back into the house, but before I can take a step, something slams against my temple, and I collapse to the ground.

I can taste the dew on the grass; I must be face down on the lawn. I am slightly coherent, but everything spins, and I have to close my eyes. I feel someone dragging me away by the ankles. There is a screeching laugh, and then everything goes dark.

CHAPTER THIRTY-THREE

ALEX

The next morning, I head downstairs and notice that Cam is not up yet. That is strange; Cam is an early bird. I am shocked that he isn't already here dressed and ready, having some breakfast.

I pour some cereal and milk into a bowl. I'm sure he'll be down soon. I turn on the TV and watch some cartoons as I finish my cereal.

After twenty minutes, I still don't hear Cam shuffling about. I decide to go upstairs and check on him. I knock on the door. "Cam? Wakey wakey, eggs and bakey."

I wait a few seconds, but there is still no sound. I decide to be a snoop and slowly enter the room. I call his name a few more times, but once the door is fully open, I notice that there is no one here. *Where has Cam gone?*

I check around the house a few more times with no luck. I head outside and check around the yard. Maybe Cam wanted some fresh air? I notice something on the front lawn and move closer to get a better look.

There in the grass is a single green sneaker. Cam's green sneaker. My heart starts racing; Cam wouldn't go anywhere with one shoe. I run back into the house and call the only person who will share my anxiety.

"Eve! Cam's missing!"

Her voice is slightly raspy; I don't really want to ask about how her night went last night. I know she was out hunting and was most likely successful. I don't want any vivid images in my mind.

"I found one of his shoes on my front lawn. Where would he go in such a hurry without a shoe? What if someone took him?"

I start crying; I can't help it. I'm so afraid that Cam was trying to track down Henry on his own and something horrible happened to him. I don't need two zombie friends. One is quite enough to worry about.

"Okay Al, listen, here is what we're going to do. You drive around town, see if you can spot anything strange. I want you to pop in and check out Cam's old house. I know the cops said they didn't find anything there the other day, but it's worth a shot. If you notice anything strange there, do me a favour and call Officer Han or Gomez. Do not go in there by yourself! I'm going to check out the cemetery. Call it a hunch, but I think zombies like hanging out there. It sure makes me feel strangely at ease."

We hang up the phone, and I plan to start my mission immediately.

I am almost out the door when my mother stops me.

"Where are you going in such a hurry?"

I try to act calm. "I need to go meet with Eve for a bit."

My mother looks a bit concerned. "Please don't get into any trouble. I don't need my daughter going to jail. Those cops seemed very interested in you and your friends the other day."

I hug her. "Don't worry, Mom. We're not criminals."

I don't think that puts her at ease much, but I turn to leave anyway.

I jump in my car and try not to speed away in a suspicious manner.

***

I park in front of Cam's old house and notice the cops are already there. It is too late to pretend that I am just driving by. They will know that I came here for a specific reason.

Officer Han and Gomez are right out front, and they spot me. They start to walk towards my car. I fear they will arrest me and take me to the station for questioning. I do not have time for that!

Officer Gomez leans into the driver's side window and smiles at me as she removes her sunglasses. "Good morning, Miss Dashkov. What brings you here? Before you answer, here's a fun fact. About 60% of all criminals return to the scene of their crime. Cool, huh?"

She says it in such a mocking manner that I'm sure my face matches her sarcasm.

Officer Han walks up behind her. "Now, now Martina, down girl. She's just about to tell us why she's here. Right, Alex?"

I nod, although I don't quite know what I am going to tell them. My head races with a whole bunch of lies I can tell, but ultimately my mind settles on the truth.

I burst into tears. "Cam is missing. I don't know where he is. I found one shoe."

I lift the shoe up for them to see. "I thought he might be here. I don't know. I just want to find him. Please help me."

Officer Gomez stands back, clearly affected by the sudden outburst of emotion. Officer Han is the first to comfort me. "Don't worry, Alex. We'll find him. I just need you to tell me what you know. When did you see him last?"

"The last time I saw him was before bed. I don't know when he left the house. I'm sure he left on his own, but then something must have happened in front of my house. He left without one of his shoes. I'm scared someone took him."

Officer Han looks closer at the shoe. The two officers stare blankly at each other, and then Officer Han signals to another cop in one of the vehicles nearby. "Hey, Roy, will you bring me evidence bag number 3?"

Roy obliges and brings him the bag. Officer Han opens it and reveals Cam's matching sneaker. I cover my mouth to hide my silent scream.

"Oh no! What happened to him? Is he in there?"

I jump out of my car and want to run and check the house myself.

Officer Han stops me. "There is no one in the house, Alex. We checked everywhere. The sneaker was in the basement and…" He stops there.

"And what? And what?" I'm starting to raise my voice now. I'm scared and angry; I need answers.

He continues reluctantly. "And there was some blood in the same area. We are sending the blood samples to the lab. We will see if it matches Cam's. You've helped us a lot, Alex. We didn't know that Cam was missing. We didn't know who the shoe belonged to. Now that we have a lead, we might be able to save him."

I am so terrified I am shaking.

"Officers, I'm not sure we can wait that long. I have a very bad feeling about all this."

We all look at each other in silence. All three of us know very well that something awful happened to Cam, and the likelihood of Cam being alive dwindles with every minute that passes.

CHAPTER THIRTY-FOUR

EVE

I arrive at the cemetery and immediately start sprinting towards the two grave sites that I have seen enough of this past week. I don't waste any time looking around the entire cemetery; there is something driving me towards this one particular spot. I always believed you should trust your instincts, and I do just that.

I don't see anyone or anything, but that doesn't mean I am alone. I cautiously inspect Henry's grave first. It is still dug up, and it now has caution tape around it. I shudder at the thought of someone falling in accidentally.

After a few minutes of searching, I sit on the ground, a bit baffled. I really thought I would find something here. As I'm seated, I look over at Cam's mother's grave. There is something different about it; the dirt is no longer disturbed. It looks as though someone has filled the hole. Perhaps this was done for the same reason? They definitely don't want people falling into an early grave. I chuckle. "Early grave, that's funny." As I enjoy my little laugh, I feel something below me. I freeze and listen carefully. What was that?

Next, comes a muffled sound from below. I place my ear to the ground; there it is again. I follow the sound to the newly filled grave. My eyes grow wide. "Oh my God! Cam!" I scream.

Why didn't I think of this before? The freshly filled hole must have Cam in it! That sicko Henry decided to really finish him off this time.

I begin frantically digging dirt with my bare hands. My strength and speed only allow me to dig as fast as a rabid dog, which is still not fast enough. He could be losing air; he could be dead soon; he maybe has seconds. I shed tears as I continue to dig frantically.

What else can I do? I look around for a shovel, but there isn't one anywhere. As I dig, I start to yell, "Help, please help! There's someone down there!"

The muffled sound underneath me stops. "No no! Don't you die on me! Cam, stay with me! I'm going to get you out. Just please hold on."

It's almost as if my prayers are answered when I see Alex, Officer Han, and Officer Gomez running towards me. I could kiss them all, even Officer Gomez! I have no idea how they knew to come, but I am so happy to see them.

"Oh thank God! Please help! He's down there! I could hear him banging on the lid and screaming for help. He's buried down there."

Alex slides down next to me and tries digging with her bare hands too. I can see Officer Gomez calling for back up and explaining the situation.

Officer Han heads over to his car. He starts it up and begins backing up towards the grave site. Han Solo gets out of his car and opens up his trunk; he has a shovel and throws it to me. I catch it and begin digging bigger loads of dirt out of the way. He grabs something else out of his trunk. It appears to be a chain with a hook attached to it. Han Solo hooks it up to the hitch on his car and brings the chain towards us.

"Eve, if we can find a corner of the casket, we can attach the hook to it and I can try and use my car to drag it out of the ground." That sounds like a plan.

I continue to dig on the same side until I make a hole deep enough to feel around in. I tap the ground with my hand and feel a hard surface. "Here! There's part of it."

I drop the shovel, and Alex and I clear more dirt away with our hands to expose the casket for Han to see. He has a little axe and makes a hole in the casket so that the hook will have something to grab onto. As soon as he has a big enough hole, he puts the hook in place and returns to his car. Han starts it up quickly and hits the gas. His wheels are spinning, but the coffin hasn't budged.

I keep digging with my shovel, hoping I can help dislodge the coffin as Han's car pulls at it. This has to work; I don't want to think of the alternative.

Han backs his car up a little to give him some more space to rev up. He hit the gas, and we all prayed as we watch the grave. As the chain tugs at the casket, the dirt shakes, and the casket shoots halfway out of the ground. "Thank God!" That is good enough.

I grab Han's little axe and begin to hack away at the bottom of the coffin. We can drag Cam out that way. I hack away at the coffin until wood blasts apart, splinters of it everywhere. I hope they won't notice that this sort of force isn't natural for my stature.

The end of the casket is off, and I can see feet. "Help me grab him out!" I yell over to Officer Gomez.

She grabs one ankle and I grab the other. We both pull until Cam is halfway out, then we try to gently take the rest of his body out. He doesn't need further injuries; he has been through enough.

It takes all four of us to place Cam on the ground. Officer Gomez yells that she sees another body in the casket. With the help of Officer Han, she drags out Cam's half-built mother. They both retch at the sight of her. Alex and I are shocked. It is almost as if Henry is expecting a big family reunion.

My interest returns to Cam; his body doesn't seem in bad shape. There is just a gash on the top of his head. I'm so happy to have him out that I forget to check if he's breathing. Officer Gomez is already ahead of me. She is checking for a pulse. After a minute, she shakes her head. My stomach lurches. "No, no, he's not dead. Move!" I shove Officer Gomez out of the way and check for myself. There is no breath on my hand when I place it over his mouth. I place my ear to his chest, and it is silent. I scream in agony. I can't lose him.

I begin CPR. I can hear the ambulance in the distance. Help is on the way, but I need to be doing something productive before they arrive. I give Cam a breath of air and pump his chest and repeat. Air, and then pump again. It isn't working! I sob as the paramedics move me out of the way. They set up their defibrillator as fast as they can and attach it to Cam. The machine shocks him once, and his body jolts, but nothing happens. I close my eyes tightly and pray for the first time in years. Please God, just let Cam live.

I hold my breath as they prepare for the second charge. Cam's body jolts viciously again, and this time, he gasps and opens his eyes. Alex and I begin to breathe as well. I hug her so tightly I may have crushed her bones; she lets out a little yelp but does not back away.

The paramedics place Cam on a gurney and roll him into an ambulance. I'm not leaving Cam's side again and insist on riding in the ambulance with him. I tell Alex I will meet her at the hospital and that she should probably fill our parents in on what's happened.

CHAPTER THIRTY-FIVE

CAM

I wake up in another hospital bed. This can't be good. I feel much more awful than the last time I was in here. I feel very numb and out of it.

The first person to greet me is Eve. She's staring down at me, and my heart beats faster, which makes my chest sting a bit, and I place my hand over the sore spot. Eve runs her fingers through my hair, and I feel instantly at ease. She has such power over me, but I can never admit to it.

Next, Eve starts crying. She presses her forehead to my hand. "Cam, I thought I lost you."

I stroke her cheek with my free hand. "I'm still here."

She nods and tries to control her sobs. "Your dad took you?" Eve asks as she tries to gulp back her tears.

"Yes, he did. He smacked my head with something outside of Alex's place and then took me to my old house. I only remember bits and pieces, but I think I remember seeing my mother? And I definitely remember being put in a coffin. That asshole buried me alive!"

Eve takes a big breath before speaking. "He buried you with her."

This whole thing is so strange. "I thought zombies were supposed to be mindless. My father plotted to take me and bury me with my mother. How can a zombie do that?"

Eve shrugs. "This is going to sound stranger still. I think he just wants his family back together."

The weight of what Eve is saying hits me like a bus. My eyes well up with tears, but I don't dare let a single tear fall. Men don't cry; my father taught me that.

"Cam, your father loved you. He had a messed up way of showing it, but even after death, he can't stop thinking about his family. What does that tell you? I think it's time to end this. I don't think Henry will put up much of a fight now that we messed up his little get-together."

I want this all to be over. Both my parents are dead, and I don't understand why I have to keep revisiting this incredibly painful fact.

"So when can I get out of this place so we can get to work?"

Eve looks at her watch. "Well, it's midnight. The nurse said sometime in the morning."

Eve makes room for herself in my bed and closes her eyes.

"Well, aren't you going home to sleep then?"

She opens one eye and raises an eyebrow. "Where else am I going to go? This is where I want to be." She closes her eyes again and gets comfortable.

I am touched, not that I expect anything different from Eve. I know that I am important to her; I just want to be everything to her that she is to me.

When I notice she is sound asleep, I whisper my true feelings into her ear. "I love you more than you can imagine."

I feel better after saying it, even though she didn't hear me. I close my eyes and doze off.

CHAPTER THIRTY-SIX

EVE

While Cam is giving his statement to the police, I find time to wander around in my thoughts. Something in me has changed. I want Henry dead so badly it's all I can think about. I am consumed with hatred. I don't want him hurting Cam again.

I have fed recently and feel powerful. I could tear his head off with my bare hands or kick it off like a soccer ball. I catch myself smiling as I think of Henry's demise. Something evil has risen in me, and it doesn't bother me one bit. I am starting to embrace my darker side. I'm not human anymore; it is about time I start accepting that.

Once the police leave, I ask the nurse when Cam can leave. She says she will go ask the doctor. The nurse returns an hour later and tells Cam he is free to leave. She tells him to take it easy over the next few days and come back if he feels even a little strange. Cam promises he will and begins putting on his normal clothes. I pretend to look away but find myself peeking as he changes. I am finding him really distracting at the moment. I can't help but stare at his perfect abs as he puts on his shirt. Cam catches me looking. *Damn.* He smiles at me and finishes changing.

I don't want to give him any ideas; it won't be smart for us to be together now. If I want to keep him alive, I should keep him as far away from me as possible.

***

We get in the car and pick Alex up from her house. She has a large duffle bag with her. This makes Cam laugh out loud. I guess the tiny woman with the large bag is quite a sight.

"Alex, are we robbing a bank, or have you started some boxing training I don't know about?"

She punches Cam in the arm when she nears the vehicle. "Shut up! I thought I would bring some weapons. I packed a few crowbars, a shovel, a nail gun, a baseball bat, and some knives."

I look at Alex. "Good thinking, girl. You will both need to protect yourselves. You might even need to protect yourselves from me."

They both say, "Never!" in sync with each other. This angers me. They need to see me as a threat and have their guard up.

I raise my voice so they will understand my seriousness. "No, you don't understand. I can't always control the virus. It does what it wants, and if it wants to rip you to shreds, it will!"

The car goes silent; I hope that means that I have gotten through to them.

We go back to the only place I can think of. It's daytime, but the cemetery has heavy gray clouds above it. We get to the grave site, and I sit on the ground. I shiver at the thought of Cam slamming his fists inside of a buried casket. That was only a couple of days ago, and here we are again.

Alex and Cam sit beside me. Alex hands Cam the baseball bat, and she takes the crowbar in hand as her weapon of choice. She doesn't offer me anything; she knows I won't need anything extra.

After thirty minutes, I can tell that Cam is getting antsy. "So now what?"

I give him a look. "Now we wait. Do you have a better idea?"

I guess I shouldn't be getting snappy with him. I know he just wants to bury the past in a very literal sense.

After a few hours, I begin to get a bit frustrated. What can I do to draw him out? I'm sure he will be here. Where else would Henry hide? I have a rather gross idea enter my mind, but it might do the trick.

I ask Alex to hand me one of the knives in the duffle bag. She looks at me sideways. "What are you gonna do with that, Eve?"

I don't answer the question. I just tell her to trust me. She hands me the knife, and I cut into my arm deep enough for the blood to gush. I hear Cam and Alex scream, but I ignore them; they'll get over it.

"Hey, Henry! I know you're out there!" I yell out.

Then I take my gushing arm and start smearing blood all over Mrs. Jackson's tombstone.

"Well if you're not here, I guess I can just bleed all over your wife's tombstone. You won't mind, I'm sure."

Still no sign of him, but I can swear I hear some bushes rustle slightly behind me. I guess I will have to be a little meaner.

"Hey, Henry! Your stupid wife called. She's dead tired of your drinking. Get it? 'Dead tired.' Pretty funny, right? I'll be here all week."

I hear a growl in the distance. Oh, he is nearby alright. It is working. I need to egg him on just a bit more and then he will make his appearance. I am certain of this.

I try to think of the worst thing I can do to piss Henry off.

I take hold of Cam's shirt and push him to the ground. "Just go with it, okay?" I say to Cam, but he still looks terrified as I hold the knife above his head.

I begin to yell again. "Henry, your son's gonna be my next meal. I will make sure there is nothing left of his face. That's my favourite part."

I wait a few seconds before the next blow. "Well, I guess you care less about your son than I thought. Are you just going to sit back and watch him die? What a poor excuse for a father you are! You just keep failing him, don't you?"

That last one must burn a bit because the growl in the distance intensifies and gets closer.

I whisper to Alex, "Get ready. He's coming."

I stay put, still holding the knife over Cam.

It goes oddly quiet. He must want to use the element of surprise before he attacks. I stand, trying to sniff him out, but I am too late by then; he is already behind me.

I get a quick glance of him before he knocks me to the ground and sends the knife in my hand flying. He's so strong and so putrid smelling. I try to hold his mouth away from my flesh; I don't know what being bitten again will turn me into.

I don't want to be a full-fledged zombie-like Henry, with all the rotting flesh and growling; it doesn't sound appealing.

Henry keeps trying to chomp at me as I keep trying to shove him off. Alex hits his back with a crowbar, but he doesn't release me. It only angers him further, and he smacks her with one arm, sending her soaring backward. Henry notices the crowbar on the ground; he releases me and grabs it. I try to crawl out of the way before he figures out how to use the thing. It doesn't take him long; he slams it down on my back with such force I feel one of my spinal discs crumble.

I scream in agony, and that sends Cam into action. He hits his father in the head with the baseball bat. It sends Henry stumbling back a bit, but it isn't hard enough of a blow to kill him.

"Hit him again, Cam," I grunt through a clenched jaw.

Cam tries, but Henry catches the bat and throws it away. He continues towards Cam.

I need to get up, but after a few more tries, I realize I can't. I will have to wait for my spine to heal itself before I can stand again.

I glance over at Alex, who is also trying to rise. I guess she hit the ground pretty hard. She looks a little disoriented.

"Alex! Help Cam! I can't move."

She nods and grabs the nail gun. She shoots a few nails at Henry, causing him to howl with annoyance, but he still continues to walk towards Cam. Henry grabs Cam's head and licks his face; it almost looks like a kiss. Alex runs up to Henry and smashes the whole nail gun onto his head.

"Take that, you deadbeat dad!"

Henry turns and grabs Alex by the throat with his other free hand. He's so strong he raises her in the air.

Henry has both my friends in his hands, he holds all the cards, and all I can do is watch.

"Leave them alone, Henry! Pick on someone less human, huh? Come get some!"

I think he gives a zombie laugh. He knows there is nothing I can do.

Alex is starting to turn a bit blue. I just keep screaming, "Stop! Stop!"

I feel dizzy from screaming so hard.

Alex keeps fighting; she claws at him and tries to kick her feet. Cam is trying to break out of his headlock and get to Alex, but he isn't having any luck.

My fear intensifies when Alex stops struggling. I watch Cam with a brief glimmer of hope. His foot finds the crowbar. He is struggling to break free. Cam is able to twist his arm away, and I hear a loud *snap* as Henry's arm falls awkwardly to his side. I hold my breath and pray.

Cam doesn't hesitate; he knows Alex will be dead if he doesn't do something right now. Cam takes the crowbar and spears it up through Henry's chin all the way out the backside of his head. Henry's hand releases Alex, who collapses to the ground and desperately takes in air. Henry cascades to the ground with no further movement. It is finally over.

Cam sits beside his father's body a little breathless as well. He looks Henry over, making sure he is dead. He notices something in Henry's pocket and pulls it out. He briefly sobs and then places the object in his pocket. He tries to compose himself and crawls over to Alex.

"Are you both okay?" I yell over since I can't see for myself.

Alex nods, still trying to recover.

Cam starts walking towards me now that he knows Alex is okay. "Can you stand, Eve?"

I shake my head. "No, not yet. He crunched my back pretty good."

Cam lifts me off the ground and carries me over to Alex. He's about to put me down, then rethinks it. He looks into my eyes with longing. I return the gaze; I can swear my pulse is racing as he places his lips on mine. I feel all those things you should feel when the right person kisses you. Sparks, fireworks, and however else they describe it.

When it ends, I'm left a little beside myself. Cam places me on the ground next to Alex and doesn't speak another word. He has unfinished business to attend to.

Alex and I watch as Cam lifts his father and places him in the grave that has been waiting long enough to receive him. Cam pulls a shovel out of Alex's duffle bag and begins covering his father in dirt. Each pile feels permanent, and that's a good thing. We will never have to worry about Henry again.

Alex and I hug as we watch Cam say goodbye to his family for the final time.

CHAPTER THIRTY-SEVEN

EVE

It is time to head back to school. It feels like we have been home longer than a little over a week. However, I am glad this god-awful week is over and we made it out alive.

The cops notified Cam that his father's body had been returned, and they promised him that they would continue to search for the grave robbers. I'm not so sure they will ever discover that zombies are to blame. That will be way too far out of the box to even consider.

Cam and I never speak about the kiss we shared, but Alex brings it up whenever she can. Alex keeps harassing me about dating Cam, but I can't wrap my head around any of that right now. I have too many issues, and a relationship will add too much chaos to my already spinning head. I haven't actually seen much of Cam over the past few days, which is probably for the best; he has been really busy studying.

Back to school means midterms and facing Dr. August's slew of tests. For a moment, I thoroughly consider zombie hunting as a viable career choice. I can do that for the rest of my life; it doesn't sound like too terrible an idea. I just don't want to deal with reality. I still don't want to believe that I will never be the same again.

***

I have a midterm the day after we return to Guelph. It is a math exam in the MacNaughton Building. A big concrete building with many windows, it looks too modern and out of place here. I hate the building but hate math more. The course is part of my program, and I have to take it. I'm not a terrible math student; I just find it a little boring. Dr. August always tells me how important mathematics and collecting data is to the study of anthropology, but I really just want to find cool stuff.

The exam takes me a couple of hours to complete. I would have been done sooner, but the stupid professor decided to add an essay question at the end, which throws me for a loop. I don't expect to write a short essay on "the importance of math in everyday life," but my professor is kind of a hippy math lover, so it isn't unusual for him, I suppose.

After handing my test in, I make my way to Dr. August's office. I have a date with science next.

I arrive solo this time. No Alex or Cam to back me up or calm me down. Dr. August said he wanted a very quiet environment for testing. I have no idea what is in store for me, but my spirits are very low. I don't have much faith that this virus can be cured.

As I walk into Dr. August's office, I notice that he has already set up everything for the tests. There is something that looks like a dental chair in the middle of the room and a tray of tools and test tubes beside it. I am never fond of visiting the dentist, so this is a bit off-putting.

"Oh hello, Eve. Would you have a seat, please? I'm just going to finish my preparations."

That's what I was afraid he was going to say.

I have a seat in the chair, and it begins reclining. This is starting to feel very much like an alien abduction as a spotlight blinds my vision from above. Dr. August comes to sit beside me after a few moments.

"Now, Eve, the first part is very simple. I need some blood samples."

I give him the thumbs up in a very bemused way. He cleans the skin where the needle will be placed and then pokes the needle in my arm and attaches the collection tube. Nothing comes out.

"That's strange. Let me try another vein."

Dr. August tries a few more veins with the same result.

"Eve, it appears that the wound heals immediately, making it impossible to withdraw blood in this manner."

I roll my eyes. "Dr. August, the wound is too small. A bigger wound takes longer to heal and you can get more blood."

I grab a scalpel off of the metal tray and slit my wrist. "See, now it's torrential. Grab your little test tube and go for it."

He turns a bit green at the sight of all the blood pouring out but doesn't hesitate to drip some of it in a few test tubes before it heals.

Once the wound is closed, there is nothing but dry blood on the surface of my arm. Dr. August grabs a moist towel and rubs the blood away. Underneath is a perfectly unharmed wrist.

"Remarkable," Dr. August says as he stares in disbelief. "You know, Eve, if we could control how the Azrael Virus worked, we could save so many lives. People could even grow back missing limbs."

He is getting that crazy mad scientist look in his eyes; I need to bring him back down to earth. "Listen, the virus is unpredictable and could even be used as a weapon if given to the wrong people. These sorts of suggestions come with consequences. Consequences that I don't want to have to think about."

Dr. August looks down at my wrist as he replies, "You're probably right. I just think it's a shame that some good can't come of this."

His comment irks me. "If something seems too good to be true, then it is probably more dangerous than anyone can even imagine. Just think of Pandora's box. Good and evil are often infused together. The only safe way is to stave off any curiosity here."

I hope Dr. August will listen and not try anything crazy. He will be putting me at risk too, which I'm sure he will never want to do, but I suppose the idea of winning a Nobel Prize is tempting to such a scholar. I truly hope I can trust him.

"Okay, let's move onto the next test, shall we? This is a fun one, I promise. I wanted to see how you react to different foods. You mentioned that it was becoming difficult to keep down food. It makes you feel sick, yes?"

I nod, and Dr. August continues to explain the test. There are three metal serving platters with a dome covering each of them. He reveals each meal one by one. I feel like I am watching *The Price Is Right* as he addresses each "prize."

"I have prepared some lasagna, some chicken salad, and the *piece de resistance*, raw beef."

I pick up a fork and try a small piece of the lasagna; it tastes like manure in my mouth. I begin to choke and spit it out immediately.

"I don't think that one is going down, Dr. August."

He frowns. "That's one of my best dishes. I've never had anyone spit it out before. How heartbreaking."

He succeeds in making me laugh. I'm sure it is tasty to the ordinary palette, but I am craving something a little less cooked. The salad is next; I pick up a few leaves and some chicken and chew on it slowly. It doesn't taste as bad as the lasagna, and I am able to swallow it. Dr. August waits with anticipation; I don't know what he expects to happen next. We sit in awkward silence, and then my stomach grumbles so loudly it scares both of us.

"I guess I'm getting a bit hungry." This worries us because we both know what that will mean.

I reach for the last taste test. It looks amazing, and I drool over it. It's cold and squishy as I hold it in my hands. I take a bite of it, and it's heavenly. I am quickly sent into a frenzy and tear into the raw steak like an animal would do. Dr. August stares with his mouth agape, but it doesn't concern me until the steak is gone.

"Sorry, I can understand how gross this must look," I say as I lick the blood off my fingers.

Dr. August smiles. "No, this is good. Raw meat seems to satiate you."

My stomach rumbles again, this time, louder, and it starts to hurt. I grab at my stomach and grimace.

"Eve, what's happening? What are you feeling?"

I'm finding it hard to concentrate; it feels as though a bus has hit me. "It hurts, it hurts."

I get out of my dental chair and begin looking around, I don't know what for, but my gaze settles on small cage next to Dr. August's desk. I go towards it and see that there is a little mouse inside. He is happily sipping on his water feeder. I immediately open the latch and grab him; he is down my throat before Dr. August can say, "No!" He runs over to me and opens my mouth, but it is too late. I've already crushed and devoured the mouse.

"I feel so much better," I say as I rub my tummy.

Dr. August stares at the empty cage and whimpers. "Marty? Oh no, Marty. You ate Marty." He looks at me with disbelief.

I don't really know what to say, so I just reply, "Oops."

Dr. August sits at his desk to think for a moment.

"Okay, what I think is happening here is that you need living meat. That's what your body craves. When you eat food that is cooked or less than recently dead, it only makes you hungrier."

That seems like a good theory. I will either throw up my food or eat it reluctantly, and my body will ache with desire for something human.

"Here's what I think we should do, Eve. I think you need a few pets, and by pets, I mean animals that you wouldn't mind eating. We need to stop you from eating humans, so this might be a good alternative. Try that for a few days, and then I want you to come back and let me know how that is going. I think that's enough testing for today. Poor Marty didn't even know he was a part of the experiment today."

I would feel bad about eating Dr. August's pet if he wasn't so darn tasty. I leave without a word; I figure I should at least let him mourn his tiny rodent friend.

***

I return to my dorm room a few hours later with a cage full of hamsters. Alex comes over to see the cage, and she is beside herself with cuteness overload.

"Oh yay! They are so cute. What should we call them?"

I place the cage down on my bed. "How about we call them dead, dead, deader, and deader still?"

Alex looks at me, confused.

"Al, I have to eat them, so don't get attached, okay?"

"Eww, you're going to eat them? That's so gross. Please make sure I'm not looking when you do."

I sigh as I take a hamster out to play with. "Trust me, I don't want to eat them, but Dr. August said this might be the only way to stop me from eating people. It's a little easier to swallow, I mean, forgive myself for eating animals."

Alex understands, but I can tell it still creeps her out.

"What's Cam been up to?" I am avoiding him since our kiss, but I still care about how he is doing. He has been through so much tragedy; it is hard not to cry when I think of him.

"He's okay. He's been acting a little weird. I think you guys need to address the elephant in the room and move on. He can't concentrate on his studies. I'm sure he's just thinking about your hot lips."

I toss a pillow at her with my hamster-less hand. She chuckles as it misses her.

"Well, when are you going to tell him how you feel, Eve?"

I shrug. "I don't know how I feel yet. I love Cam, I want to be with him, but I'm realistic enough to know that we couldn't make each other happy. He needs a normal girl. I would feel forever guilty if I took away any possibility he had for a normal life. I want him to be happy."

It hurts a little bit saying that out loud. Of course, I want Cam all to myself, but it feels so selfish I can't bear it.

Alex comes over and takes over playing with the hamster I was holding.

"Listen, Cam is a big boy. He can decide what he wants. I think you should be honest with him. He seems so miserable right now."

Maybe Alex has a point.

"Okay, I'm going to go talk to him right now. I have to just get this over with."

Alex smiles in support of my decision. "Go get him, Eve!"

I leave the room with a smile on my face. I can't wait to tell Cam that I love him; I can't wait to kiss him again. For the first time in these few miserable months, I feel a bit more human; I feel a jolt of hope.

CHAPTER THIRTY-EIGHT

CAM

My eyelids feel as heavy as rocks. The piles of books and scribbled notes around my bed make me dizzy.

Yes, I still handwrite all my notes like I have been living under a rock all these years.

The truth is that I can't absorb as much off of a glowing screen; it doesn't work for me. I get many looks from students with their cute little laptops, possibly even sneers of disapproval. Snobs, all of them, I say. Why do they take such offense to my style of learning? "Screw off," I mutter to myself as I think of some of the faces in my classes.

Mark looks up at me. "You talking to me, man? I swear I didn't do anything! I did not drink the last beer in your mini fridge, Nah-uh!"

I have to laugh. I know he took it, but I don't care in the least.

"Nah, man it's cool. I didn't mean you. I'm just talking to my pile of notes. I'm so not in a studying mood right now. I don't think I've learned a single thing in the past hour."

"So stop studying, Cam. Let's go get some beers, or we can go find us some lady friends?"

I shake my head and blush; my thoughts immediately go to Eve. I have been trying so hard not to think of her. Mark reads my mind so easily; am I that transparent?

"Seriously, man, you got to stop thinking about that girl Eve.

She seems to unravel you. You sure you want a relationship like that? She has you wrapped around her little finger. One day I'll be asking someone, 'Hey, where's Cam?' And they'll say, 'Oh, he's become Eve's new backpack,' or worse her new purse! Dude, that *cannot* happen! You're a man, not a purse! You get what I'm saying?"

I laugh so hard at this comparison it hurts. "What? A purse? Man, you are ridiculous!"

Mark points at me and says, "Hey, man, I just call it as I see it."

We have just returned to our studies when there is a knock at the door. My heart pounds. I want it to be Eve, and I want it not to be Eve at the same time. I signal Mark to get the door; he sighs with resentment. He knows I am being a coward.

When Mark goes to answer the door, his eyes widen, and he remains silent.

"Uh, Cam, I'm going to hit the gym for a bit. I'll be back in like an hour."

I'm curious as to who is at the door, and I'm even more curious as to why Mark bolts so quickly. After Mark fumbles out the door, I look out into the hallway and find Claire dressed provocatively. Claire is wearing a very short trench coat and perhaps nothing else. Her heels are six, no seven, inches tall, and they make her legs look like they go for miles. I have to admit my mouth hangs open a bit as she stands there.

She forces her way through the doorway and into my arms.

"Claire? I thought you never wanted to see me again. I thought..."

She tells me to hush before I can finish telling her off, and she shoves me into my reclining chair. When I'm seated, she turns her back to me and speaks. "I realized that I forgive you. You said you'll never love me, and I forgive you for saying that."

I start to feel more scared than turned on; this girl is truly nuts. I think she might be hearing voices in her head. I thought I was clear that I have no interest in her, and somehow here we are again. How can I convince Claire to leave me alone? Insulting her doesn't work, ignoring her doesn't work, and breaking her heart doesn't work. Suddenly I have an idea; I haven't tried being a pig. Claire thinks I am Mr. Perfect; well maybe I can try my hand at being the complete opposite.

"I don't need your forgiveness, sugar tits. I just want you to shake your fat ass for me so I can shower you with dollar bills. Are You going to stand there all day? Or are you going entertain me? I'm a little bored with your talking, sweetie." I smile a little, thinking this is so insulting and misogynistic that Claire will slap me and leave.

As I sit there smiling and oh so proud of myself, Claire silently drops the trench coat to the ground. She's wearing nothing but a pink lace bra and panties to match. This girl clearly has no respect for herself.

"Cam, I was hoping you would say that. I came prepared to entertain. I will do anything to be with you."

I can see the pure insanity in her eyes. She really might do anything. *Heck, if I asked her to kill my roommate, I'm afraid she'll do it.*

She begins to approach me slowly. I'm trying to think of something else, a plan, my next move, anything! My plan clearly fails because I don't come up with a single idea.

She holds the armrests on my recliner and brings her face towards me. She's about to kiss me. I pull my head back and yell, "Stop! This is so not right. Claire, what has gotten into you? We don't belong together."

Claire pouts in a very sexy way. "Why don't you let me show

how we can be together?" She winks and continues moving her lips towards my face.

I try to keep her at a distance with my arms, but she eventually uses her full body weight to take me down. The chair topples over, and I'm on the ground with Claire on top of me.

I'm about to kick Claire off of me when I hear a gasp at the doorway.

There stands Eve.

She looks as though she has shrunk. Her hand covers her mouth, and her eyes are wide with disbelief.

"Oh God no, Eve, this isn't what it looks like."

As I say it, I think about all the movies where men use that line, but it never makes it look any better. I'm sure this looks as terrible as it makes me feel. I only feel worse as I lay there looking into Eve's eyes; she looks crushed. I want to cry at the sight of her.

Eve backs away from the entrance silently and is soon out of sight.

I have to go get her.

"Claire, get off me right now! I don't believe in violence against women, but so help me God, I will punch you straight in the tit!"

Claire crosses her arms and refuses. She smirks a little, calling my bluff, but I'm not bluffing. I get an arm free, wind it up, and punch her square in the nipple. She gives a loud scream and topples over. I scramble to my feet and run out the door in the direction Eve went. I spot her in one of the corridors. I call her name. She looks back at me and then starts running in the opposite direction. I start sprinting; there is no way I am going to let her get away without hearing my explanation.

Eve is so much faster these days, but since she hasn't been feeding enough, I figure she will ultimately wear herself out.

I eventually catch up to her. I grab her and force her against one of the walls in the hallway. "Eve, stop."

She keeps pushing me away and won't look at me. I know she's crying. She doesn't want me to see it. She never wants to show weakness to anyone, especially not to people who hurt her. Unfortunately, I am the one hurting her right now.

"Eve, please. I didn't call Claire over. She showed up and pretty much attacked me. She's crazy. You know that."

Eve sobs louder and tries to break free. If she fed on a human recently, I'm sure she would have been able to tear my limbs off, but luckily for me, that isn't the case.

"Cam, let go. Go back to Claire. You should be with Claire. It's okay."

I give her a baffled look. What is that supposed to mean?

"Eve, I don't want to be with Claire."

Eve begins to talk through her sobs. "But you should be with someone normal."

I laugh at the thought of Claire being described as normal. "Claire is the freak here. She is so not normal, believe me!"

This does not comfort Eve; she looks so beaten down. Her sobbing stops, but her voice is so delicate and woeful. She whispers, "She's more normal than I can ever be. You deserve someone human, someone, who won't try and bite your face off."

I tuck a finger under Eve's chin and bring her face up to meet mine.

"How do you know that crazy hot mess wouldn't try to bite my face off? Huh?"

Eve gives a little laugh. She tries to speak again, probably in an attempt to continue convincing me of how I shouldn't love her, but that sort of talk is years too late. I have been in love with her too long to feel any differently now. I have only ever been waiting for her.

I pull Eve close, and before she can protest any further, I kiss her again and again, for as long as she'll let me.

CHAPTER THIRTY-NINE

EVE

I am on cloud nine for the next few days, even though I am eating hamster for breakfast, lunch, and dinner. It isn't quite as tasty as humans, but it seems to be keeping my hunger at bay. Cam might have something to do with my success too; I feel more like myself.

I can still feel Cam's lips on mine as I enter Dr. August's office. It is time for round two of testing. I wonder what he has in store for me today.

When I enter the office, I can see that Dr. August has crafted a plastic tent. I can only assume today will be very messy.

Dr. August appears in scrubs and throws something at me in passing. I unravel the package; it's a hospital gown. Guess I am right about the messy part.

"Okay, what exactly do you have in mind for today? What's with the Dexter tent?"

I place the hospital gown on and begin pulling my clothes off from underneath it.

Dr. August yells from the other end of the room, "We are going to test your healing. Hope you don't mind. There may be a little blood."

My gown is on, and I enter the plastic tent. There is a medical table inside. This is going to be chilly. I slowly make my way onto the metal slab. I stare at the top of the tent until Dr. August appears overhead.

"How are you feeling, dear? Are the hamsters working out?"

"Yes, actually, they are. I don't feel hungry. I don't feel sick. Maybe I'll buy some guinea pigs next."

I laugh a little, but Dr. August doesn't share in my joke. He seems a bit off today. I wonder if it is because I ate his pet?

"I'm sorry I ate Marty. I know that's not funny. I'd be pissed if anyone ever ate my dog, Winston."

Dr. August takes off his glasses and seems so serious it scares me.

"Eve, honestly, it's okay. Marty was helpful to our experiment. Let me ask you something."

I don't like the sound of that, but I signal for him to continue.

"What if we can't fix this? I mean, I will try my best, but there is a chance this is permanent. Have you thought about leaving?"

I sit up on the metal table. "What the hell, Dr. August?! I'm scared out of my mind here, and you're being negative all of a sudden! I don't want to think about the alternatives right now. Where would I even go?"

He can see I'm ready to blow, and his tone changes slightly.

"No no, Eve, I'm sorry. I just, I just think you need to be away from here and safe if we can't cure this. Trust me, I want to cure this for your sake and for the sake of anyone else affected by the Azrael Virus. I just want you to promise me you'll disappear if people start finding out. It won't be safe for you anymore. Do you understand me?"

He shakes me as he says this. He sounds desperate.

"Of course Dr. August, but I'm being as cautious as possible. I want to stay under the radar."

He nods and then starts sifting through his tools again.

The first tool he pulls out is a knife.

"Now, Eve, I'm just going to make little incisions on your arms and legs and time their healing. Ready?"

"I guess so," I snort.

The incisions don't hurt very much; they just sting a little. I don't bother looking. I've seen enough of my healing, and it is as normal as breathing to me now.

"Okay looks good, Eve. Each incision healed in about eight seconds. Now we need to try something a tad more drastic if it's okay with you."

Do I really have a choice?

Dr. August pulls out a gun and begins placing a silencer at the end.

Where the heck did he even get a gun like that?

"You're going to shoot me? Really? That's gonna suck. You know that, right?"

Dr. August looks at the gun and then back at me. "Well yes it might hurt, but we need to know if your body can heal bullet wounds just as quickly. I promise to only graze you with the first one."

I feel a little queasy knowing we might have to do this multiple times.

"Have you ever even shot a gun before?"

Dr. August looks a bit confused. "Of course, I play video games all the time."

Oh God, is he serious?

"Now, Eve, I need you to get off the table and come and stand over here by this wall. There is a foam wall here that will absorb the bullet."

I stand in front of the wall and close my eyes. I think it will be better if I don't see what is coming.

I don't hear the bullet, but I feel a tear in my left arm. I open my eyes to find a chunk of my arm missing and a wall sprayed with blood.

"That was a good clean shot actually." I'm impressed. It hurts a lot, but I can tolerate it.

Dr. August and I watch as the wound begins to seal.

"Amazing! Thirty seconds! That's just incredible!"

Dr. August cheers as he wipes the dry blood from my arm. I feel a bit pleased with myself. It definitely is a cool trick.

"For the next shot, I'm going to have the bullet lodged in your body. I want to see how your body will handle a foreign object."

I ask Dr. August to aim for my legs. I don't feel comfortable with a torso shot yet. I will have to work up to that. I close my eyes again. This time, I scream as the bullet hits; I'm sure it has shattered bone. I crash to the ground and moan in pain. Dr. August runs to my side and inspects the wound.

"Well, it looks like the bullet is definitely lodged in there. I don't see an exit wound."

"No shit, Sherlock!"

I don't mean to be rude, but I always curse when I get hurt. I mutter a few more choice words as Dr. August pokes around the wound for signs of healing. This will take a bit longer since I have to rebuild bone as well.

Dr. August times about a minute before we start to see some progress, and after two minutes, we see the bullet emerging. It looks like my body is trying to spit it out. Dr. August looks pleased. "Just as I thought, your body will reject the foreign object. You would never need to extract items."

"So you're saying I'm self-cleaning?"

Dr. August nods. "Precisely."

These experiments are starting to get to my head. I feel very indestructible like I have Wolverine's adamantium body. I can do anything, and this kind of power is deliriously tempting to use at any opportunity, but I have promised Dr. August I will play it low key.

"Okay, Doc. What's next?"

I am excited to see the next test and clap my hands together to show my enthusiasm. I feel I can handle anything he throws at me. Dr. August walks towards an object covered by a sheet. When he removes the sheet, I think I let out a slight shriek. It's terrifying sharp metal teeth are gleaming back at me.

"A chainsaw? Are you friggin crazy?"

Dr. August shrugs. "What? You can heal. Aren't you the least bit curious if your limb will reattach or grow back? That knowledge would be of great use to you."

I am starting to think Dr. August might have lost a few marbles along the way because he seems so calm despite how insane his idea is.

"And what if it doesn't do either? What if I'm left without a limb? I don't know if I can go through with this one! It's too risky."

Dr. August looks a bit disappointed, but I don't care. It isn't his body we are hacking apart today. He comes up to me and takes my hand, inspecting it closely. "What if we take a finger? If we start small and you see your healing working, you might feel confident enough to try a limb?"

What a psycho! I want to punch Dr. August, but he has peaked my curiosity.

"Fine, let's try this finger."

I hold up the middle finger on my left hand. Dr. August raises his eyebrow and looks a bit dismayed. *Good, I'm glad I've offended him.* It makes me feel a little better. I hold out my finger, and Dr. August goes to retrieve the chainsaw, which looks a bit drastic since it's going to be slicing something so small in comparison.

He revs the chainsaw, sending shivers down my spine. Is there anything more terrifying than that sound? It reminds me of many tacky horror movies that I've seen. Although it seems the tackier the horror movie, the more gruesome and terrifying it is.

I decide to close my eyes; it has worked for me so far. The grinding of the chains is approaching; it is so loud, it can't be far off. Soon, I am screaming. The slice isn't as quick as I hoped. I feel the blade dig in and then continue scraping the bone until the top of my finger pops off.

I keep my eyes closed tightly during all this, but I can feel the blood spraying out of my finger and Dr. August retreating, trying not to get blood all over himself.

When I finally open my eyes, I can see the stump where the rest of my finger used to be. My first thought is a very superficial one; I think about how horrible my next manicure will look. Such a girly thought, but that's what will bother me if it doesn't grow back.

With gloves, Dr. August retrieves the rest of my finger and brings it over to me. We both wait to see if my finger will grow back. We wait close to five minutes, and nothing happens. I can see Dr. August sweating a little; this makes me feel a little less optimistic.

"I'm going to try holding the finger against the wound and see if it will reattach."

I keep the fingers on my right hand crossed as Doctor August aligns digit to the stump. I really want this to work.

Dr. August holds the finger in place and starts counting the seconds. When he gets to ten seconds, it is like a magnet has turned on. My finger latches back onto the open wound. It is healing so rapidly it makes Dr. August jump back a bit. The healing hurts more than anything I have yet experienced; I can feel that it is taking a lot out of me.

In two minutes, the finger has fully reattached. It is odd seeing it again and being able to move what wasn't there just a moment ago. I feel very weak and tell Dr. August I need to lie down. The room is spinning a bit, and I have to close my eyes.

When I open them again, Dr. August has already torn down the plastic tent and is cleaning up the rest of the test area. How long have I been asleep? I rise from the metal table feeling very stiff; it isn't exactly the most comfortable napping spot.

"Dr. August, can I go now? I'm going to finish off my nap in my room."

He dusts himself off and walks over to me.

"Are you feeling better? Do you have enough energy? I'm a little worried that we may have starved your body today."

I rub my head, not quite understanding his meaning.

"Eve, you've been healing most of the day, and I'm a little worried that your hunger will reach peak levels since you're so exhausted. I think you should go have a snack to prevent yourself from attacking people. I hope you still have some hamsters left?"

"Don't worry, Doc. I've got plenty of hamsters to choose from." I wink at him.

I just want to get back to my bed, so I change as quickly as I can and then bid farewell to Dr. August. He seems very nervous about allowing me to leave but just tells me to be careful. I will see him again in another couple of days for more testing.

I begin walking towards my dorm, staring at my finger in

amazement. I want to share this new finding with someone. This makes me think of Cam. I change directions and begin walking towards Cam's dorm. I may have skipped all the way with a stupid grin on my face; I do get a few looks from people. Stupid love, it makes you act like a complete idiot.

Just as I arrive in front of Cam's building, who do I see? My favourite person, Claire. She can only be here for one reason, and it makes my blood boil. She sees me and almost snarls. We stare at each other for a little while. I am trying so hard not to attack her, but clearly, Claire doesn't have the same sort of control. She runs at me, screeching and clawing. She grabs my hair first. *Typical girl fight move.* When she tries to pin me to the ground, it only makes me angrier. I'm starting to lose my cool. My stomach growls; I think it almost says, "Eat that bitch."

Claire is yelling and telling me off. I'm just taking the abuse and hoping she leaves before my hunger takes over, but she doesn't seem the type to back down. I'm calm until she screams, "You stole him from me. He doesn't love you! He never loved you. We are supposed to be together. If I get rid of you, then there will be nothing to stop us from being together."

I snap. I can actually feel my eyes glowing red. Claire must see this change because her eyes go wide with terror. She wants to back away, but it is too late. I have her in my grip, and I'm not about to let go. Does she want to get rid of me? She has no idea who or what she is dealing with. It is time to end this little psycho's reign of mischief.

I grab Claire by the hair and drag her into the nearby gardens. I don't want any witnesses. She is screaming, but I figure if anyone is around they would have come to save her already. I guess it is my lucky day. I throw Claire down in between some rose bushes. Some thorns nick her arms, and speckles of blood appear. My hunger intensifies at the sight of it. I'm like a bull drawn to a Matador's cape.

I'm trying to fight the urge to take a bite out of her; maybe I will be satisfied with slapping her around a bit? I smack her face as hard as I can, and this halts her screaming momentarily.

When she recovers from the brief sting, she scowls at me and whispers, "I knew there was something wrong with you. I was right."

Fear takes hold of me. She knows, and she might tell others.

I have to figure out a way to get rid of her.

I growl in her face, and this makes her eyes grow wide. She maintains eye contact with me, but I can see one of her arms shuffling about in one of the bushes.

What is she up to?

Before I can figure it out, a pair of garden shears come flying at my face, stabbing me in the neck.

The pain is excruciating. I hold the wound with one hand, and Claire gets ready for the next blow. She stabs me in the chest and knocks me on my back. I can't believe she is winning.

Claire climbs on top of me, grinning like Charles Manson. She holds the shears up, ready for another blow. As she brings her arm down, I grab hold of it and tear into it as hard as my teeth will let me. She lets out a blood-curdling scream, and I continue to chomp at her delicious arm meat.

She drops her garden shears, and now I have the upper hand. She has no way to protect herself. Not from me, I am unstoppable!

I push Claire onto her back and continue tearing at the flesh until I see a big rock. She stares at the rock and then back at me; she knows what I'm about to do. She wants to squirm away, but I have her now. All zombies love brains, but it can be very hard to get at them. I will need to open her skull up like a coconut. I grab the rock and raise it above my head, ready to smash. I feel no guilt; I feel no pity. I only feel my hunger.

CHAPTER FORTY

ALEX

I have been waiting for Eve for what seems like forever. She is supposed to meet me for dinner, well, mostly to watch *me* eat dinner. I hate eating in front of Eve. It is like eating cake in front of someone on a diet. She can't have whatever I am having, and I know she wishes she can eat what she used to. Hamsters are definitely not cutting it.

Maybe Eve is with Cam? It is about time those two got together. Although, under the circumstances, I feel Cam should be cautious. A kissing session may lead to a snacking session. I want to believe Eve can control the virus, but I know full well she can't. Hopefully, she will learn to.

I wander out of the dining hall and start walking towards Dr. August's office. Perhaps the tests have taken longer than anticipated.

When I get there, Dr. August's office is locked, and I don't hear anyone inside. *Nope, not here, I guess the testing is over for today.* My next stop will be Cam's dorm. I'm sure she will be there; new lovers are usually inseparable.

As I head towards Cam's dorm, I hear something. It sounds like a squawking bird at first, but as I approach, I realize someone is screaming.

It's a ghost town on campus around dinner time; I look around for a sign of anyone at all. I don't really want to investigate on my own.

The screaming gets louder, and I make the split decision to start sprinting towards the sound. *Probably a dumb decision.* As I run, I hope that someone will come to my aid in the same way someday. Being a good Samaritan has to count for something, at least grant me some good karma if I'm going to put my safety at risk.

My feet are slapping on the concrete hard. I can't get there fast enough. I reach the source of the noise. The screaming is coming from the gardens outside of Cam's residence. I'm frozen for a moment; I'm not sure I want to see what's happening, and I'm even more terrified that no one can see me once I enter. I will be concealed by foliage and darkness.

I hear another piercing scream. I drop my bag and enter the garden as ready as I am going to be. As I round the corner past the gateway, my eyes flood with disbelief, and the only thing I can get out of my mouth in time is, "Stop!"

She halts, holding a large rock above her head, and turns to look at me. I see her drenched in blood, but the body beneath her is still moving. I can still save her.

The woman staring back at me is not Eve. Her eyes glow a devious red, and the veins in her face are blue and swollen. Her mouth is lion-like with teeth exposed and triumphant. She tilts her head to look at me; there is a cracking sound as she looks at me sideways. It is such an inhuman movement, so grotesque, I have to hold my stomach and tell it to stay with me.

This is what the virus has created. I have to be cautious around my best friend; she may appear vaguely familiar, but her eyes are foreign. She is hell-bent on smashing someone to pieces, and I don't want that to be me.

She begins to approach me, and I slowly start inching back. I can see the woman on the ground more clearly now. She is trying to crawl away slowly. It's Claire! I can see that her arm is bloody; I gasp and stare at Eve. "What have you done?"

Eve stares back blankly and snarls at me. Out of the corner of my eye, I can see Claire backing away as quickly as she can. That coward! I came to save her ass, and her first impulse is to take off when Eve is distracted. *What an ungrateful bitch!*

"Eve, calm down. It's me, Alex. I want to help."

I hold my hands up, showing that I mean her no harm, but that doesn't soothe her. She's like an animal ready to pounce on its prey. If I run, I'm dead. If I stay, I'm most likely dead.

Eve comes close to me and sniffs me like I'm a delicious steak dinner. I close my eyes and pray. I know I can't outrun her or overpower her; all I can do is hope she can fight the virus. I feel her breathing on me; I tremble but refuse to open my eyes. I want to pretend that this is not happening.

Without warning, I am violently shoved to the ground. The wind is knocked out of me from the unexpected fall. I feel Eve pressing on top of me. She growls loudly in my face, and it causes me to open my eyes. I shake as I look into her burning eyes. I miss her baby blues; the unnatural red looks almost as if a fire has been lit inside of her and isn't quite as friendly as the sapphire eyes she once possessed.

"Eve please, please stop. I'm your friend. Remember? Your best friend. We went to prom together because we couldn't find dates. We used to sing Madonna songs before bed when we had sleepovers. We got matching haircuts one time because we wished we were sisters."

I feel Eve's grip loosening slightly; maybe she is coming around. I continue talking in the hopes she will come back to me.

"I was the first person you told when you found out your mom had cancer, and I was right there with you the whole way. I will never leave you, Eve."

Eve starts twitching. She takes her hands off me and lifts them to her head, pressing so hard on each side that it seems like she is going to crush her skull. She shakes her head and holds it between both hands. Her inner struggle is anything but easy.

I slip away from her reach and watch her shake and hit her head. Eve grabs her hair, ready to pull it out, and screams into the air with such an ache in her voice that I want to hug her. She starts crying and lays on the ground, wrapping her legs into a fetal position.

"I'm sorry, I'm so sorry. What have I done? I'm sorry."

Eve keeps repeating her apologies over and over again.

My fear vanishes; all I want to do is comfort her at this point. I rush back over to her and hold her. "Eve, it's okay. Can you stand?"

She nods in my arms.

"Good, because we need to get out of here. We're in a lot of trouble, Eve. We need to disappear."

She understands and gets to her feet quickly. I take her hand and lead her away from the scene of the crime and, unfortunately, away from Cam. We will need to call him later, once we are clear of this place.

Eve and I race to the parking lot where my car is parked. We get in, and I've never sped away so quickly in my entire life. I feel better once we're off campus grounds.

Eve looks like a wreck. She is gnawing at her fingernails, and her eyes are so wide I begin to wonder if she has any eyelids at all. "Eve, did you bite Claire?"

Eve searches her memory for a second before answering. "Yes.

I think I did. I tried really hard not to, but she attacked me and the virus took over."

Eve rubs the blood off her neck with her sleeve. The wound Claire inflicted has already healed. I feel sick to my stomach thinking about what Claire might become.

"Eve, we need to let Dr. August know what happened. Claire is infected now. She's going to start feeding soon."

Eve starts cursing, which is not helpful, but I guess she needs to get it out. I try to refocus her. "So what's the plan?"

She picks up her phone without answering me. "Hi, it's Eve. Something bad happened after I left your office... I bit someone."

The other end of the phone is silent for a few seconds. I know Dr. August is freaking out on Eve's behalf.

"We left. I'm with Alex. Yes, the victim got away."

I'm not sure what he's saying, but I can hear his voice rising in horror. He knows as well as we do that Claire will start attacking others, and we can't even begin to understand how the virus will manifest in her. All the victims of the virus have had very different experiences. If Claire is anywhere near as powerful as Eve, it will be difficult to kill her.

Eve hangs up the phone. "Dr. August said we should stay away for a few days and he will see if he can locate Claire."

Eve looks distraught, and I know there is nothing I can say to comfort her, so I simply listen to her. "Alex, I think I need to go away permanently. I need to go where no one knows me and where I can't hurt the people I love. I've caused you and Cam nothing but problems since we returned from Egypt. Oh my God, Cam!"

Eve cuts her sob story short and pulls out her phone again. The phone rings, and no one answers. Eve hangs up and tries again, still no answer. Eve throws her phone into the back seat in frustration.

"Al, we need to go back."

I raise my eyebrows. "No, we're not going back. You heard Dr. August. We need to hide out. They'll take you, Eve. They'll find out!"

"You don't understand, Al. This is Claire we're dealing with. Do you remember what Claire wants more than anything?"

I pull over to the side of the road and hit the brakes.

"Oh my God! You don't think? Shit! Cam!"

Eve has a point. Cam is still Claire's obsession. He might be safely in the library studying or at the pub with Mark, but we can't know for sure unless we check it out.

As I drive furiously back to campus, Eve continues to try calling Cam. He won't pick up his cell phone, and no one answers the phone in his room. Eve and I begin to imagine the worst.

As I reach the parking lot and find my spot, a looming sense of doom takes over. I have a feeling something terrible is going to happen tonight, and unfortunately, I am rarely ever wrong.

CHAPTER FORTY-ONE

EVE

My legs are on fire, moving as quickly as they can towards Cam's dorm. He needs to be okay or I will never recover. Why didn't I stay and track down Claire immediately? Is my own safety that much more important than Cam's? I don't care in that moment if anyone learns about my secret; they can cart me off and do experiments on me all they wish as long as Cam is unharmed.

We finally reach the residence and climb the stairs with such ferocity that I fear the steps may shatter beneath our feet. I can't be bothered to wait for the elevator. I know my legs will be faster. I reach the door before Alex. I knock on the door and wait. I see Alex coming down the hall; she finally catches up, panting.

"Oops, I forgot. Sorry, Al. Didn't mean to rush ahead."

Alex waves her hand at me in a don't-sweat-it gesture and then bends over and holds her knees, trying to catch her breath.

Usually, zombies are these super slow, quickly decaying entities; I don't know how I lucked out and got the gift of speed and rapid mending.

It's only been a few seconds, but no one is answering the door. I knock again, much louder, and let Cam know it is us. Still nothing.

"He could be in the shower, I guess."

Alex can be right. I press my ear against the door and listen in, but I don't hear any water running. My stomach is in knots; I can tell something is wrong.

"Cam, Cam?" My voice sounds high-pitched and desperate. I can't wait any longer. I back up against the hallway wall on the opposite side of Cam's door, then with all my might, I run and slam my entire body into it. I make a nice dent in it, but it still refuses to open. I ram the door again, and it bursts open like saloon doors.

I scan the room and see a pair of feet hiding behind Cam's bed. *Oh God!* I run to the side of the bed, and I'm not sure I can handle what I will find.

There, I discover Mark's lifeless body. I kneel beside him in defeat. We are too late.

He's barely recognizable. His throat has been torn open, and his intestines have been ripped out and left out in the open. Claire also bashed his head in with Cam's large metal paperweight in the shape of a mummy; the mummy joined Mark in the pool of blood soaking the floor. I guess she watched enough zombie movies to know that you need to destroy the brain in order to stop them from returning from the dead.

Girl is smarter than she looks.

The scene is horrific. I hear Alex gag as she comes up behind me. She covers her mouth to stop herself from screaming or throwing up or both. I want to cry; this is all my fault. Mark was only in the wrong place at the wrong time. My mind continues to race. I imagine Claire bursting into the room as a half-zombie half-human psychopath. The psychopath part has nothing to do with the Azrael Virus; that is all Claire. Perhaps Cam and Mark were here together. Claire might have tried to take Cam, and Mark might have tried to stop her, *wrong move.* My theory seems plausible, and I share it with Alex.

"I think Claire has him. She wouldn't kill him. She'd want to keep him, like a pet or love slave or something…"

I'm rambling; I tend to do that when I'm nervous or terrified, but I am wasting time talking out loud. It will be better if we actually *do* something. While I speak out loud to myself, Alex grabs a bed sheet and places it over Mark.

"I can't see him like that anymore. He didn't deserve this. What do we do now? We need to inform the police. Oh God, his poor family. They need to tell his family. He needs a proper burial."

Alex begins sobbing. I'm about to go over and comfort her, but my phone decides to interrupt us. When I pick up, Dr. August doesn't even say hi.

"Have you found her yet?" His voice sounds heavy with fear.

"No, but we've found her first victim. We came to find Cam, and we found his roommate instead."

Dr. August's voice begins to tremble a bit. "Is he…has he been taken care of?"

I know what he means. He wants me to make sure Mark won't become a zombie and start killing others.

"Claire took care of that."

He doesn't reply right away. "Strange that she wouldn't let him rise and join her."

"I guess she likes to do things solo…Listen, I think she has Cam. He's disappeared, and I have no idea where to start looking."

"Eve, I have been reading up on zombie mythology in order to help you with your…umm…condition."

More like a curse, but good save.

"Now from what I've read, zombies have a superior sense of smell. If you can smell living flesh, you can certainly sniff out one of your own kind."

I didn't think of that. I suppose we smell differently from the living. Although I'm not rotting, I have noticed a difference in my natural scent.

"Good idea, Doc. I'm going on the hunt. I will call you when I find something."

Dr. August tries to say something else, but I hang up before he can finish. I am much too eager to get started. There is no time to waste. I don't know what Claire is up to. For all I know, Claire wants a new undead boyfriend all to herself. I can't let that happen.

"Alex, I'm going to hope to hell my nose will lead me to her, or Cam is as good as dead."

My eyes well up with tears at the thought. Alex comes over to me and hugs me. We both look back at Mark's covered body as we leave the room. My heart is heavy knowing that I can't save him; he was a great guy.

"Mark, we're coming back for you. I promise you. You deserve a better resting place than a dorm room floor."

It is strangely comforting talking to the dead, just like visiting a cemetery. I guess it is a bit of denial as well. I want to talk to him like he is still alive.

✳✳✳

We walk around campus trying to find Claire's scent. I don't really pick up much. I smell her in the garden, but of course, I would; that's where she became infected, by me. I hang my head in shame as we pass the garden. We continue walking, and I let out a snarl when I sense something foreign.

"This way, Alex. I think I have her."

I follow the scent all the way to the cafeteria. It seems like a good place to hide out. No one will be in the cafeteria at this hour.

I tell Alex to stay close behind me as we enter.

Once inside, I notice all the lights are out. Something is definitely lurking in here. Even after hours, the cooks usually leave the lights on in case anyone wants to use the space as a study area. I feel Alex clinging to my shirt. She is sharing the same thought.

We venture further into the cafeteria, and we're not able to see much, but I feel a rush of wind to my right. I push Alex to my left side and turn to face the source. I still don't see anything, but I know there is something in here with us for sure. My nose flares; one of my kind is among us.

My senses are on overload. I want to attack in every direction. I hear something shatter in the kitchen and head that way.

"Eve, I can't fight this feeling that we're being watched."

I pull Alex closer to me. She screams when we feel another gust of wind to my right. I pause and sniff the air. My eyes grow wide. This is an ambush.

"Alex, get down!" I yell.

She doesn't hesitate and throws herself on the ground under a table. I am able to block the first attack. I am holding the head of another student as she chomps at the air. She looks familiar, possibly from one of my anthropology courses? And then it hits me. "Oh God, Nina! What has she done to you?"

Nina looked a little like herself but very veiny and bloody and definitely not as friendly as I remember. She moves like a real zombie, slowly and without thought. I don't want to hurt her, and in my hesitation, another zombie takes the opportunity to attack me from behind.

They jump on top of me and try to tear my head off. They will do anything to get at Alex, who ironically is the dinner they have been waiting for. If they need to go through me first, so be it; food is their only desire.

As I try to fight off the two students, I see another zombie exiting the kitchen. I better do something quick, or Alex and I are finished.

I decide to give into the virus and all its power. My strength immediately intensifies. I grab a hold of the zombie on my back and throw him to the ground. Alex smashes his head in with one of the chairs closest to her. She smiles victoriously, but the zombie that grabs her from behind quickly erases her grin. Her scream is blood curdling. I grab Nina and snap her neck.

"Sorry, Nina, nothing personal."

I rush towards Alex, who is trying her best not to get bitten. When I reach them, I bite the zombie's hand so hard that he's forced to release Alex. He lets out a monstrous growl.

Yup, he is definitely a regular mindless zombie, and he is super pissed that I took his food away.

I move back with Alex in hand, and as I look around, I can now see that the room is full of zombies. Claire was a very hungry girl.

"Al, I think we need to make a run for it. I can't fight off all these zombies and keep you alive at the same time."

We start to back out of the cafeteria slowly as the zombies watch us. As soon as we are outside, I look around for a way to contain the zombies. I see an iron fence and tear one of the bars free. I bend the bar around the two door handles, creating a temporary lock. The zombies begin pushing against the door. I can see them smashing their faces against the windows; their fingers claw desperately at the glass, their eyes starving for flesh. I can sympathize with their hunger, but I don't want everyone on campus to become a meal tonight.

"Let's go to my car. We should call Dr. August and let him know what's going on."

I agree with Alex, and we make our way to the parking lot. Once there, we get inside and lock the doors in case there are any more surprises stumbling around. As soon as I'm back to my senses, I pick up my phone and make the call.

Dr. August doesn't speak but listens.

"I'm afraid I have more bad news, Doc. Claire seems to have created a mini army of fucking deadites!"

Dr. August is now freaking out on the other end, making it harder to continue explaining.

"Whoa, whoa, hang on. I managed to contain them in the cafeteria, but that won't hold forever... Doctor August, tell me what to do next. I don't know what to do."

As I try to formulate a new plan with Dr. August, I hear Alex trying to get a word in. "Eve...Eve, you need to see this."

I ignore her at first, but when I hear the terror in her voice, I decide to check it out.

"Umm, Doc, I'm gonna need to call you back."

As I look through the windshield, I can see a hoard of zombies approaching us.

That's no mini army.

As we watch speechlessly, one of them appears at the driver's side window, and Alex lets out a shriek. The other zombies will be on us in a matter of seconds. I see no point in making a run for it.

"Alex, I know this is a fairly new car, but I think it's time to scuff the paint a bit."

Alex is shaking, but she understands. She turns on the car, spilling light onto all the zombies surrounding us. They are ugly and rotting. I think I see one zombie's ear fall off as they approach. *Gross!*

Their arms are stretched out in front of them with longing; some of them are beginning to thrash against the car. Alex is finding it hard to compose herself. I can see beads of sweat forming on her forehead as the zombie at her window begins beating against the glass even more violently. He finally manages to smash through the glass. This sends Alex screaming in motion.

"Screw all of you! I'm going to squash you all, like bugs under my shoe!"

It is a little odd seeing Alex this aggressive, but that's what it is going to take to stay alive.

Alex shoots the car backward and then throws it in drive, taking down the first row of zombies. It is slightly comical seeing them shoot into the air and burst into pieces. Once Alex clears a good chunk of them under her tires, she throws the car in reverse and squashes a few more that have been following us. Luckily, zombies aren't that smart. They don't think to take cover.

"Al, there's one more over there. Get him!"

She doesn't hesitate to slam her foot on the gas, and we go flying towards the motionless zombie. He is hit with such force that he splits in half. The zombie's torso hits the hood and then glides up the windshield and off into the air. He leaves a nice big bloody streak in the process.

"Ewww, gross!" Alex exclaims and then uses the wipers so that we are able to see again. There doesn't seem to be a single zombie left.

CHAPTER FORTY-TWO

CAM

My eyes find it hard to focus. The room is dark and unfamiliar. I think I see a small rag doll in the corner by the window. *Where am I?* My disoriented state makes it hard to recall what happened in the moments before. I know my right temple aches quite a bit; my guess is someone knocked me out. I can only focus for a few seconds at a time. I try to stand and get a better look at my surroundings, and that's when I notice that I can't move. My hands are laced behind my back, and my legs seem to be tied to the chair I am sitting on. I shuffle about to see if I can wiggle free, but the ropes are on there tight. I begin saying, "What the fu…" and I am cut off by a dark image coming towards me.

"Who's there?"

The figure doesn't answer; instead, it begins laughing in a terrifying and sinister way. Sweat begins to bead at the back of my neck and run down my spine. It makes my entire body shiver.

The figure moves an arm into the light. The arm is small and delicate but grotesque at the same time. Its nails are blue, and the skin seems so abnormally transparent that I can see every vein. The arm reaches towards my face. I try to back away but am only able to turn my face away freely. The cold hand strokes my cheek in a loving way. My mind decides this must be Eve; perhaps the virus has done something strange to her.

"Eve?" I question.

The hand retracts quickly, and the dark figure paces the room. Why won't she answer? What is wrong with her? I begin to panic.

"Eve, let me help you."

The figure halts and then races towards me. Before I know what's happening, her face is lit up by moonlight, and she is only inches away from my nose.

"Why did you have to go and mention her for? She did this to me. That bitch bit my arm, and now I'm hideous. I will rip her spine out next chance I get."

Claire is foaming at the mouth in a very literal way as she spits out each word. Clearly, I am dealing with a whole new level of psychopath, and if she is as powerful as Eve, then I will need to tread lightly.

"Claire, what am I doing here?"

She laughs again in that repulsive way.

"Cam, you should know why you're here."

I shake my head with confusion. *I have no fucking idea why I'm here.*

"Oh, silly Cam. I'm going to make sure we're together forever. Now that I'm stronger, I can get rid of Eve, and then I will make you into something just like me. I've already made so many like us. I thought I would test out how to make the perfect zombie. It seems the less I bite, the more human you'll remain, but with a few upgrades. Unfortunately, I was really hungry at first, so I may have eaten more students than I meant to."

Claire pouts as if she expects me to feel sorry for her. My stomach is turning, threatening to explode.

"Claire, I don't want to be like you and Eve. I want to be human."

Now Claire is the one who looks confused.

"Why wouldn't you want to be super strong and super un-breakable? Oh, I get it. It's a joke. You're joking, Cam. You're funny."

Her laugh makes me want to throw up; it sounds like demon laughter. Claire begins to stroke my face. She's leaning in closer, and she looks so hungry.

"Claire, don't do this."

She's so close that I fear she is going to take a bite out of my cheek. Instead, she settles for licking my face.

"Mmmm, that is delicious. Sorry, I had to have a quick taste. I don't know how Eve does it. I get so hungry so quickly. I don't want to eat until Eve gets here. I know she'll come for you, and then I will destroy her. She messed with the wrong girl."

I shuffle in my chair with rage. I won't let her hurt Eve.

"No, you will leave Eve alone. I will stay with you. You don't need to hurt her. If she shows up, I will tell her that I want to stay with you."

Claire looks touched and places her grotesque arm over her un-beating heart.

Claire moves over to the window and keeps watch. I take a deep breath now that I've been given some space. I try to think of a way out of this, but I don't have any bright ideas. If only I can signal to Eve that this is a trap. I know Eve will eventually come here, wherever here is, and I suppose I would do the same if it was her.

I close my eyes tightly and think of her smile; my God, it is breathtaking. I won't let anything happen to her; she is mine to protect. I try to quietly fiddle with the ropes around my wrists while Claire is distracted. Perhaps I can find a way to loosen them enough to slip free. I mean, if magicians can do it with strait jackets, surely there is a way for me to break free.

CHAPTER FORTY-THREE

ALEX

We burst into Dr. August's office out of breath.

"Doctor, we need your help. Something awful…"

Eve stops talking once she notices we are not alone. Dr. August is seated at his desk, and there are three men in suits sitting in the chairs across from him. It seems as though we have interrupted a very important meeting because the three men don't seem at all amused when they turn to sneer at us.

I quickly interject. "Something awfully important to talk to you about on our upcoming test. Can we speak to you real quick?"

Dr. August rises from his chair and addresses the three men. "Will you please excuse me for just a moment, gentlemen?"

They don't seem pleased, but they nod. It's creepy how they seem to mirror each other.

Dr. August leads us into the hall, and his tone quickly changes from that of a calm and collected man to that of a terrified one.

"Girls, you should not be here. Those men are from CSIS. Eve, if you hadn't rushed to hang up on me, you would have known this."

He seems very ticked off with Eve. She fidgets with her hands, looking ashamed, and apologizes.

"Sorry is not good enough, I'm afraid. They are on a bit of witch hunt, and your panicked entrance looked a bit suspicious."

Eve and I exchange confused glances, and I venture to ask, "Who are they hunting?"

Dr. August's eyes move to Eve.

"Do they know about her? How can they know?"

Dr. August looks behind him before answering my question; he most likely fears the men in his office may be listening in.

"They have eyes everywhere, and I'm sorry to say, Eve, but they found some of the data from our tests. They know I'm studying someone, but they don't know it's you. They will find out soon enough, and you will need to run. They will track our trip to Egypt and knock on every volunteer's door until they find the person they are looking for. I've been trying to convince them that I was running tests on Vincent's blood again, but they aren't buying it."

Eve's eyes are wide, but she's trying to stay calm. "We will need to worry about that later. There are a bunch of squashed zombies in the parking lot, and we still haven't found Cam. I'm afraid CSIS is going to want answers for that too."

Dr. August looks nauseous. "Yes, that will be hard to explain, won't it?"

Before we can continue the conversation, one of the men appears at the door.

"Excuse me, ladies, why don't you come on in and wait? Our business here is almost finished, and we are in a bit of a hurry."

Something smells fishy, but what other choice do we have? If Eve and I flee, won't they suspect something and come after us? We silently decide to follow Dr. August back inside. Eve and I sit in the love seat just on the other side of the door.

Before heading back to his seat, the CSIS agent introduces himself. "Oh, how rude of me. I really should introduce myself. I am Mr. Williams." I shudder; he must mean "Agent" Williams. I remember his name from Dr. August's story; this is the man in charge.

Agent Williams holds out his hand and waits for us to introduce ourselves. I almost want to give him a fake name, but I'm sure he can always check on that, and then lying is always suspicious. *Why lie if you have nothing to hide, right?*

Eve takes his hand first and introduces herself. I extend my hand out next and simply say, "Nice to meet you."

Agent Williams looks a bit taken aback by the half-introduction, but I don't feel he needs to know my name, and I know he won't bother asking for it now; it will be a bit awkward. We are both hiding some of our cards now. I can tell he has instantly become suspicious of me, but I don't care. Perhaps that is a good thing. It will lead him off Eve's trail.

Agent Williams is not terribly old and is quite handsome. However, his grin is something sinister; I can't explain it. I shiver as he smiles at us and then begins walking towards his seat. He is almost in his seat when he turns back to look at us and asks, "Just out of curiosity, ladies, when is your test? If it's tomorrow, I shall try and be quick. You will need your study time."

Yup, that definitely sounds like a trap.

Eve and I glance at each other briefly. I shake my head at her slightly, trying to say, "Don't answer," and then of course Eve foolishly answers for both of us. "Yes, it's tomorrow. We are slacking a bit, I guess. We should have asked our questions earlier."

Agent Williams's smile fades. I guess that is the wrong answer because Dr. August hangs his head in defeat.

"You know what's funny, ladies? Dr. August here had told me that his schedule was clear for the next week. He was going to come and have a visit with us, actually. I even took the time to peruse his schedule to be sure it would be a good time to visit him tonight."

He waits for a retort, but we aren't prepared with an explanation.

I'm a little afraid of what will happen next. Agent Williams walks closer, and his men follow behind him.

Oh shit, they know! I'm sweating, trying to think about how to get Eve and me out of this. I don't want them to take my friend. Plus we still need to find Cam. We don't have this kind of time to waste.

Agent Williams is uncomfortably close to us now, and the other two men are stationed behind us. They are most likely anticipating our attempt to escape. I examine the agent on my left; my eyes focus in on a gun hiding under his tailored jacket. How do they hide those guns so well? It feels a little like we are stuck in a James Bond film and this is the showdown between the good guy and bad guy. The only problem is that I don't think we are going to be the victors, and I am pretty sure these CSIS guys are the ones with a license to kill.

"So which one of you has been Dr. August's test subject for the last little while? Huh?"

Agent Williams' voice sounds curiously calm. Is he attempting to lure us into confessing everything by treating us like toddlers?

"I'm not going to hurt anyone. I just want the truth, and it seems Dr. August has been hiding some of it from me, which is not very nice."

He shakes his finger at Dr. August before returning to look at us. *How condescendingly rude!* The hairs stand up on the back of my neck; I don't trust this guy one bit.

After about a minute of silence, Agent Williams starts to pace the room. He pauses and grins. I don't like that look. He is up to something. I can hear Eve starting to growl to my right; I know she senses something, but now is not the time to show her true colours.

Agent Williams walks towards Dr. August, takes out his gun,

and quickly grabs him and pulls him to his feet. He places the gun against Dr. August's head.

Eve juts forward. "Stop! What the hell are you doing?"

The agent closest to her quickly pushes her back. This angers Eve, and she shoves the agent back. He looks stunned by the force Eve exhibits.

I whisper to Eve, "Stop it."

She backs off but retains her scowl. I feel dizzy. I want to protect Eve and Dr. August and save Cam and somehow save my own ass. How am I going to achieve this?

"Ladies, I will ask you again. Which one of you has been his little lab rat? I will kill him. He's only mildly useful and absolutely replaceable. So let's start talking, huh?"

I grind my teeth with pure hatred as I stare at Agent Williams. I realize that he is totally and utterly serious. One of us better say something soon, or Dr. August will have a nice bullet hole where his eye used to be. I look over at Eve, and she instantly knows what I'm about to do. She shakes her head and whispers, "No, no, Al!" but my mind is made up.

I stare at her with worry in my furrowed brow and simply whisper back one word. "Cam."

She and I know very well that if anyone could save him, it would be her. I will never stand a chance next to Claire. Eve needs to get out of here. Saving my own ass will have to wait.

"It's me. I'm the one you want. Dr. August has been protecting me this whole time. I was scared, and he was trying to help me."

I look over at Dr. August, hoping he'll keep his mouth shut and play along.

Agent Williams lowers his gun. "Now was that so hard? Thank you, darling, for being honest."

Just when I think I've given him what he wants, he raises his gun over Dr. August's head and lowers it with a thud against the doctor's temple, knocking him out instantly. Eve and I both cry out as we see Dr. August drop to the ground.

Now is her chance. "Eve, get out of here."

She looks at me with resistance. "No, Al. There's another way."

I elbow the agent next to me so hard that it winds him. "Go!" I yell, and I jump on top of the other agent. Very quickly I am pulled to the ground and held down.

Everything moves in slow motion. I see Eve running towards the door and looking back at me with a horrified glance. She continues out the door until she is out of sight. She made it. Thank God, she made it. The last thing I remember is convulsing on the ground and jolts of pain reaching my every extremity, then everything goes black.

CHAPTER FORTY-FOUR

EVE

I keep running until I am outside, hidden by shadows. I witnessed my friend being tasered by two strange men who believe she is the infected student. I keep replaying the image of Alex seizing on the ground. It looked like they were killing her. How could I leave her? I pull at my hair and pace in a circle until I can compose myself.

In the middle of my panic attack, I hear something rustling in the bushes. I turn to see another zombie student. She isn't going to attack me; there is no food to get at this time.

We are the same. Dead. Unfortunately for her, she looks it. Her eyes are unnaturally pale, and her skin is flaking. There is blood around her mouth. *Oh God! Who has she been eating?* As I look at her, I think of Cam. What if this is his fate and he's wandering the campus somewhere?

Everyone I love is in danger because of me. So many students have been killed tonight, and this one is no different. I can't let her live and pass on the virus. That is irresponsible.

I pick up a rock near the bushes that is usually used as decoration and bash her head in. While I repeatedly slam the rock against her skull, I think about the family that will never see her again, and I feel disgusted with myself. I find myself wishing that I am the girl whose head now resembles scrambled eggs. At least then it will all be over.

I am exhausted and emotional as I stare at the former zombie, former student, former human. I don't even know where to begin looking for Cam. I collapse to the ground. The pressure to succeed is too much. Alex sacrificed herself so that I can save Cam, and once I do so, I'm sure she's counting on me to save her. I can't let them down, but I am immobilized by my distress.

Lying on the cold grass feels so good. I try to think like Claire. If I am a psycho-stalker, where will I hide?

As I try to think up a plan, images of Alex being tasered, Doctor August with a gun to his head, and Mark's lifeless body keep flashing back and forth in my mind. My body begins to build up with rage. I can feel myself shaking with anger. The virus is taking over in a whole new way.

My back arches on the ground as I try to fight back and keep a clear head. Something is changing in me, and it is terrifying. I fight for as long as I can but eventually let the virus take me.

My body rises off the ground without my consent and head in a direction that I haven't selected. It is auto-pilot time, and I am just along for the ride whether I like it or not.

Before I know it, I am in front of my residence. My body feels as heavy as a stone wall; every step feels powerful. My eyes feel fiery; they burn with purpose as I enter the building. Soon I am in front of Claire's dorm room door. I don't bother to knock; I just begin to slam my body against the door until I am through.

CHAPTER FORTY-FIVE

ALEX

When I wake up, I find my cheek pressed against the cold floor, and I am lying in a puddle of drool. I feel disoriented but manage to slur a few words. "What did you do to me?" It comes out as more of a mumble.

I try to rise, but my body feels stiff. As I lay there, Agent Williams brings his face closer to mine and smiles. I want to tear that smile off his face.

"What did you say, dear?"

Before I can repeat myself, his two minions pull me to my feet. They drag me across the floor and throw me into a nearby chair. I don't have the strength to sit properly, and I begin to spill over the seat, which causes them to hold me in place.

Now that I am upright, I can see that Dr. August is sitting at his desk. He looks distraught, but I'm glad he no longer has a gun pointed at his head. I see Agent Williams grab a book off of Dr. August's desk. He's flipping through the pages looking for something specific. When he finds it, he shouts out, "Ah ha! Here it is."

He puts the book down in front of Doctor August and asks him to read a passage. Reluctantly, he begins to read.

"The subject seems to heal at a rapid pace. Wounds heal in a matter of seconds, leaving no identifiable mark or scar."

Dr. August's eyes grow wide as he watches Agent Williams approach me. He reaches into his pocket and pulls out a switchblade.

It glistens as bright as his smile as he approaches me.

"Shall we run the test again? I need to be sure it's you."

This man loves being in power; I can tell he thrives off of it.

Agent Williams holds the knife over my thigh. I scream and try to move away, but I am held down in place. "Please don't! I can't heal right now. It only works when I feed, and I haven't eaten today."

Agent Williams ponders that for a second but decides to plunge the knife into my thigh anyway. The pain is excruciating, and I am screaming so loudly it causes the two agents holding me down to jerk backward a bit.

He watches as the blood pours out of my leg. He shrugs as he looks at me.

"It's not healing. Why isn't it healing?"

I'm in too much pain to answer anyone. I see Doctor August appear behind him, and he grabs Agent Williams' gun and points it at him. "Leave her alone," Dr. August says.

Agent Williams drops the knife and backs away. "Now, now, Doctor, there's no need for that. I've finished my experiment. I guess she's not the one we're looking for. Perhaps that other girl, Eve? Was that her name? Perhaps she was the one we should be looking for."

Agent Williams backs up towards one of the other agents, who hands him something. I want to warn Dr. August, but he moves so quickly that everyone is surprised by the sudden "bang" that fills the air.

I look over at Dr. August as he drops his gun. Blood starts to flood his sleeve, and he crumbles to the ground, yelling in pain. This is quickly turning into a blood bath.

My screams along with Dr. August's are filling the room. All

I can hear between screams is Agent Williams shouting at us to shut up.

I try to calm myself and put pressure on my leg, which is still bleeding. Surprisingly, Agent Williams grabs the first aid kit on the wall, pulls out some bandages, and begins to bind my wound to the best of his ability. Why is he bothering to mend me if he is intending to kill me? He doesn't bother to do the same for Dr. August, who is leaning against his desk holding his arm.

"What do you want from me?" I cry out, sniffling like a baby.

"I want what any other government agent wants. I want information. Can you give that to me? If you can, then I promise you I will disappear like this has all been a bad dream. Now where is Eve?"

Does he really think I will hand over my best friend? And then it dawns on me; I *can* give him some other information that might peak his interest.

"The woman you are looking for is Claire Madison. She is our dorm leader..."

I continue to tell him about how we found Mark's body and how we believe she kidnapped our friend Cam. I eventually get to the part where she creates multiple zombies, and this confession sends Agent Williams into a fury. I'm sure he is pissed that he will now have to stage a rather large-scale cover up. There are multiple families to contact about their child's death, bodies just strewn across campus, and a violent zombie on the loose. That is a lot for Agent Williams to swallow. I hope that he will focus on the cover-up mission and forget all about Eve.

Agent Williams turns to his men and asks them to go and check on the situation in the parking lot. He whispers something about wanting to start with a physical clean up before working on the explanation for the whole incident.

As soon as the men have their orders and take their leave, Agent Williams begins screaming at Doctor August.

"Do you have any idea how much work you've created for me? Why couldn't you have told me about the girl sooner? This whole mess could have been prevented. Did you think that you could save her? You couldn't even save Vincent. What makes you think you can help her?"

Dr. August's retort is short, but it's brave. "I won't let you kill her," he utters and spits at Agent Williams.

He curses at Doctor August and kicks him in the leg, adding insult to injury. I'm still too weak to move; I am only able to watch and hope that he won't hurt him any further.

"You're a bad man," I whisper.

I didn't think Agent Williams would hear me, but somehow he does. His focus is now on me. He walks over to me with a murderous look in his eyes.

Agent Williams leans into my face, leaving almost no space between us, and yells, "What did you say? You think I'm the bad guy here? Really? You're looking at the man in charge of protecting this goddamn country, and right now I'm not doing a very good job, am I? I will do anything to make sure that people are safe, and I will make up whatever story I have to so that people will believe they are safe and can go about their daily lives without looking over their shoulders."

He has a point, but I don't really appreciate his technique.

Agent Williams sighs and picks up his phone. I hear him mention something about a cleanup crew and staging a fake fire. Looks like I am going to witness the creation of a conspiracy theory.

As he talks on the phone, I try to think about anything else but the pain in my leg. I wonder if Eve has found Claire and Cam. I pray that Cam is okay, but I fear for Eve. I'm not so sure she will be safe after all this. All eyes will be on campus. I'm sure they will have spies everywhere looking for leftover traces of the virus. I don't want Eve to become their little experiment. I hope that Agent Williams will believe that Claire is the only zombie girl in existence, and if he does, then maybe, just maybe, Eve will be able to return to some slightly normal way of life.

CHAPTER FORTY-SIX

CAM

My wrists are raw from trying to free my hands from the ropes Claire bound them with. She continues to stare out the window, and I know she is determined to eliminate the only woman I have ever loved. She wants me all to herself, but why? She doesn't even know me very well. She has no idea that my mother died, leaving me heartbroken at a young age, and that my father continued stomping on my heart by drinking himself into a monster. She doesn't even know the simpler things about me, like my favourite colour, or my favourite sport, or my favourite team for that matter. She doesn't care about any of that. The only thing she is interested in is whatever fantasy she has created in her head. Perhaps I am Prince Charming? Don Juan? Casanova? Whatever she is thinking is pure fiction. If only I can make her see that it isn't me that she loves; she is in love with a figment of her imagination.

I venture to ask, "Claire, why do you love me?"

She turns to look at me with a bewildered expression.

"I love you for so many reasons, silly."

That isn't really an answer, so I try again. "Can you tell me some of the reasons why you love me?"

She laughs it off without a real reply.

That's what I thought. She's in love with a work of fiction.

I decide to ask a question she might know the answer to.

"Claire, what colour are my eyes?"

She looks over at me, and her smile fades. With a furrowed brow, she answers, "Why, they're blue, silly. Of course, I know that!"

I shake my head and smirk. "Nope, they're not. If you love me, shouldn't you at least know my eye colour? I mean, at the very least?"

I can see I've pissed her off. She has a scowl on her face and is now walking towards me rapidly. She grabs my face and stares into my eyes. She's squeezing my face so hard I think my jawbone is going to snap.

"So they're brown. Oops."

She's not very sorry about her inaccuracy; she shrugs it off and then begins to untie my hands. *Is she going to let me go?*

Once my hands are free, I rub them and try to get my circulation going again. Claire grabs my hands so suddenly and violently, it feels as if the bones are going to shatter.

"Claire, you're hurting me."

She doesn't release me.

"I'm not trying to hurt you, Cam. I want you to feel how much I love you. That's how much it hurts when I'm not near you. Do you feel it?"

I'm about ready to scream; I just agree with her and hope she loosens her grip. The virus has made her strong, just like Eve.

"Claire, please."

She stares into my eyes, but it's like she's looking through me, not at me. The new Claire is even scarier than the previous one.

Just when I think my wrist is going to snap off, I hear a big bang at the door. Claire steps back and snarls. I automatically scream, "Eve!"

A few more bangs and the door splits open like that scene from *The Shining*. Shards of wood fly through the room. A piece just misses my face, but Claire gets a rather large chunk lodged in her shoulder. She doesn't bother to pull it out; she is fixated on the door. Eve pulls the rest of the door apart and makes her way inside.

I'm happy to see her, but I'm not sure I like seeing her in full zombie mode. Her eyes are red; she is twitchy and looks ravenous. Claire has a similar look to her; she glares at Eve as if she can tear her apart just by staring.

I struggle with the ropes at my ankles. I don't think standing between these two is a smart move. As soon as I'm free, I back up behind Eve. Claire twitches her neck to one side in preparation for battle. The crack in each vertebra makes the hairs on my arms stand. She then pulls the large piece of door out of her shoulder and chucks it to the floor. The blood gushes out until the wound seals itself, leaving only stains on her blouse.

As I wait for someone to make the first move, I wonder if they will even be able to kill one another. They are both indestructible with the Azrael Virus coursing through their veins.

I look from one woman to the next in anticipation. Finally, Claire decides to sprint towards Eve, and Eve doesn't hesitate to rush with great speed towards Claire. They crash into each other like two pieces of steel. Claire grips Eve's head between both of her hands; it looks as though she is attempting to tear it off. Eve grabs Claire's waist with a bear hug and slams her to the ground. Eve begins to rain elbows and punches down on Claire's face.

Every dent Eve makes heals so quickly. It's as though the battle never started. Claire screams like a banshee with each blow; she tries to get Eve off of her by using her legs. Eventually, Claire is able to wrap both legs around Eve and twists until Eve grunts in pain and steps back off of Claire. Eve is holding her side. I think Claire might have snapped a rib, but Eve will heal soon enough.

I look around the room for some kind of weapon so I can assist Eve or at least hand her something helpful. I spot a three-legged side table and smash it on the ground to break off the legs. I say, "Catch," as I throw two of the legs to Eve. I save the last leg for myself.

Eve holds the two legs up like jousting lances and runs with them towards Claire. The two legs make contact in Claire's shoulders, and she shrieks as they pin her against the wall. Claire is snarling as she tries to break free, but she's pinned so firmly to the wall that she just dangles without progress. Eve uses all her strength to hold her a few inches off the ground. It seems like Eve is enjoying Claire's shrieks of pain because she is grinning.

Claire gives one final scream and then does something unbelievable. She holds onto the two table legs lodged in her shoulders and uses them as gymnast parallel bars to kick Eve away. Eve goes flying to the other side of the room, landing on her back. Claire is now wriggling to the end of the parallel bars lodged in the wall. I feel as though I may throw up as I see her gliding away from the wall through the holes in her shoulders. She looks demonic as she uses the blood to slide her way down the table legs. Once she reaches the end of the legs, she drops to the floor, but the holes in her shoulders are still there, and I can see through them.

I gasp, "Oh, dear God," and then look over at Eve, who is already on her feet.

Claire looks around the room for something. Her gaze lands on her bed; it is one of those fancy cast-iron beds. Claire grabs one of the rods at the end of the bed and pulls it off effortlessly, then proceeds to walk towards Eve.

Eve and Claire keep eye contact, and this does not work to

Eve's advantage because she doesn't notice Claire aiming at her knees with the iron bar. Claire's wind up is quick, and she makes contact with the right knee, sending Eve to the ground. She then raises the bar, ready to slam it down on Eve's skull.

Now it is my turn to take action while Eve is immobilized. I hold the table leg tight and run at Claire, striking her head as if it is a baseball. Her head does not come off, but I manage to smack it hard enough that it is now facing backwards, leaving me looking at the back of her head. I drop the table leg in shock. She turns her body so she can see me. She has a pout on her face.

"Cam, why did you do that?"

She tries to reach her head so that she can snap it back around the right way. I try to hold it, but as she does this, I throw up all over her floor. I've never witnessed anything quite so grotesque as someone putting their head straight again.

Once I'm finished throwing up, I look up and no longer see Claire. *Where is she?* I look behind me, and of course, there she is, still pouting. She grabs me by the neck and raises me in the air. Eve is desperately trying to crawl towards us, but her knee hasn't healed yet, and she looks on with sheer panic.

Claire smiles with satisfaction as Eve crawls towards her. She then takes her foot and kicks Eve in the face. This knocks Eve back a bit. Claire continues to carry me by the throat over to the window. I am trying to break free, but her hands are like a vice. I feel as though my throat might snap. It's so hard to breathe that I'm gasping. Claire holds me out the window, and I can feel the night air on my skin, but I'm unable to take it in. This is it. I am going to fall to my death, and Claire has won.

Claire looks away from me for a moment and speaks to Eve in a demonic voice.

"If I can't have him, no one will have him."

She loosens her grip on my neck slightly, and I grab her arm and won't let go. I refuse to have it end this way. I will fight till the end.

I can see Eve rising through the window. She is limping; she must be healing if she can stand now. I feel a prickle of hope in my chest as I watch her rise. Azrael Virus or not, Eve is a very determined girl.

I see her back up, and the next part happens so fast that I can barely recall what happened. Eve sprints towards us, and then somehow I land back in my bedroom on my back. I get up as quickly as I can. I still feel something around my neck, and when I go to touch it, I feel cool fingers and gag a bit, realizing that Claire's arm is somehow still attached to me. I quickly peel it off finger by finger and throw it across the room. The fingers continue twitching as the arm lies there.

I realize that Eve must have torn off the arm and thrown me inside, but where are they now? I glance at the open window.

"Oh my God, they fell out the window?" I say.

I run to the window and glance down. Sure enough, the two zombie girls lay below. They aren't moving, but there is no threat of them being dead since they already are. I'm sure they have broken their spines with the fall, and the quickest one to heal will have the advantage.

I feel helpless as I watch. I won't make it downstairs in time for the battle to resume, and even if I do, what can I really do to help? I see Claire rise first; perhaps her missing arm will put her at a disadvantage. She won't be able to retrieve it and re-attach it unless she comes up here.

"Come on, Eve, get up!" is all I can say as I watch on in horror.

Claire waddles over to Eve. I guess one less arm has thrown off her balance a bit. Once she reaches Eve, she uses her remaining arm to drag her out of the bushes and onto the concrete below. Then Claire disappears into the trees. *What is she up to?* I try to glimpse through the trees. I know there is a maintenance shed there. I hear a lot of banging and assume that Claire is trying to break into the shed.

The next sound I hear is probably one of the most terrifying sounds known to man, unless you are in the landscaping business, in which case it just sounds productive. Through the trees, I hear it winding up, *brum brum brum*, and when it finally gets going, each buzz of the blade slices a hole in my heart. I keep praying, "Eve, please, please. Get up, get up, get up!"

I don't want to witness the love of my life being cut into pieces.

Claire finally makes an appearance with the chainsaw overhead. I scream out, "Nooooooo!"

Claire looks up and laughs that creepy laugh just for me. She is heading towards Eve, who is still unable to move. The chainsaw is just inches away from her when it stops working.

There is a God!

I laugh out loud with delight. "Ha ha, you bitch! Leave her alone. Hey, Claire, I hate your guts. I hope you burn in hell."

She places the chainsaw on the ground and scowls at me. She's drooling with rage. I can't even understand how she got that chainsaw working in the first place. My questions are soon answered as I see her attempt to restart it. She holds the saw to the ground with one foot and pulls the starter with her remaining arm. The chainsaw attempts to start, but nothing happens. This doesn't stop Claire from trying again and again.

To my horror, she does get it going again. She squeals with

delight. I'm sure she would clap with joy if she could. I step on the arm lying next to me with all the force I can muster. As I dig my heel into the arm, blood squirts out. I curse at it, "Evil, bitch, die already!"

When I glance back down, I see Eve wiggling her fingers. She is beginning to heal, but I am doubtful she will fully heal before Claire makes it over to her. I chew on the insides of my mouth as I watch. The saw roars above Eve's still body. It comes closer and closer to her, wiggling out of control since Claire is only able to hold it with one arm. I hold my breath with despair in my lungs.

Before the saw reaches her face, she jolts upright and lifts her arm in front of her to protect herself. The chainsaw quiets slightly as it tries to tear through the flesh and bone of her arm. Blood sprays everywhere, and Eve's screams are piercing. I am positive people will hear and come outside to look, but to my surprise, no one appears. As the saw makes it through bone, it halts again. What luck!

Eve screams as she glances down at her dangling arm. She has no time to reattach it now. She tears off the rest and leaves it on the ground.

She stands prepared to continue the brawl, and Claire is just as ready. Eve runs towards Claire and kicks her in the chest with both legs, sort of like a flying ninja. Claire's knees buckle, and she falls to the ground. Eve is quickly on her feet again and pounces on top of Claire, grabbing her by the hair with her one able hand and smashing her head into the ground countless times. Claire tries to fight back, but Eve has her pinned real good this time. I can see blood beginning to pool out of Claire's head, but Eve isn't satisfied until her head splits open like a cracked egg. Claire is no longer moving, and her wicked eyes stare up at the sky without motion. The blood stains the pavement; it is more like a black ooze.

Eve falls backward, exhausted. When she can gather more strength, she grabs her arm and holds it in place waiting for it to reattach. It looks like a painful healing process because Eve grimaces more with every second that passes. I decide I no longer want to watch; I want to be next to her. I race out of the room and head for the stairs. I don't think I have ever sprinted down a flight of stairs so quickly before.

Once I'm outside, I see Eve's arm has fully reattached, and she is wiggling her fingers and flexing her arm trying to get sensation back. As I approach her ready to embrace her, I realize that her eyes are still red. This is not a good time for a hug. I realize my mistake as she rises and glares at me with desire. She licks her lips as I try to back away.

I attempt to call her out of her trance. "Eve, you don't want to eat your boyfriend. Remember me? It's Cam."

Her head twitches as she battles with this knowledge, but the virus seems to be winning. She has to feed.

Eve is about ready to pounce on me and devour me whole, but just then I hear people coming. She knows there is a buffet arriving. As they round the corner, she looks in their direction.

They don't notice what they're walking into right away but look scared when they finally come close enough to see Claire's demolished body. One girl screams and runs away. The other two are frozen in fear. Eve races towards them and takes them both down. In a fury, she tears into both men. I see blood squirting and organs flying.

"Eve, no! Stop!"

I wish I can stop their gruesome murders, but very quickly the deed is done. Eve smashes their skulls in when she's done feeding. She won't have them rise again and terrorize the campus. Eve is still in there somewhere.

Eve sits in a puddle of their blood. Her eyes have returned to their normal shade of blue. She begins to sob out loud uncontrollably. The switch from zombie mode to somewhat human must be miserable, especially when she notices what she's done.

I run to her side and hold her, blood covered and all. I think I may have surprised myself, because even after everything I have just witnessed, I don't care.

"Cam, I'm a monster. I hate myself. I can't do this anymore. I want you to do me a favour."

I don't like the sound of that. "What kind of favour?"

She looks over at the chainsaw and simply says, "Please."

I shake my head furiously. "No way, you're not leaving me!"

I press her tight to my body and hold her as she continues to sob.

CHAPTER FORTY-SEVEN

EVE

A s Cam holds me, I have an epiphany. I don't share that epiphany with him. I keep it to myself, and no, it doesn't involve suicide. I will have to do something even more drastic, even more painful.

I squeeze Cam back as hard as I can without hurting him. He smells like Cam, which is a combination of sweat, deodorant, and fabric softener. He would always lend me his sweaters in high school, and I would sniff them because his scent was so comforting. Perhaps I loved him then, but I was too stupid to know it or act on it. I love him so much more than I can ever tell him. There is no point now. I will be gone by morning.

We sit in a magical embrace, and I absorb every second of it. It feels as though time has stopped for us. I hear nothing but his beating heart, which is so beautiful I could cry. I miss my own beating heart, but I know I am still capable of love, because this is heartbreaking.

When it's time to break our embrace, I kiss Cam gently and tell him, "We need to go and help Alex."

I explain the situation with the agents in Dr. August's office and how they tasered Alex, thinking she was me. Cam's horrified expression says it all, and we are on our feet and running in no time.

As we're running, we pass the parking lot. I forgot to tell Cam about the zombies that Claire created. He stops to gaze at the carnage. There are flattened bodies strewn everywhere. In a corner of the parking lot, there is a large van parked, and I can see agents placing the bodies in the vehicle. I guess it is time to clean up before too many questions are asked, or worse, the media catches this all on video and plasters it all over television and the internet.

I place my hand on Cam's shoulder. I know he is in shock, but we have to keep moving. He turns to look at me; I can see in his eyes that he is wondering if I did this. I simply say, "Claire," and he looks relieved.

We race towards Dr. August's office. There are now agents stationed outside the door. Cam and I stop in the hallway, staring at them as they stare back.

"Cam, I'm going in there, and I'm not sure what I'm going to find. It may be better if you wait…"

Cam presses his finger to my lips and shakes his head. "I'm not leaving your side. Good or bad, we're going in together."

He kisses me hard. I want to faint under its power, but Alex is counting on us to save her ass, so I shake myself alert and ready.

We continue walking towards the guards, and they ask us to halt. One of them even takes out a gun to stop our approach. I glare at them. "Gentlemen, we don't need to get violent here. I just want to see my friends. Take us in."

The other agent takes out his gun and aims it at my face.

"We have been ordered to keep everyone out, ma'am. We will use force if necessary."

I put my hands in the air and back away. This isn't going as planned. I don't want to hurt them, but soldiers always listen to their orders, and there will be no other way in but through them. I charge at one of the agents and take him down. I hear a bang and feel warmth flowing down my back. I punch the agent on the floor so hard that he goes unconscious, then I run my hand along the source of my pain. As I bring the hand back into sight, I can see there is an excessive amount of blood.

I turn back and snarl at the other agent, "You shot me? Really?"

He then drops his gun. Cam takes this opportunity to punch him square in the jaw. The agent crumples to the ground. "Nice one, Camy." We high five and then make our way to the door. I hold my ear up to the door first, but I don't hear anything. The silence scares me.

I look at Cam and whisper, "Okay, on the count of three we bust in. You ready?"

He nods. When I reach three, we blast into the room.

There doesn't seem to be anyone around. I see blood surrounding Dr. August's desk. If it is already too late, I will never forgive myself.

As I am examining the trail of blood, I hear Cam grunt and then hit the ground with a thud. I turn in a panic and see Cam shaking on the ground. Behind him stands Agent Williams with his damn taser gun. I plunge to the ground next to Cam. I can't do much for him, but I stroke his hair to let him know I'm still here.

"Now I know what you're thinking. That was a bit unnecessary? I guess it was, but I have to play it safe. We have zombies on the loose, you know?"

I scowl at Agent Williams. My eyes are welling up with tears, but I fight them back. I'm not going to let this bastard see me cry.

"Where are Alex and Dr. August? What have you done with them?"

Agent Williams uses his famous smirk again.

"Well, the doctor will be coming with me. He has work to do, and he hasn't been so productive here, so I think we will make sure he stays in one of our labs permanently. As for your little buddy..."

He points to a dark corner of the room, and two men drag Alex out into the center of the room. I can see blood on one of her legs, and she still seems pretty out of it. When they lay Alex next to me, I grab her and hug her. I am just thankful she is alive. Alex gives me a weak smile.

I sit between two of the people I care most about in this world. They are in pain, and I am the only one who can make it stop.

I stand to face Agent Williams. "I want you to let these two go. I'm the one you want."

I feel Alex grab my ankle. I look down at her, and she's shaking her head. "Eve, you don't have to do this!"

I shake free of Alex's hand and walk towards Agent Williams. He looks intrigued.

"I was under the impression that I wanted some girl named Claire. Are you Claire?"

I shake my head. "No, sir. Claire's dead. I killed her."

Agent Williams looks confused. "Why did you kill her?"

I take a deep breath before laying all my cards on the table.

"I killed her because she was infected with the Azrael Virus. I was the one that infected her, and unfortunately, she proved to be much more dangerous than I could have ever imagined. I am the one Dr. August has been studying and trying to help, but I guess I'm beyond help."

Agent Williams signals to his minions. "Restrain her."

Before they can continue their approach, I tell them, "I wouldn't do that if I were you."

The men seem a little afraid. Their fear makes me hungry, even though I just had a rather large meal.

I turn to look back at Agent Williams, who must be watching my fiery eyes because he looks a little afraid himself.

"Agent Williams, I wasn't finished yet. If you think you can take me without my permission, you must be out of your damn mind! I'm going to come with you willingly. I want to continue my tests with Dr. August, under your supervision, of course."

Agent Williams looks skeptical. "So you are just going to come quietly then?"

"Yes, that's the plan. I go with you, and you let these two go. They're not infected. They just have the misfortune of knowing me. I promise you they won't tell anyone about what took place tonight. They never even told anyone about me. They are excellent secret keepers."

From behind me, I hear, "No, don't!" It's Alex shrieking. I can see her attempting to get up.

"Eve, why would you want to go with them? Are you out of your mind? Do you know what they'll do to you?"

I hear the sadness in Alex's voice, but I ignore it. I know this is the very thing they were trying to prevent, but it is the only alternative I see.

"Al, I need to do this. I need to find out what I really am. Plus Agent Williams can contain me and keep me where I can't hurt more people. Everyone will be safe again."

Alex is unsteady on her feet, and I wish she will just give it a rest entirely. My mind is made up.

"Eve, how do you know they won't use you to hurt others? And forget what they might do for a second. What about us? What about your family?"

My un-beating heart stings as I think of leaving my mother and father. I shed a tear as I think of how they'll react once they find out I've gone missing. I imagine my mother sobbing in my empty room and my father becoming so silent that people will forget what his voice even sounds like. This is the mental picture of hearts breaking. This image angers me, and I end up yelling back at Alex.

"Don't you think I've thought of everything? I know this is best! I have to do this. Don't think for a second I haven't thought about you guys. I'm doing this for you. You can have your normal lives back. Be grateful!"

Alex is crying. I don't really want to leave on bad terms, but it looks as though it is going that route. I look down at Cam, who is unconscious. I am glad I won't have to say goodbye to him. It would be too difficult. The short time that we shared together is most likely to be the highlight of my life. I will have to hold onto that.

I stare at Alex, knowing this is the last time I will ever see her.

"You will forget me. Forget our history, forget our friendship, and forget my name. I don't exist. Got it?"

Alex whimpers but manages to get out a few last words.

"Is that what you want me to tell Cam? To tell your parents?"

I ponder this for a moment. "No, tell them the truth… I'm dead."

Alex sobs harder. I can't watch. I turn to leave and step over Cam to show Alex that I am truly serious. Our friendship is over; it is for the best. As I leave, I feel Agent Williams and his minions following close behind me.

My face is like stone as Agent Williams points to their vehicle. We walk towards the dark limousine, and he opens the door for me. I step inside readily. He sits across from me in the car and stares at me. I can feel his confusion as well as his eyes on me as we begin to drive away.

"What?" I reply irritably.

"Why are you doing this, Eve? What do you really want?"

I grab Agent Williams by the collar; he is shocked but shows no fear.

"I want to work for you. I want you to give my life purpose again. I will do anything you ask. Just promise me you will leave my friends alone. Let them live their lives in peace, and I will give you whatever you ask of me. Are we clear?"

He smirks and says, "Of course. I'm glad you will join us. This makes my job much easier."

I know immediately that I hate this man, but whatever chance I have of finding out what I truly am and perhaps finding a cure depends on him.

As we continue driving, I doze off. This is the first time in a long time that I am able to shut my eyes and not worry about the virus. I know that if it acts up, CSIS will be there to take me down. I am no longer a threat. The rest is beautiful in a very literal sense. For the first time since the incident, I am dreaming something semi-blissful.

***

I am sitting in a field of golden wheat on a sunny day. My hair glistens in the sunlight. I see someone walking towards me. The approaching body is out of focus until it comes closer. Coming towards me is Cam. My excitement wills me to rise and run to him. I run through the glittering wheat fields and crash into him. He holds me in his arms so tightly. I sense him sniffing my hair and running his fingers through it playfully. We say nothing, but our smiles say it all. The embrace is warm; it feels so real.

I continue holding him blissfully but feel a chill rising between us. I furrow my brows. Where has Cam's warmth gone? The body I am holding is unpleasantly cold. I slowly break the embrace and glance up, trying to see his face. His face is frozen in a terrified stare. His skin is now a bluish gray. I shake him, trying to revive him, but his eyes sink back into his head, leaving black holes. His mouth widens, and he shrieks at me. This is not Cam. I fall to the ground, and the horrid monster drags his feet towards me. I am crawling backwards as fast as I can and feel the ground crumbling beneath me. It feels like an earthquake. As the ground shudders, it splits between Cam and me. The crack in the earth swallows Cam, and he falls into the abyss. The crack is getting larger and larger. I try to escape it, but it eventually swallows me as well. I feel myself falling into the darkness and scream as if there is someone who may hear me, but no one will be there to save me.

***

Agent Williams shakes me awake.

"Eve, are you alright?"

I shake him off. "I'm fine. Why do you care, anyway?"

"You were screaming, and I need you to be okay, for testing, that is."

I think I may have seen a glimmer of kindness from Agent Williams. Does he actually care about me? I shrug it off. Most likely he is hoping his lab rat won't die on him before he can administer some tests. I should be very cautious with this man; he has a lot of power.

"Agent Williams, I'm fine, just a bad dream. I have had many of those lately. You'll get used to it, and perhaps you can study them as well."

The limousine stops, and I find myself feeling anxious about what my future will look like in this private camp. Will I be tortured or treated with respect? Either way, I chose this fate, and I have to live with it.

The car door opens, and another agent greets Williams. We both step out of the car into a very white parking lot. It looks like the ceilings are made completely of lights. Blinding lights actually. Do they really need it to be this bright? I squint as I follow the agents through a sliding doorway.

We walk through the winding hallways until we reach a metal door. Agent Williams scans his ID card, and I follow him inside. This is a door to a gigantic laboratory. It is a scientist's playground.

As I scan the room, I see something familiar, and I am so grateful I can cry.

"Dr. August!"

I run over to him, and despite the nurse tending to his wound, I hug him as hard as I can. He squirms in pain, but his eyes are content. He is happy to see me, but there is also an air of concern in his body language. He knows what I am giving up to be here. He pats my hand, trying to comfort me. This gesture is more appreciated than he knows.

I feel Agent Williams behind me.

"You will be working with Dr. August. I thought that someone familiar would increase testing productivity since you already have a rapport with him."

I am more than happy about the arrangement than I let on. I don't want Agent Williams to see my jubilation, so I simply nod.

"Good, glad you're on board. Testing begins tomorrow. Let me show you to your sleeping quarters."

I wink at Dr. August, who gives me a brief smile as I exit.

I'm following Agent Williams for what seems like an eternity.

Every hallway looks the same. They are dim with many doors. There are red beams of light on the floor that give this place a spaceship feel. I don't care much for the colour red anymore. When we reach my room, I am standing in front of a white door with the number eleven on it.

"This is to be your room, Eve." He allows me to enter first.

The room is very sterile. Every wall and even the floor are white. My bed is small but seems to be comfortable when I sit on it. There is a small night light and a book shelf. I go over to the shelf and glance at the titles. There's a little Shakespeare, Byron, Hemingway, Woolf, and then Stephen King? An odd assortment, but I will most likely read any of them.

I notice a small door next to the bookshelf. Inside is my bathroom. As expected, it is also white. There is a shower, toilet, and sink, but no mirror. This is feeling more like a prison cell than a bedroom. I know why they don't have mirrors in prison—it's so people won't smash them and kill themselves with the shards or try and attack others with the glass. Glass is a weapon for the desperate.

My first question is an obvious one. "Why can't I have a TV?"

Agent Williams laughs at my observation. *He laughs like such an a-hole!*

"Part of the experimentation process is removing you from all outside stimuli. They may distract you, and we need you focused at all times. A clear mind makes for a successful test subject. There are books for your entertainment. Studies have shown them to increase brain function. Television, not so much."

I silently mimic him and make faces as he looks through my little library.

"Agent Williams, what is your first name? I'm getting awfully sick of calling you that, and since we'll be working together for an indefinite amount of time, wouldn't it be nice to be on a first-name basis?"

Agent Williams raises an eyebrow. "No. I like to keep things professional. The only people in here that know my first name are my superiors, and even they don't call me by my first name. You will continue to call me Agent Williams."

I stick my tongue out at him.

"Very mature. I will take my leave so you can get some rest. See you in the morning."

He shuts the door behind him, and I hear a *click*.

I wait five minutes after he leaves and then decide to check the door handle. I want to know if I am as free as they have led me to believe. I turn the handle slowly and then realize I can't turn it any further. I push on the door. It's locked. So this truly is my prison cell. Not very hospitable. I will have to mention it to Agent Williams in the morning. I growl and then throw myself onto the bed.

I lay there thinking of the people I love and if they'll manage without me. My thoughts automatically go to my mother. She will be devastated. How can I do this to her? I choke back tears as I pull the locket out of my shirt so I can look at it. In my head, I keep telling myself that this is the right thing to do, but my stomach is still full of regret.

I don't think I will be able to sleep. I feel much too guilty and depressed. While I lay there feeling sorry for myself, I hear a hissing sound. I glance around and notice a gas entering the room from the floor. It is moving quickly. I stand on the bed looking around. I am cornered; there is nowhere to escape to.

"What the fuck is this shit?" I yell into the mist as I choke on it.

I start to lose control of my body, and I goes limp. The last thing I see before closing my eyes is Cam's smiling face.

CHAPTER FORTY-EIGHT

ALEX

As I sit there watching over Cam, I don't know how I will find the strength to tell him the truth. I don't want to believe it myself. We failed to protect her. She walked right into their hands and out of our lives.

"How could you, Eve?" I whimper.

"What's that, Al?"

Oh shit, he is coming to.

"Take it easy, Cam. You won't feel too great at the moment."

He rubs his face and slowly tries to sit up.

"What happened? My head is spinning."

"You were tasered by those asshole agents."

He looks around, and his eyes go wide. He tries to stand but is still too disoriented.

"Where's Eve? We need to find her."

He keeps trying to stand, but I grab his arm and pull him back to the floor. This is going to be difficult.

Damn you, Eve, for leaving me with all the dirty work.

"Cam, she's gone."

Cam looks stunned but undaunted. He clearly doesn't understand me.

"I know she's gone. We need to go get her! We can't waste any time!"

I start sobbing again. I can't help it.

"No, Cam, she left with them. She chose to go with them. She wanted to keep everyone safe, and she hoped they would quarantine her or something."

Cam still looks confused. He doesn't want to believe me, but this isn't a lie or a joke. These are the facts.

He begins to yell at me. "Al, why didn't you stop her? How could you just let her do that! They're gonna kill her!"

I can feel his pain. The ache in his voice is choking me. There's nothing positive I can say, so I stay quiet and let Cam get it all out.

Cam smashes a lamp on Dr. August's desk before continuing his rant.

"Damn that piece of shit Claire. It's all because of her! She wanted to get rid of everyone I cared about. Before she took me, she killed Mark. I saw him die, Al. That bitch didn't want me to have any friends left. And now because of her, Eve is gone too. I have nothing now! Nothing!"

I am crying so intensely that it's hard to catch my breath. It's a wonder I get the next few words out.

"You have me."

Cam looks at me with tears in his eyes. He comes over to me and hugs me so violently that I fear I may break in his arms.

"I'm so sorry, Al. Of course, I have you. I didn't mean… I'm just…" He sighs in frustration.

"It's okay, Cam. I know you're hurting. I'm hurting too. I wanted to help her so badly. Now we're never going to see her again."

My voice cracks. This is a very harsh reality to swallow. My best friend all these years is gone, forever. Who am I going to talk about boys with? Surely not Cam! Who is going to come shopping with me? Who is going to scream like an idiot when N*SYNC finally does their comeback tour? These are all stupid things, of course, but it's the little things that make up a friendship. It is as if I have lost a part of myself.

"Alex, you're bleeding."

I look down at the wound in my thigh. "Oh yeah." I am so distraught I forgot about the pain in my thigh. Cam puts his arm around me and helps me limp towards the door.

"Come on, Al. I'm gonna get you to a doctor."

I'm not sure I need one, but then again I have never been stabbed before, so what do I know? I hold onto Cam. The pain in my heart makes it harder to walk than the wound in my leg.

As we limp away, I ask Cam to fill me in on what happened with Claire. I want to think about something else for the moment.

We both find joy talking about Claire's demise. She wasn't very pleasant as a human and even less so as a zombie. The details are gruesome, especially the part about Mark's death, and although it is painful to hear, it's better to get it all out.

Cam puts me into the passenger side of my car and then hops in on the other side. He is very quiet on the ride to the hospital. I have a feeling he may never be the same again. I watch his face as we drive. His expression goes from anger to sorrow over and over again. He slams his fist on the steering wheel a few times, and I don't bother asking him what that is about. I know it hurts. His girlfriend, his best friend, left without so much as a goodbye. I know that this will haunt him for the rest of his life. He will always wonder why, and he will always wonder where she is. I just hope he won't try to go looking for her; it will only lead him to dead ends and more pain.

While in the car, I think I see Cam wipe away some tears streaming down his cheek, and that says it all. He isn't ready to let Eve go, not now, not ever.

TWO YEARS LATER...

CAM

I drive up to her house and park out front. I'm having trouble finding the strength to go inside. This house is full of amazing memories and painful ones.

The clock in my car says 2:15 pm.

"Holy shit! I've been sitting out here for forty minutes?!"

I guess it is time to mosey on out and make an appearance. I know Alex is already inside. She has been texting me asking, "Where are you?" and "Are you close yet?"

I have no idea why Mr. and Mrs. Brenner called me here today. I want to turn the car back on and drive away.

I turn up the music on my iPod instead and try to calm my nerves. Entering this house means revisiting all my feelings for Eve. Just as I am beginning to move on, they are pulling me back in. Why can't they just tell me what they want over the phone?

My palms are sweating, and I keep rubbing them on my jeans.

"Okay, Cam, it's go time. Just get your ass to the front door and see what they want."

I know talking to myself really doesn't seem all that healthy, but I do it often, and for whatever reason, it helps me keep my cool. I finish listening to my Rolling Stones song before making my move. It seems like bad luck to leave in the middle of a song, especially when it is rock royalty.

As I get out of my car and begin towards the house, I keep

telling myself that I owe this to Eve. She will want me to check in on her parents. I feel a little guilty that I haven't done it more frequently. I've been avoiding them for almost two years, and none of it is their fault. It is me. I am hiding, but I guess I can't avoid the past forever.

Alex and I used the staged "fire" on campus as a cover for Eve's disappearance. It was an easy alibi to use because it was one that CSIS had already crafted in order to conceal the existence of zombies. I still remember Mrs. Brenner's screams when I called and told her that Eve had been one of the ones caught in the blaze.

My legs wobble beneath me as I think about what I did to her family, of what Eve forced me to do. The lies and the pain are excruciating. I can't help thinking, *Fuck you, Eve, for making us all suffer,* but that is just me being bitter again. I still ask myself from time to time why we were so easy to leave behind. Why was I so easy to leave behind?

I knock on their door and hear barking on the other side. As the door opens, Winston races towards me and attacks me with excitement. I kneel to receive his kisses.

"Good boy, Winston. I missed you."

I get up to meet Mr. Brenner. "Hi, sir. How are you?"

He doesn't crack his usual smile; I guess he is a little pissed off that I haven't made an appearance in awhile.

"I'm okay, Cam. Please come in. We're sitting in the living room. Want anything to drink?"

I shake my head. "No, I'm good, thanks."

I make my way into the living room, and Alex is sitting next to Mrs. Brenner, who is looking a little worse for wear. She looks so skinny and pale. My heart sinks as I begin to understand our meeting here.

Mrs. Brenner's smile glimmers as she greets me. "Oh, Cam, it's so good to see you. Please have a seat."

As I hug her, I can feel her bones through her loose-fitting clothing. I try to be gentle with my embrace. Mr. Brenner joins me on the sofa facing Alex and Mrs. Brenner. Winston also joins us, planting himself by my feet.

"Now, Cam, I have already told Alex the news, and I thought you should know too."

Mrs. Brenner takes a deep breath before continuing. Alex doesn't make eye contact with me. She seems like she's barely holding it together herself.

"I don't want to keep you in suspense, so I'm just going to spill it out real quick here. I went and saw my doctor a few months ago, and unfortunately, my cancer is back, and it has spread."

I bite the insides of my cheek and try not to let any tears fall. I want to be strong.

"What forms of treatment have they offered you, Mrs. Brenner?"

She smiles, but it's a little dimmer this time.

"Well, they suggested chemo, and that's what I've been doing, but they told me before the treatments started that it most likely wouldn't do anything."

I don't understand. "So what other treatments can they offer?"

Mrs. Brenner goes quiet, so I turn to Mr. Brenner, and he simply shakes his head. I know the answer in my head, but I refuse to believe it. I need someone to say it out loud.

"Mrs. Brenner, there has to be something else. Did you get a second opinion? They have so many experimental drugs right now. Maybe you would be a candidate for some?"

Mrs. Brenner smiles through her tears, and even though she

looks sorrowful, her smile still beams just like it always has. She signals with her finger that I should come closer. I kneel in front of her, waiting for a reply. She ever so gently takes my hands into hers.

"Cam, honey, this is it. There is nothing else they can do for me. I am lucky that I get to say goodbye. Everyone has to go someday, and I accept this exit. It's better than some other options out there, I guess. I mean, I've really been blessed. I had survived it once already, but now it's my time, you know?"

I feel my eyes drying up and stinging; they are wide open in shock. There is nothing I can possibly say to this. I'm not ready to say goodbye. This is a lot to digest. I think what shocks me further is this woman's undying positivity. Her daughter "died," and she is slowly dying too. She will be forced to leave the people she loves, and she feels lucky?

I feel a huge pain in my stomach when I ask my next question. "How long?"

I look into her kind eyes as she answers, "Three months, maybe six if chemo can hold it off a bit."

I embrace her as she sobs. I feel her tears drenching my shirt, and I hold her, feeling emotionally obliterated by the news.

Eventually, Mrs. Brenner breaks the silence. "Okay, everyone, that's enough sadness for one day. I have some things for you both."

Mrs. Brenner pulls out a bag from behind the sofa.

"Alex, this is for you. It's some of Eve's things that I want you to have. There's no need for me to hold onto them since I will be seeing her soon anyway."

The mere mention of an afterlife makes me jitter. Alex looks just as uncomfortable.

Alex slowly takes a few pictures out of the bag. She giggles as she looks at them. She shows me one picture of the three of us back in high school. We were such nerds in our superhero tee shirts. The next thing Alex pulls out is Eve's favourite teddy bear. Alex hugs it tightly. I bet it still smells of her, but I resist the urge to sniff it.

"Mrs. Brenner, I can't take this. It's been hers since she was little."

Mrs. Brenner refuses to take it back. "I know that, and I hope it brings you as much comfort as it brought me."

Now it is my turn. I'm not sure I am ready to see what Mrs. Brenner has for me, and I'm not sure I want a part of Eve laying around as a painful reminder either.

Mrs. Brenner pulls a small envelope out of her pocket and hands it to me. It says, "For: Cam," on the front.

"Now, Cam, I haven't opened it since it was addressed to you. I found it sitting in one of her drawers when I was clearing out her clothing for Goodwill last year. I've been very curious to see what it is, so go ahead, open it."

I open it very slowly. There is no note, only something small in the corner of the envelope. I shake it out into my hand. It is a red stone.

Alex and I stare at each other in silence.

Mr. Brenner chimes in. "A rock? What is the rock about?"

I can tell they are waiting for an explanation, but I can't very well tell them that among other mysterious powers, this rock may or may not ward off zombies. It may also have other powers that we are still unaware of.

I quickly think up a lie. "Oh right, I gave this to Eve when we went on a school trip to Ottawa. I told her it was the prettiest rock I had ever seen. I guess she wanted to return it to me for luck. We always thought it was a good luck stone. Silly, right?"

Mrs. Brenner pats my thigh. "No, that's not silly. It's important to have beliefs. It's those beliefs that get you through so many strange things in life. Well, I certainly hope it brings you much luck in the future, Cameron Jackson."

I smile at her. I like the sound of my full name. She says it so affectionately, and it reminds me of Eve. She would always tease me and call me Mr. Cameron Jackson. I recall this memory fondly; I still miss her most days.

Mrs. Brenner asks us to stay for dinner, but Alex and I make up an excuse so we can leave. Alex and I need to talk, and today has already been too heavy, but I promise Mrs. Brenner that I will return next week for a dinner date. That makes her happy, and it makes me feel better knowing that this is not goodbye, not just yet.

Alex and I get into the car and drive off. We don't speak until I stop the car at our favourite park, the one we always visited with Eve. The last time I was here was that day Eve got hit by a car. I replay the strange incident in my head as I look around the familiar space. Once I finish rummaging around in my thoughts, I pull the rock out of my pocket and hold it out so we can both look at it. It is such a stunning red; it seems to have a glow about it.

"Al, why do you think she left me this? When did she even get this? Didn't Dr. August always have it on him?"

Alex looks too petrified to touch it. "Maybe he gave it to her? Maybe she wants us to guard it? But we don't even know what it does...hmmm."

I shrug as I look at it. "Do you think we can find her using this? Maybe she wants us to find her and this is…"

Alex places her finger to my lips. "Shh, I think you're getting ahead of yourself, Cam. She wanted to leave to protect us, remember? And the rock might protect us from something, just like it protected Dr. August. She wouldn't want us to find her. Trust me, Cam. If you'd heard the way she spoke that night she left, you would know that she's never coming back."

I shove her finger away. "You mean she wouldn't want to know her mother is dying? I think she'd want to know, Al. Maybe this thing is a way to contact her in case of an emergency?"

I speak into the rock as if it were a microphone. "Hello? Hello? Eve?"

I stop after a few more tries. *Well, that made me feel like a total idiot.*

"Cam, snap out of it! That rock's not going to lead you to her. The fact that she left it for you means that she had been planning to leave for awhile. She was always going to leave, Cam. She had already made up her mind."

Alex's words cut deep, but she is right. Eve decided to leave long before we knew about it. She didn't need our permission, and I'm positive that given the chance, she would have just disappeared without any explanation. This rock proves she was planning this. I feel like a fool. Why did she bother to start anything with me if she knew she was leaving?

I think Alex can read the hurt on my face. She grabs me and hugs me tightly.

"Cam, I'm so sorry. I just want you deal with reality. These are the facts. She did love you, though. I know she did!"

I laugh. "Love me? Yeah right! I'm not sure we meant anything to each other."

Alex looks at me, confused. "Don't act like you wouldn't take her back in a second if she reappeared right now. You love her too. Don't play macho with me. I know you better."

"You see, that's the funny thing, Al. Love isn't enough, is it? To keep two people together forever, it takes a lot more. It takes respect, patience, sacrifice, and trust. Eve didn't respect me enough to tell me the truth, so it's over. Do I love her? Yes. Would it ever work? No. I see that now. All those years I spent waiting for her to see me as more than a friend were wasted because we were never meant to be anyway."

Alex looks away. I can tell she's upset.

"Cam, you don't mean that."

Just as she's about to continue yelling at me, the stone begins to glow brightly. It looks as though it is on fire. We quit arguing and watch it in stunned silence. What is this thing? Eve clearly wanted us to have it, but why? We are so consumed with watching the stone that we become oblivious to what is going on around us.

When I look up, there is an odd fog in the air. It was a clear night only a moment ago. I can see the moon, but now white clouds surround our car.

I drop the stone behind me when I see some dark figures through the windshield. They are surrounding the car. I can't make out what they look like, but their eyes burn like fire.

Before I can start the car, they are on top of us. One is banging on the roof of the car. I can see dents forming with each loud bang. Another one smashes Alex's window, and glass goes flying everywhere. She's screaming and trying to fight the figure off of her. I try to help, but it drags her out of the passenger side window before I can grab hold of her.

My last resort is the red stone Eve left me. It better have some sort of magic! I try to reach for the rock; I can see it glowing in the back seat. I stretch my arms as far as they will go, and I am just inches from it.

"Come on, rock. If you have any way of protecting us, now is the time!"

As I'm reaching for it, I notice a face in the rear window. I freeze as I stare up at the familiar face through the glass.

"Eve?"

She looks vicious, almost evil, and she doesn't seem to recognize me. She gives a sly grin, and black ooze pours out of her mouth. I hear Alex's frightened screams in the distance, but I am powerless to stop it. I can only stare as Eve punches through the glass and grabs me by the collar.

I look into her fiery eyes. "Eve, what have they done to you?"

TO BE CONTINUED...

A NOTE OF GRATITUDE FROM THE AUTHOR

I would like to first and foremost thank CHBB Publishing for giving a debut author this incredible opportunity to bring Eve Brenner into your homes. Without their support and tireless work, none of this would have been possible.

A special shout out to fellow authors Stephen Kozeniewski, my unofficial consigliere, Jeremiah Israel, my rock star muse, and Elise Walters, my spirit animal. Thank you for your support, you blurbs and kinds words. It means the world to me that such talented authors took the time to read my newbie book, and heck, they actually liked it! (So much yay!)

I know this next thank you is uncommon, but not unheard of; the fans are the ones that truly get wheels moving! I must thank all my twitter followers from the bottom of my heart. I didn't forget about you, and you know who you are! The ones who were there from the beginning, helping to promote me and my blog. My very loyal followers, you helped make this dream come true in more ways than you can understand. Thank you for your support, kind words, and re-tweets. PZ loves you guys!

The next set of thank you's are for my family. They have been encouraging me and my artistic endeavors since my very first sketch, very first poem, very first dream. I would like to thank my mother, who is my biggest cheerleader. There is nothing that woman wouldn't do for her kids, and she is the kindest angel you will ever meet. A bonafide superhero with no cape.

My younger brother has always told me I was talented, even when I didn't believe it. He helped create www.poeticzombie.com and has become my advisor in many ways. He is very keen and social media savvy, so I thank him for pushing me out of my comfort zone and into social media where I can meet other brilliant minds who might also enjoy my work and geek out with me.

I want to thank my husband, who spent many nights comforting me as I sent out endless queries for my book. Those nail-biting days without answers could only be managed with the support of someone far less worried than me. Thank you for being carefree and confident when I couldn't be.

I want to thank my little son, who inspires me every day. He inspired me to bring my books to the public. I thought to myself, *How could I one day ask this child to go for his dreams if I couldn't do the same?* So here I am, little guy. Momma wrote a book!

To my extended family, thank you so much for your support and love. It feels good knowing you have my back always! Without you guys in my corner, I'm not sure where I'd be.

To my friends who supported this book before I ever wrote it. You guys support my madness no matter what it is. You never cease to amaze me with your loyalty, love, and sage advice.

Much love to you all. Hope you continue to enjoy The Zombie Girl Saga.

A.Giacomi

A.Giacomi is the author of the wildly entertaining Zombie Girl Saga. She is an educator, writer, and artist from Toronto, Canada. She is a zombie enthusiast, a wife, and mother to two small human children.

For more on **A.Giacomi** visit her on:

Twitter **@thepoeticzombie**

Facebook **A.Giacomi**

or her official Blog **WWW.POETICZOMBIE.COM**

*Be sure to add THE ZOMBIE GIRL SAGA to your to read list **on GOODREADS***

61670394R00174

Made in the USA
Charleston, SC
25 September 2016

30030 1517